BEST INTENTIONS

Also by Erika Raskin

Close

BEST
INTENTIONS

ERIKA RASKIN

St. Martin's Press
New York

BEST INTENTIONS. Copyright © 2017 by Erika Raskin. All rights reserved. Printed in the United States of America. For information, address St. Martin's Press, 175 Fifth Avenue, New York, N.Y. 10010.

www.stmartins.com

Library of Congress Cataloging-in-Publication Data

Names: Raskin, Erika, author.
Title: Best intentions : a novel / Erika Raskin.
Description: First Edition. | New York : St. Martin's Press, 2017.
Identifiers: LCCN 2017009301| ISBN 9781250101228 (hardback) |
    ISBN 9781250101235 (e-book)
Subjects: LCSH: Domestic fiction. | BISAC: FICTION / Contemporary
    Women. | GSAFD: Suspense fiction.
Classification: LCC PS3618.A765 B47 2017 | DDC 813/.6—dc23
LC record available at https://lccn.loc.gov/2017009301

Our books may be purchased in bulk for promotional, educational, or business use. Please contact your local bookseller or the Macmillan Corporate and Premium Sales Department at 1-800-221-7945, extension 5442, or by e-mail at MacmillanSpecialMarkets@macmillan.com.

First Edition: August 2017

10 9 8 7 6 5 4 3 2 1

BEST INTENTIONS

PROLOGUE

Sometimes I can barely remember how I got here. The past seems to have shaken loose, faded into overlapping lines on an old Etch A Sketch. Other times every detail comes into sharp focus.

Even the irony.

Like how one of my phobias used to be public scrutiny. That was before, of course. Now Nancy Grace screeches my name nightly and the Twitterati come up with clever hashtags to attach to it.

#SocialWork
#AHelpingProfession
#NoReally

My best friend is a reporter. She keeps telling me this is nothing, that I need to prepare myself for the correspondents who are packing their bags for the trial. They'll come to Virginia, she says, because the case has it all. Malpractice. Adultery. Class. Race.

And murder.

As an added bonus, the political climate has swung back to the right and it's widely known that my father is a liberal Jewish congressman from New York. Which is pretty much a losing trifecta in certain circles. In fact, just yesterday the Tea Partying governor was quoted as saying that the rosy red apple never falls far from the tree. He seems to have forgotten that his wife and I were first-grade room mothers together. Though she and I never crossed the cordiality zone, we did spend a lot of time together organizing events like the Christmas extravaganza and the underappreciated, labor-intensive Teacher Appreciation Day.

I tell myself that concentrating on everything but the horror of what happened means that I am coping. I tell myself that if I don't look down, I'll be able to maintain my balance. But the tightrope is swinging wildly.

And mostly I'm just waiting for a hard wind to blow.

CHAPTER ONE

If I were writing up case notes on the events that brought me here, the record would start with last year's Spring Fling—which is pretty sad, since I'd been looking forward to the annual party for a very long time. The function was supposed to mark the end of Elliot's training, the start of his full-fledged career as an obstetrician, and a new level of participation in family life. Instead of celebrating, though, I was once again making small talk with a babysitter and trying not to cry. My husband was an hour and a half late.

"Sorry about the mess," I apologized, pitching a couple of Barbie amputees into the hot-pink convertible by the couch. By the time my youngest was born, I had realized I could either have a really clean house or a relaxed and happy home. I wasn't coordinated enough to do both. I threw another Barbie leg into the car.

Elliot finally called. "Hey. Sorry. We're getting hammered. I'm still waiting for Anesthesia so we can get a section started."

"But you're not on tonight, El."

"I know, Marti," he said with exaggerated patience. After twelve years of marriage, *what* was said was a lot less important than *how* it was said. Tone trumped content every time.

"Okay."

"Look, Clark had a headache and I told him I'd cover. I'll meet you as soon as I can."

"Okay," I repeated. I knew there was only a fifty percent chance he'd make it.

It was exciting at first, watching Elliot's career unfold. Very early on, he decided that he wasn't going to be just good, he was going to be the Best. And he was. Extra hours of research earned him rare coauthor credit in a prestigious medical journal while he was still a student. As an intern, he was chosen to represent the department at a weeklong convention in San Diego. He won the coveted role of chief resident, followed by the only slot in the three-year fellowship program in high-risk obstetrics (an honor that meant Elliot waved off his classmates as they graduated and started real jobs, while he stayed behind and extended his eighty-hour-a-week training). My pride had long since faded into weariness. Emergencies, late-night meetings, and co-workers with headaches all meant the same thing. Elliot was never home, never on time, never available.

"We're just going to meet at the restaurant," I said to the sitter.

"Cool." She pointed to the family photograph on the mantel. "How long ago was this?"

"Couple years now. Nina was probably seven, Poppy three, and—"

"I was stuck in the middle," Simon offered without looking away from the TV screen. "As usual."

The photo was very Kennedy Family Vacation. The five of us were beaming, our hair lifting like wings above the clear water behind us, arms tangled around orange life jackets. The kids' blue eyes matched their dad's. Summer freckles had hatched on all of their faces. I looked Mediterranean next to them. Elliot had some rare time off that day, and we drove to Maryland for a sailing trip with his parents. He and I held hands while the kids raced around a little island searching for shark's teeth and sea glass.

"It was a great trip," I said. "Except on the way back to Annapolis, I got so sick my father-in-law banned me from his boat."

"Permanently," Nina said from the sofa, giggling.

"That means fo-evah," Poppy explained in her mysterious Brooklyn accent.

I kissed the top of her silky head and asked her to pay it forward.

I eased the van out of the too-tight parking space, then glanced over at the house with its old wrought-iron gate. It sat cheek-to-cheek with other brick homes built in the century before last, all illuminated by gas lamps. The setting was so authentic looking that our block had been used in location shots for two Civil War movies and a TV show. (Which was cool at first and then just a pain in the ass.)

My favorite, not-yet-overhauled Richmond gas station came into view. Its windows were adorned with handmade signs offering "Fresh" Milk and "Free" Coffee with "FILLUPS!" When we first got down to Virginia I'd been confused by the random italics, quotation marks, and exclamation points that sprang up willy-nilly. But then I realized they weren't grammatical guideposts but cheery decorations, and I loved them all.

I turned onto Broad Street, the former dividing line between historic gentrified Church Hill and historic impoverished Church Hill. There I slowed for a group of well-heeled diners heading to the latest trendy restaurant that had appeared in our neighborhood.

Two hours late, I pulled into Ting's parking lot.

"Crap." The only open space was next to the green Dumpster. I gave it a wide berth in case any rats were lying in wait (nothing like having a rodent phobia in this city) and hurried into the restaurant. Once inside, I observed the milling crowd from the landing above the sunken dining room.

All the scene needed was a Discovery Channel narrator.

I watched as a couple of Talbots-clad wives worked a cool breeze through the room. Snippets of their conversation rose above the din.

"This is going to be my last year on the women's committee. I swear the Pink Ball just about does me in."

"Oh, you say that every year!"

"I almost strangled the caterer yesterday—"

The matrons' identical foil highlights caught the light as they nodded hello to a couple of casually dressed female gynecologists wearing matching Birkenstocks. All four of them gave the side-eye to a resident who'd ditched her scrubs for a plunging neckline and fuck-me pumps. The men, too, were interesting. From my vantage point I could see hands patting and hugging, occasionally lingering a tad too long on a bare shoulder or back.

I could have stayed in that spot all night, but then I saw Colby.

She was in the corner, surrounded by admirers. Of course. My southern-belle best friend was born a perfect ten (a fact I generously overlooked) and attracted attention just by being. With her auburn hair and russet eyes, Colby looked every bit the on-air reporter everyone assumed her to be. But she was a print journalist, a rough-and-tumble investigator who used her looks only when it helped her get a story.

I stared hard enough to get her attention. She frowned and pointed to her watch. I smiled and pointed to the bar.

I was midsip when Colby goosed me, sending a tidal wave of alcohol over my skirt. "Whoops," she said, bending nonchalantly, using her cocktail napkin to pat the wet spot.

"Colby—stop! It looks like we're shooting a porno."

She bent in closer to inspect the damage. My light gray skirt had turned transparent. "Here, put my shawl on so no one sees your aversion to bikini wax."

I handed over my glass and put on the soft, flowing jersey. It was infused with gardenia, her signature fragrance. "Thanks. Sort of."

"Well, anyway, that's what you get for being late. I've been dying here for weeks. Where were you?"

"Waiting for Elliot."

"Hmm," Colby said, employing our most meaningful expression. Hours of conversation were condensed that way. "Hmm" was sarcasm, understatement, and shorthand for *say no more*.

I drained what was left of my drink. "What's new?"

"Nothing."

Her expression made me tense. "What's the matter?"

"It just looked like Charlie was coming down with something. But he's not."

"You sure?"

"Yeah. I took him in. The doctor told me to stop being such a nervous Nellie. He said we're almost at the five-year cure mark and I'm going to need to remember that kids who've had cancer still get regular viruses."

"Easy for him to say."

"Right? Dumb-ass."

When Colby should have been enrolling Charlie in nursery school alongside Simon, she was taking a crash course in lumbar punctures, T cells, and sterile precautions. Throughout that dismal time, she'd clutched her child in one arm and fought back death and disease with the other. She was my hero.

Suddenly, a British accent carried above the din and with it a nervous energy that rolled through the room.

"Oh boy," Colby said. "Cover your mouth, darlin'. The shit is about to hit the fan."

I turned and saw Mrs. Hill-the-First, the recently replaced wife of the OB-GYN Department chairman. She was facing off against her ex and his pregnant trophy.

"I hope she shoots the tiny son of a bitch," Colby said.

Nigel had had an affair with Leslie (the sexy nurse of my own nightmares), ironically resulting in an unplanned pregnancy. Things might have settled down when he chose Leslie and their unborn child over his existing wife and four children, but Natalie Hill wasn't disappearing graciously.

"Yikes."

"Hush now, Marti. I can't hardly hear."

The volume in the room had been turned up, with murmurs of "You look nice" and "What are your plans for the summer?" as Nigel's obliging subordinates tried to make enough small talk to cover the fight. I thought Colby might shush them, too, but Natalie compensated by shouting. Her drink was rocking violently over its banks.

"I hope this happens to you, my dear. After you've given him the best years of your life. He'll probably have time to squeeze in one more marriage after this, don't you think?" Natalie rotated to address the crowd with upper-class inflection. "Do you know how the grand doctor left us?"

"She really is out of it," Colby whispered. "Everyone remotely connected to the hospital knows."

"It was after we'd come back from the Bahamas. It was a lovely trip really. Blue skies, white sand. The older boys parasailed. On the last night Nigel presented us with gifts. New phones for the children. A gold watch for me. For my retirement, I suppose." She laughed bitterly. "It wasn't a week later, I was uploading the holiday photos, actually, when he came home early with his announcement. Pronouncement. Decree." She paused, leaned in toward Leslie. "Tell me, dear, did you celebrate the pregnancy test? Call your parents with the happy news? Mention that Nigel already had a family?"

I couldn't see Leslie's face, but holsters of sweat had darkened the pale yellow fabric around her arms. Suddenly Natalie threw the last of her drink at her ex-husband, triggering a simultaneous gasp from the audience. Nigel calmly took out a handkerchief and wiped his face. He may have been reaching for Atticus Finch, but a blue vein pulsed in his temple and his mouth shrank to a thin hyphen.

"He looks like a small penis," Colby whispered.

Nigel took hold of his ex-wife's arm and guided her toward the exit. Up on the landing, Natalie turned around and cried out, "This is *my* life you're in, Leslie." She was bum-rushed through the door.

"That was painful," I said.

"Dignified with the accents, though. Very PBS."

"I'll never get over how fast the divorce went down."

"He guaranteed her a chunk of money."

"I know. But still."

Nigel returned alone. "My friends, I beg your indulgence. Obviously, Natalie is not well. But"—he clapped his mini-hands together—"let's all continue with the celebration. It's nearly the end of another academic year and we need to pay homage to our residents and fellows who are completing their training."

"Too bad Elliot is missing the oh-mage," Colby said, talking over Nigel. "How are y'all doing?"

"I don't know. I just can't wait until he becomes an attending. I am definitely in countdown mode."

"You have been for years."

"What makes you say that?" I smiled. "I need a refill. Want anything?"

"Nah. I saw John on his way back to the food table. I want to head him off at the pass. He's gone for seconds three times."

I was trying to do the math when two men in tortoiseshell glasses, lightweight suits, and wedding bands came over. The shorter one spoke first.

"Excuse us. We were just having a discussion about this morning's editorial on that euthanasia case and wanted to get a real live reporter's opinion."

I unfurled my hand toward my friend, Vanna style.

"Why, I'm flattered," Colby drawled, all sorority and sweet tea. "I didn't write it, mind you," she went on. "But the paper's argument rests on the line between no heroics and actually withholding sustenance." She tried to bring me into the discussion. "Marti, what do you think? When should doctors turn everything off?"

"After a really bad haircut?"

"Seriously," she prompted.

"I guess I don't think prolonging a vegetative state makes sense. Death with dignity and all."

Colby nodded, but I was more aware that the guys had shifted their postures, disposing of a corner of the conversational square. They'd made a triangle and I had been lopped off.

Colby said she needed to go check in with the General.

"The General?" one of the tortoiseshells asked.

"John. It's short for general anesthesia," Colby explained to appreciative laughs. Really, she could have said anything and the goobers would have eaten it up. Colby threaded her way through the crowd and planted herself at her husband's side. They were like jigsaw pieces from different puzzles. Chubby, plain John put his arm around his gorgeous wife.

Of all the couples I knew, the Kusiks were the happiest.

I excused myself and went for a refill. The bar line stalled, mooring me directly in front of the women's bathroom, from which a sickeningly sweet smell wafted each time the door opened. I concentrated on the unfamiliar man in front of me. He was a couple inches south of six feet, with salt-and-pepper hair, a thick mustache, and hipster glasses. He wasn't WASPy handsome like Elliot, but he certainly was cute. Craggy-face cute. Tommy Lee Jones in his heyday cute.

When he made it to the bar, he turned and asked what I was drinking. I blushed. He must have been aware of me examining him. "Diet Coke and vodka."

"Wow. I haven't heard a request for one of those since college. Of course back then it was Tab and vodka."

"The Dark Ages," I said somberly.

He passed me the squat glass with a lime buoy bobbing up and down. "Win Phillips," he said, extending his other hand.

"Marti Trailor."

"Doctor?"

"Wife."

"Mrs. Doctor."

"Right." We smiled at each other; our eyes met long enough to warm my face. I had to look away. "Win's an interesting name," I said, trawling for the lime. "What's it short for?"

"Nothing. My parents were very competitive." He held out his hand for the green wedge. I placed it in his palm, feeling bewildered by the intimacy of the act. It was as if he had bent down to tie my shoe. I wasn't accustomed to this much notice. He put the fruit on an abandoned dish and we continued walking.

"What's Marti short for?"

"Martha. Though my brothers call me Martyr." He smiled and then I blurted, "I'm a social worker. I mean, besides being a doctor's wife."

"Really?"

I nodded.

"Where do you work?"

"Oh, I don't."

Win laughed and I blushed again. What, I thought, is wrong with me? Why did I tell him that? "Well, I did have a job a couple of years ago at a family service agency. But then I had kids."

The truth was I had the kids when I had the job. Which was how I lost it. I could never find any help. Whenever a throat was sore, or head lice took up residence, I had to use up my sick days. And that was before the chicken pox struck. Six weeks of calamine lotion. First Simon, then Nina, followed by Poppy. Then my job.

"I'm a social worker, too," Win said as he set his drink on a table and pulled out a chair for me. "Can you sit for a minute?"

"Sure," I said. "Where do you work?"

"Actually, I just moved here from Michigan. I'm heading up the new New Moms program at Richmond Medical."

"What's that?"

"It's kind of an experiment. We got a grant for social work and OB to work together on infant mortality. We're—and I'm not sure why I'm using the first-person plural since I still have to hire someone—going to be offering counseling services, networking, and job-training hookups. Stuff like that."

"You're kidding." I almost levitated. "My thesis was on infant mortality and poverty. Then after I graduated I helped write a congressional position paper on how to make prenatal care more accessible." I was trying hard to control my excitement. Poppy was set to start kindergarten in the fall and I had recently begun to float the idea of returning to work.

"Tell me more about this position paper," Win said.

"It was about the best ways to improve OB services for poor women. Real ways to increase access to care. Things like transportation, babysitting. Stuff like that. I actually interviewed a lot of agency directors from around the country and compiled that information."

Win nodded thoughtfully.

I had already decided against mentioning that the congressman who got me the job was my father. Dad, whom Fox News once misidentified as Chuck Schumer, was a dyed-in-the-wool arranger. Over my protests, he put in a call to a colleague.

"You'll take this opportunity and put it to the betterment of others," my father instructed. "The only time the old boys' network is valuable is when it doesn't help old boys. You'll do good work."

He was used to people submitting. So I did.

"Hey," Win said. "You seem like a good person to ask. I had a tour of the hospital a couple of days ago. What's the story with that VIP wing?"

I rolled my eyes. "Basically it's a way for affluent people to be hospitalized without having to brush up against the masses. When the VIP wing was announced, people started calling the hospital RichMed. RichWhiteMed. There was an online petition against it. But it didn't go anywhere because the plan got support from unexpected places. Like some of the black city officials."

"Interesting."

"The argument was that unless Richmond Medical could provide special amenities to self-paying patients who could afford a thousand dollars a night in a hotel-like private room, they'd just migrate out to the suburban hospitals and take their checkbooks with them."

"So poor people would lose out in the end."

"Right. Thus the separate wing. I know other places do it, too. But it's gross. They even have their own chef up there."

"I wandered over earlier. Even their elevator is nicer. Got any other pointers?"

I thought a moment. "Don't see *Gone with the Wind* in a theater. It's like *Rocky Horror* with a rebel twist—people throw popcorn when Sherman's name comes up." I smiled. "And never, ever confuse enthusiastic good southern manners with friendship. That should cover it."

He laughed. "Have you ever thought about coming out of retirement?"

"Once or twice."

He threw his head back and roared.

"What's so funny?"

"It's just that I wouldn't be surprised if you had your résumé in your purse. Next to the cigarettes you've got hidden in there."

My eyelids stretched wide of their own accord.

"I knew it." He laughed. "You've got the telltale signs."

"Which are?"

"Substitute thumb insertion between smoking fingers, incessant foot jiggle. How about helping me get the program rolling?"

Before I could answer, the scent of gardenias filled the air and a perfect manicure reached across me. "Hi there. I'm Colby. Marti's best friend."

They shook hands. "Win Phillips. Her future boss, I hope."

"For a second I thought you were going to say her future husband." She grinned. "Which would have been less surprising."

"Colby!"

She ignored me and smiled at Win. "Nice to meet you. I'm glad someone's finally going to make an honest woman out of this slacker. Marti, I don't believe you mentioned anything about a job."

"Fast-breaking news," Win said.

"Well then, it's a damn good thing I got over here." She produced her most engaging smile, flashing white teeth. "Being a reporter and all."

"The *Richmond Daily*?" Win asked.

Colby nodded.

He raised a brow. "Interesting editorials."

"The paper is just to the right of Ted Cruz," I said. "I only have a subscription because she gives me one for my birthday. Every year. Just once I'd like a pair of earrings."

"I'm sure we could rig a couple of sections up to your little lobes, darlin'. Hey, listen to this. You know that piece on the architect I've been working on?"

"Yeah?"

"He asked me to read him his quotes a few days ago. He okayed them and I submitted it. Then he called this afternoon and said he wanted to make some changes. I told him I'd see what I could do, but my editor might not go for it. And the guy goes, 'Oh, come on. We're hardly talking *The New York Times*.'"

"Uh-oh." I laughed. "What did you say?"

"That we weren't talking Frank Lloyd Wright, either."

Win asked Colby if her husband was an obstetrician.

"No, an anesthesiologist. He does a lot of OB cases—which is how we always get invited to this delight. John and Elliot have known each other since med school."

"Elliot's my husband," I explained, feeling sort of funny that I hadn't mentioned him.

Win was about to say something else when he looked toward the door and saw the hospital's director of social work, Joel Levine, struggling with his coat. A large man who seemed to be caught in his own clothes, Joel looked a little panicky. Win stood and said, "I don't think it would be very good form for me to just watch. Marti, call me Monday through the hospital switchboard. I don't know the office number yet. Colby, it was a brief—but I hope informative— pleasure."

Then he walked toward the door.

"Who was that?" Colby asked, sliding into his chair.

"My new boss."

"Hm," she intoned.

A waiter passed with a bowl of wrapped treats and Colby smiled. "Tight-lipped fortune cookies are pretty appropriate for a gyno dinner."

"You are seriously disturbed."

"Hello, beautiful women," Elliot said from behind.

"Hi!"

"Hey, you," Colby said, standing and giving him a hug. "I kept your seat warm."

I studied his face when he sat. The crease between his brows was practically smooth. He looked happier than he had in a long time. I pulled his hand to my mouth, kissed his familiar fingers. "You are about to become an official attending physician. You did it, my love."

"We did it," he corrected.

Which made me feel a little teary. "I am so proud of you, El. So proud and so excited for this new chapter." I kissed his hand again. We sat in a comfortable quiet as the other guests began to leave. It wasn't until we got up to go ourselves that I remembered my news. "Hey—something amazing happened before you got here."

CHAPTER TWO

The second time I met with Leland Powell, we were in a glass-walled conference room, high above the James River. Leland's secretary served coffee in cups with matching saucers and pretended not to study me. The elegant office imparted an account of a man who seemed to take great delight in life: casual family photos snapped on ski trips and European holidays, one with a dozen grandchildren in matching Christmas attire; formal pictures with state leaders of both parties, always a handshake and a smile; a candid shot of five men on a sailboat holding forth a trophy. I'm pretty sure one of them was Chappell Wycliff, the city prosecutor.

Leland told me to take him through the past months as slowly as I could.

"Tell it to me like a story," he said softly. "Start from the beginning."

The first time I met Leland was in a cinder-block conference room at the regional jail. A caged fluorescent bulb and a soot-covered skylight lighted the space. It was there he convinced me to relinquish custody of my children. "It's temporary. To prove you're not a flight risk."

I shook my head.

"Mrs. Trailor, if you don't get bail, you won't have them anyway."

Which was when I vomited down the front of my prison shirt.

He came to my side of the table and handed me his cashmere scarf to clean myself.

"Take a moment," he said. "Then we need to get back to work."

The day I was to start at New Moms began so badly that I seriously considered bagging the whole thing. Actually, the downward slide kicked off the night before. Elliot was choosing his clothes for morning rounds, carefully matching a new tie to different shirts, while I studied myself in the mirror. My recent haircut had devolved into a bearded pyramid. "I guess my quest to become Julianna Margulies continues."

"Doesn't she have straight hair?"

"Now she does," I said, trying to pull my frizzy curls into a bedtime scrunchy. "Which is why she is my hair hero. Although, maybe she wore a wig for that show—"

"Marti?" Elliot's tone was strange.

My pulse picked up. "El?"

"Do you think you'll be spending a lot of time up on Labor and Delivery?"

"What? Why?"

"I've been questioning the wisdom of two Trailors at the same hospital."

"Is it a name thing?" I asked seriously. "Do you want me to go by Maxwell?"

His sigh was quiet but seismic.

"I don't know what I'm supposed to do with that, Elliot."

"Never mind. I shouldn't have said anything."

We went to bed in silence and I awoke alone, jaw aching from being clenched all night. An old Eagles song was on the radio: "Take It Easy." Elliot used to play it. He used to try to teach me guitar. We'd end up hysterical every time. He'd named each of my fingers things like Lennie and Yogi Berra and expressed profound sorrow over their unwillingness to learn.

But that was a long time ago.

I showered and dressed quickly. I'd promised the kids we'd celebrate their first Monday of vacation with blueberry pancakes, but they were up already, eating cereal and watching Nickelodeon.

"Good morning, strangely blond offspring!" I said.

"And Batman! Don't huht his feelings!"

"And Batman," I added. The dog looked up briefly and then went back to performing an act that should have been undertaken in private.

A commercial came on and Simon aimed his plastic Uzi at me. "Where's Dad?"

"At work, honey. Don't point that, please." I thought wistfully of my fleeting injunction against guns and how it had been hastily abandoned during a temper tantrum at a toy store.

"By the way," the seven-year-old added in his prematurely adult voice, "the tooth fairy didn't come last night."

Shit!

"How 'bout I front you the money—"

"Again."

"Again," I conceded. "And you leave the slacker a note to pay me back."

"Fine."

I handed him a five from my purse.

Suddenly, Poppy noticed I was wearing a skirt rather than my jeans. She catapulted from the table, throwing herself at my thighs.

"I don't want you to go to a new work and I don't want that new babysitter!"

"It's going to be okay, Poppyseed," I promised, picking her up. "Katie's great!"

My personal backup singers, the Anxieties, roused. They crooned concern about the sitter's references not really being legit, then finished with a flourish about me hiring someone shady to take a job my family didn't want me to have in the first place.

"Why can't you just start in September?" Simon asked.

"The moms who need help with their babies need the help now, even though it's summer."

"So you're going to take care of other kids?" Poppy demanded, dismissing weeks of Mommy's-going-back-to-work prep.

"Pretty much," her brother confirmed into his cereal bowl.

"You know, you don't always have to go out of your way to make things worse, Simon," Nina-the-Elder reprimanded. Her older-sister tone sometimes got snotty.

I could see that Simon was contemplating weaponizing his spoon, so I quickly put Poppy down and laid a quieting hand on the back of his neck. "All right. Hang on, everybody. Look, tonight—if everyone behaves and that includes being polite to each other—we can go out for supper."

"Where?" Poppy asked.

"Patty Cakes could work," Simon bargained.

Which would mean rush-hour traffic across the bridge to a madhouse of outrageously expensive video games and flashing overhead lights that I was sure could trigger mass seizures. "Fine."

Poppy pulled on my shirt. "Will you fix my socks, please?"

I bent down and began twisting and tugging, feeling the agitation growing in her calf muscles. "There!" I said as convincingly as I could.

"Nooo!"

"Poppy. Come on."

"They still hurt!"

Fortunately, the doorbell rang before a full-throated meltdown.

"Never mind. Just take them off," I instructed. The kids followed me to the front door, where Katie was standing on the porch like a tattooed Mary Poppins. She had a wheeled suitcase beside her.

"What's that?" Simon asked.

"Glad you asked, little man," she said, undoing the clasps to reveal two sides of magic. Paints, fabric, glue, brushes, and glitter stood strapped in organized formation.

The kids actually gasped.

"Okay, guys, I'm going to go. Be good and have a wonderful—"

"Bye!" Poppy interrupted.

"—day," I finished.

"What?" asked Nina as she eyed a package of gimp and lanyards.

"Never mind. I love each and every one of you."

It felt strange being out of the house during the day without holding a small hand or telling someone to please hurry up. It was strange, but I liked it. I noticed a trio of robins worming in our little square of a front yard and the lingering spice of tobacco that rose from the expensive lofts in the converted warehouses at the bottom of the hill. I sucked it all in, feeling a nearly unrecognizable sense of lightness.

A babysitter who was not only Red Cross certified, but also had a personality meant that I could relax. Or quasi relax. Because the truth was, ever since my very first labor pain nine years before, I could only really unwind during deep sleep. Motherhood was like an end-of-semester project. There was always one more thing I should be doing. Or could be doing. Or worried about doing. Nothing was ever finished.

I ignored the ominous scraping from the back of the van as it bumped along the few blocks of cobblestones in Shockoe Slip. Now a yup-scale shopping and tourist destination, the waterway district had been set ablaze in 1865 by the retreating Confederate army. Once a hub of tobacco and cotton commerce, the area had also housed a notorious slave market known as the Devil's Half Acre.

The still distant Fourth of July was being heralded by coordinated store decorations, each specialty shop adorned in red, white, and blue. Flags draped over best sellers in the bookstore, hung shawl-like on the backs of ancient rockers in the antique store, and sprang from cupcakes at BonBon. Matching mother-daughter navy hung crisp and cool in a boutique window, surrounded by bunches of bright poppies and white stargazers. I spent the rest of the ride debating whether I could be friends with somebody who'd twin-dress with her offspring.

At the hospital I finally found a space on the sprawling roof and realized that because I'd Ubered over for my formal interview, I didn't have a clue how to get to the office from the parking lot. Elliot may have spent the majority of our marriage inside Richmond Medical, but to me the place was as abstract as a foreign country. I studied the YOU ARE HERE map and felt a little panicky. As far as I could tell, the only way to reach the front entrance was by jumping.

"Marti Maxwell-Trailor. As I live and breathe."

I turned. "Colby! What are you doing here?"

"Dropping John's phone off. He forgot it, again. Hey, guess who stole my parking space on the B level."

"Who?"

"The second Mrs. Hill. It pains me deeply to report that she's enormous and appears to be carrying Nigel's spawn in her neck."

"Good."

"She had a Legacy Country Club sticker on her windshield."

"Which one's that?"

"The one that used to hold the Night at the Plantation dance."

"It's heritage, not hate," I said, smirking. "Are you working on anything interesting these days?"

"I'm getting ready to do something on Stocker Pharmaceuticals."

"What's the story?"

"They're holding their urology convention here. I got a call from somebody who said what really goes on makes a Vegas bachelor party look like Wednesday night Bible study."

"Really?" For years the drug companies had done what they could to encourage doctors to pimp their pills, pumps, and cures. From weekly pizzas for medical departments to expensive trips for attending physicians, payola for prescribing was par for the course. But the national press had been riding Big Pharma lately. "I thought that kind of thing was finished."

"Did you, my child? Brand loyalty will be serious business forever."

"What happens at the convention?"

"Basically it's a vice cop's wet dream. Prostitution. Drugs. My source said one year people were using catheter coke straws in the bathroom. Security is so tight they collect guests' phones at the sign-in table."

"So how are you going to get in?"

"It's supposed to be an educational dinner, urologists only. There's a bus trip out to the amusement park for the families that have accompanied the docs. Ferris wheels and laser shows in exchange for some of Daddy's time."

"What about the female doctors?"

"There aren't that many women on the rod squad. It's mostly a guy field. And it's not like a big public orgy. People disappear for a few minutes here, a few minutes there. Plus the hookers are dressed like drug reps. The conservative ones. Not like the drug reps who dress like call girls."

"Ironic."

"I'm getting a wig and glasses and appropriate PTA attire so I can go incognito as an escort going incognito as a pharmaceutical shill. This is all on the DL, of course."

"Thanks, Cole," I said sarcastically. She knew that one of my (many) concerns was that something would happen (a high fever, one drink too many) and every secret anyone ever confided in me would come popping out of my mouth like pearls off a snapped strand.

"No probs. So are you excited for your first day?"

Just as I was about to tell her what had happened with Elliot the night before, a V formation of birds flew into view and one of them fell straight down.

"Oh, my God!" I nearly shrieked. "I just saw a duck or a goose or something have a heart attack!"

"What?"

"It dropped like a shoe! Do you think it's an omen?"

"For the bird, Martha Helen. I've got to run. Call me tonight and tell me how it went."

The waiting room at New Moms had been transformed since my first visit. Light danced off a sparkling aquarium, and the old finger-wagging social work posters had been replaced with framed photographs of happy kids. A toy chest, its lid nailed forever into a safe yawn, sat on a blue carpet. Except for some random couch pillows arranged like strangers at a bus stop, the space was relaxed and welcoming.

"What do you think?" Win asked, coming out of his office. Before I could answer, he succumbed to a series of violent sneezes.

"Whoa!" I said. "Welcome to Richmond, home of the millionaire allergist, asthma capital of the South."

"Jesus—in Detroit we just said gesundheit."

"Bless you." I smiled.

"So, anyway, this waiting room is really, excuse the buzzword, intentional. At my last job one of my clients dropped out of the program because coming to the clinic was such a hassle, chasing her toddler around, trying to corral him. The freaking wall sockets didn't even have covers!"

"I hear that. Bringing excess children to a doctor's office is generally a brink activity."

"Is that a social work term?"

"No, it's a Marti term. A brink activity is any undertaking that can push you over the edge."

Win looked amused. "Like?"

"Bath time after a particularly wretched day with one's offspring. Or going to the post office. Anytime. Baking cookies for Back to School Night. Basically anything above and beyond."

Win laughed.

He reminded me of the earnest college interns who inundated Dad's office every legislative term. My first grown-up boyfriend had been gleaned from that very crop. Then, with a shock, I realized Win also reminded me of Elliot, before responsibilities and stress and long hours had worn him down. My husband, the man who for years I couldn't believe had chosen me.

"You okay?" Win asked. "You have a funny look on your face."

"I'm fine."

"Anyway, I hope that when we get more funds we can provide some form of drop-in babysitting for the mothers while they're here for other appointments," Win said before he blew his nose again. "Of course, now that I've seen some of the case files that Joel sent down, I realize that the waiting room is going to be the least of our worries."

"Why?"

"Because right now, before we've even officially opened, we have referrals for an incest victim, a twenty-year-old whose fetus has been diagnosed with a heart problem, a woman with Down syndrome, and an HIV-positive teenager in her second trimester. I also just got a call from a gym teacher. She's sending over one of her students who hasn't told her parents yet."

"Oh boy." I walked toward the aquarium, which was emitting a low murmur. A gray clam opened and shut in a steady rhythm. A fish curled into a C bobbed up and down near the air bubbles. "Eww. I think we have a casualty."

Tonya Maines was my first client. She had luminous brown eyes, the same shade as her skin. Her voice was husky and quiet. When she walked into the office, her unsnapped pants revealing a wide V, she reminded me of a little kid trying to keep her composure after getting separated from her class on a field trip. Almost immediately she dissolved into heavy, desperate sobs. She leaned into me and wept and wept.

"How pregnant are you, honey?"

"Somewheres around four or five months, I guess. I'm sorry. I don't usually act like this."

"It must be a really scary and confusing time."

"Do you think I can get something to drink?"

"Let's go grab some lunch from the cafeteria."

"That's all right. I didn't bring any money with me. Just a glass of water would be good."

"My treat. It's my husband's favorite restaurant."

"Is he a social worker?"

"Obstetrician slash gynecologist."

Her look of distaste made me laugh. Usually when Elliot's specialty came up, new acquaintances would either break into lurid descriptions of *Candida* infections or act like his familiarity with the female reproductive system made him hot.

The cafeteria was crowded. Patients in bathrobes, staff in blue scrubs, and visitors in summer pastels all vied for seats. It was a lot like high school. Certain chairs were clearly saved. Partially occupied long tables dotted with white coats were obviously off-limits to everyone else. A couple of maintenance guys in gray overalls ate their lunches standing over by the conveyer belt for dirty dishes.

I pried apart two sticky trays and led Tonya to the deli section, where I encouraged by way of example. I grabbed Doritos, a turkey sub, and a piece of pie, urging Tonya to do the same. Then I led her toward chairs at the end of a doctors' table and silently dared any of them to challenge me. Tonya looked up and whispered that she had just started to get her appetite back.

"Morning sickness?"

"I lost right close to ten pounds. Funny thing is—I didn't even know I was pregnant. It was my gym teacher who gave me the test. She kept looking at me funny during volleyball and made me stay after class."

"She had a kit in her office?"

"Yeah, in her desk."

"Like next to her whistle?"

Tonya, who had begun constructing little pink structures out of Sweet'N Low packets, laughed, knocking down the building. "Pretty much."

"Have you thought about what you're going to do when the baby comes?"

"Not really. When I went over to Kelvin's to tell him, I guess I thought maybe we could get back together. Or leastways talk about things. Instead he grabbed his jacket and went right past me out the door. I just sat there in his kitchen listening to the stove clock. I had to walk by his father to let myself out."

"That sounds awful. Could Kelvin have just been surprised, maybe?"

"No, ma'am. He's just about ready to go into the army. He doesn't want nothing to do with us. Whatever I do is going to be up to me. If I keep it or give it up."

I transcribed a mental note to investigate the rules governing paternal rights in adoption. "Tell me about your family, Tonya."

"There's my mom, the twins, and my brother. My dad left a couple a years back. After he got laid off and we lost our house. We had to move in with my uncle's family up here."

"How is that?"

"Terrible. Mama started drinking just to drown out my aunt."

"Does your mom work?"

"Yeah, she's a waitress at the Grandy Ann's. She wanted to work at that new one past Short Pump, but she didn't have anyone to carry her out there."

I nodded. Public transportation between Richmond and the whites counties was suspiciously inadequate. There might as well have been a moat.

"Would you like for me to be with you when you talk to her?"

"That's okay, Ms. Trailor. I better do it myself. But I appreciate the offer. And lunch, too." She had a blinding, beautiful smile.

At the end of the day, as I was getting my stuff together, Elliot texted to see if we could grab a coffee.

He was in a back booth, unwrapping a sad cellophane muffin. He looked up and smiled. "How was it?"

"I loved every second of it."

"I'm glad, Marti." He sighed, ran his hand over his hair. He looked fried.

"What's the matter, El? Has something happened?"

"I found Clark passed out. He OD'd on fentanyl."

"Oh, my God! Is he all right?"

"He's being taken to that treatment facility for doctors and nurses in Norfolk." He looked into my eyes. "I never would have pegged him as the type."

"I don't think there is a type, honey."

"You know what I mean. And since I'm in charge of quality improvement for the department, this is going to be my shit storm."

"You're OB-GYN's rep? Since when?"

"Since I signed my contract." He stared, then challenged, "What difference does that make?"

"I don't know, it's just such a big honor! I wish you'd share that kind—"

"Seriously, Marti? You want to discuss that now?"

"I'm sorry." The rebuke burned. Eventually I asked what would happen next.

"Risk Management will be crawling all over us again."

I nodded. A couple years back there'd been another incident involving an impaired resident. Exhausted, that young doctor had gotten two cases confused. After too little sleep and not enough oversight, he'd terminated a planned pregnancy. A confidential settlement with the bereaved parents had done a pretty good job of stifling publicity, but the accident had rocked the department. After he'd transferred to another hospital (and another specialty), the house staff had had to pick up his shifts. Elliot and his colleagues also had to squeeze into their already overpacked schedules the completion of an online patient safety program that provided such laughable suggestions as residents informing their attendings if they needed a nap.

"So now I get to run interference about Clark with the administration. Which will be stressful and time-consuming."

Great.

"Do you have to do it?"

"Of course I have to do it. Nigel chose me. It's part of my job description." He wiped the bottom of his soda can with a napkin, folded it into a neat square, and used it as a coaster. He was perched on the ledge of one of his unreachable silences.

"I'm worried about you," I said quietly.

"Don't be. I'm just tired."

"Can I do anything?"

"Shoot me." He smiled.

Sometimes I wondered who he would have been if he'd become a musician. For a while in college he had actually considered taking that path. On some level I think he would have been happier. A lot happier. The nights when he played blues guitar and harmonica at the bar near campus, when he'd come down offstage between sets, his face would be shining, his shirt soaked through, and he'd be buzzing this uncomplicated, contagious joy. We'd sit together at a little table holding hands, both of us riding the same wave, the only people in a crowded room.

"I should go, El. Pissing off the babysitter on her first day is probably poor form. I told the kids we'd go out for dinner."

"You better take me out of the lineup. Do me a favor, though, and tell Neens I recorded a gymnastics documentary for her last night?" He stood, put his hand in the deep pocket of his white coat. "Oh! This is for you," he said, withdrawing a shiny nameplate. "Note that it says Marti Trailor, *not* Maxwell."

I squeezed his hand. "Thank you, El."

We said good-bye in the lobby, his eyes already charting the path he would take back to work. I joined a huge swell of employees going toward the garage.

CHAPTER THREE

I wasn't even really awake when I stumbled into the front hallway, thinking, Seriously? Before eight? I expected a huddle of pleasant-faced Jehovah's Witnesses offering to share good news; instead two uniformed officers stood on the porch. They were wearing shower caps over their hats.

"Marti Trailor?"

My heart rate increased, echoing the fast fall of the rain on the porch roof. My voice was a whisper. "Yes?"

"We have a warrant here for your arrest. We also have a search warrant to be executed on your property and already exercised one at your office at the hospital."

"What?"

"My name is Detective C. Lee," the taller man said. "Your children are here?"

"What? Yes, of course."

"Do you have someone you can call or should we radio Emergency Foster Care?"

"Foster Care?" I repeated.

That was when the silent scream started.

My hands shook as I looked up my neighbor's number. Carter-Randolph Hayes said she'd be right over. Everything seemed to be happening to someone else. I felt once removed. The best friend of the victim, the cousin of the criminal.

The kids were distraught.

I tried to reassure them that I'd be home soon. Carter called my children into the kitchen before I was taken out.

Lee did that weird thing they do on TV, putting his hand over my head as I got into the car. In the backseat everything came into a dream-state focus: the missing door handles, the cops laughing at the radio dispatcher, the stray debris trapped like specimens between the seat and plastic covering. Three evidence bags bounced on the dashboard like they were enjoying the ride. One held a pill bottle of Xanax so old they'd turned into a fine powder; another contained a vial of newer tranks, a prescription filled right after the accident. Most of the pills were still in it. The third bag had a syringe.

When we pulled up to the police station, Detective Lee whistled. "Looks like someone in the prosecutor's office doesn't like you. They called the press in for your perp walk. Ready for your close-up?" he asked his partner.

I was startled by the stout shape and graying bobbed hair of Natalie Hill. What is she doing here? I wondered. Nothing made sense anymore. But the woman turned and I saw it wasn't Natalie at all but a photographer holding a huge camera with a little weather shelf above the lens. Just as she began to snap my picture, a few more reporters skidded around the side of the building. Ducks to Wonder Bread.

"Why'd you do it, Marti?" a man shouted.

"Will your father be coming down?" another voice bellowed.

I sped up, slipping hard on the slick concrete steps, sending a sharp pain from my knee to my brain. The policeman, not Detective Lee, helped pull me up.

"Watch yourself there," he said. "I wouldn't want a celebrity hurt on my shift."

Within weeks, I could barely remember not working. Sitting across from Larraine Biggs, I was having a hard time remembering why I wanted to work in the first place. Singularly unpleasant, the great slouch of a teenager rebuffed all my attempts to connect.

Experiencing bad feelings toward a client ("countertransference" in therapy-speak) about whom I was supposed to remain nonjudgmental and supportive was definitely not cool. Short of endangerment, I'd been trained to respect her right to her own decisions. Even poor ones. My role was to help clarify the effects of her choices. But Larraine was the total package that made practicing unconditional positive regard hard. Really hard.

"I don't know why you keep on asking me who's going to help," she said, her face getting redder. "I told you like ten times my mother lives next door. Anyways, I decided that I'm just going to try it for a while. I might not even feel like keeping it." She laughed. "If it's anything like my niece, I probably won't. Ever since that kid was born she's done everything she could to get on my last nerve."

"Larraine—you can't test-drive a baby!"

"What?"

"You don't want him to feel like you gave him up because there was something you didn't like about him."

"It's a free country last I checked. Anyways, it might be a girl, you know." She heaved her weight up. "I gotta go. My brother doesn't like sitting out there with all them n-words."

I hoped my eye twitch wasn't noticeable. I walked her out to the waiting room, where the young man was indeed glaring in our direction. "What the hell took you so long?"

"It's not my fault."

"The hell it ain't."

"I'm sorry, Wade."

"Yeah, whatever." She toddled after him. The whole thing was tragic.

I phoned the county hotline and laid out my worries to the intake worker, who withdrew every buzzword she could carry from the profession's phrase bank ("empowerment," "boundaries," and "appropriate treatment planning") while simultaneously offering no assistance.

"I hear your concerns and appreciate your sharing them with us, Ms. Trailor. Especially the piece about surrendering the child. But since you're not making an actual report of abuse or neglect, there isn't anything we can do. We do have guidelines."

Scratch a caseworker, uncover a bureaucrat. "I just want her on your radar. Her participation in our program is voluntary. She could drop out at any moment."

"Mm-hmm," the woman said, blowing me off.

"Thanks so much for your help."

I decided to ask Win for advice. I was halfway down the hallway to his office when I heard his raised voice.

"Goddamn it, Lydia! This just doesn't make any sense. These trips are cutting into alimony now. I don't have that kind of money." He paused. "Well, don't forget how I got here. I can't talk anymore right now. I'm working. I'll see you Friday."

I shifted course and went to the bathroom. Hearing Win so upset made me wonder about the end of his marriage. How did it happen? With slow deterioration or a sudden and terrifying rupture? Once when he was out on a home visit and I had to grab some papers from his desk, I saw a snapshot of him with his wife and daughter. I studied the photo for clues of the impending divide, but the three of them appeared happy. Nothing showed up on X-ray.

I stood in front of the mirror. I looked tired. The fluorescent lights didn't help. I stared past myself and into my marriage, where the Anxieties had grown even more frenzied. They hummed under every sarcastic comment and weary shrug Elliot made, frantically underscoring his discontent. His transition from fellow to faculty had barely made a ripple in our lives. In fact, with the exception of his new salary, things were worse. His exhaustion was veined with chronic disappointment that spilled over into sudden impatience. Our home was carpeted in eggshells. When Batman rummaged through the kitchen garbage and got sick, Elliot withdrew into a silent funk. When I forgot to get the car inspected, he rolled his eyes in disgust. Over the weekend, when he'd discovered a bunch of damp clothes that had been left in the washer, he'd yelled, "Is it really too much to ask that things get taken care of around here?"

Simon had flown into the kitchen, upset. "Why are you so mad at Mom all the time, Daddy? What did she do?"

Elliot had blanched. "I'm not, big guy. I'm sorry. She didn't do anything." He'd scooped our son into a bear hug. "I just didn't get enough sleep. Do me a favor and give her a kiss and tell her it's from the badmean," he'd said, using one of Poppy's words. I'd forced a smile I hadn't felt.

Back in my office, I found Tonya waiting for me. She had a long, deep scratch on the side of her cheek, scabbed over, pink against the brown. "What happened, honey?"

"I finally told my mama about the baby. She threw her hands up and her ring caught me. I'm sorry I didn't tell her before like I said I was going to. I wanted to. I really did. But I couldn't get the words out."

Tonya's sadness radiated like a fever. "You don't have to apologize, sweetie. We'll just take it from here. Does she lose her temper often?"

"No. It was 'cause she was so upset."

"How about with the other kids? Does she hit them?"

"I swear, Ms. Trailor. She's a really good mother, she doesn't beat us. But she had me when she was sixteen and always said she'd knock us to Christmas if we did anything that dumb."

"I guess we have to give her credit for follow-through."

Tonya smiled. "She felt so bad about it that she started crying. And she never cries. But I can't go back there. My aunt said she doesn't need this going on in her house. She might put everyone out."

"Do you have any other family you could live with, Tonya? Anywhere?"

"No, ma'am."

I worked my way through the short list of emergency shelters, eventually starting back at the top and cajoling the social worker at Dan Whitcomb into making space. All the while Tonya sat across from me, a patient passenger trusting the driver to deliver her. As we were leaving, Win yelled for me to text if I was going to be late.

"Yes, Mother," I trilled, making my client smile.

"Hey, hang on a second," he called, stepping out of his office. "Tonya, how old are you?"

"Just turned eighteen."

"Okay, good."

"Sir?"

"Otherwise we'd need your mom to sign a release before we could even give you a ride over to Dan Whitcomb."

Which caused a little *whoosh* of close call to pass over me. I hadn't even thought of that. "I suppose kidnapping isn't on our service menu."

"True, dat," my boss agreed.

The Daniel Whitcomb Home was named for a homeless teenager who'd frozen to death a few years back. First thought to be a pile of discarded clothes, the high school sophomore's body was discovered under a bridge, next to an empty orange juice container and a half-finished paper on the disappearance of honeybees. Agencies and private donors had been galvanized into action. But when we climbed the stairs of the rehabbed house, I saw that the initial influx of interest had waned and the place, once proudly showcased in the media, had again taken on the characteristics of its forlorn neighbors. A soda can held a bouquet of cigarette butts on the top step, and when a yellow hamburger wrapper skittered across the porch I jumped, alert to the very real possibility of being brushed by a rat.

After Tonya's intake interview, we headed up to the girls' room, where a pale blond swung open the door. A jolt of recognition brought a smile to her face. "Tawny! What're you doing here?"

"Amber!" Tonya exclaimed excitedly, turning to me. "We go to the same school."

"How nice," I said guardedly.

Crisis-fed relationships were rampant in this population. A chance morning encounter at a soup kitchen could lead to shared lodgings by nightfall, an explosive breakup a day or two later. These transient arrangements wreaked their own kind of havoc, particularly on the kids who were subjected to constant upheaval and an ever-changing cast of unvetted roommates. During my field placement, I had an adult client named Lola who described her pillar-to-post childhood in such harrowing detail that after the session ended I went into the staff bathroom and threw up.

"How come you're here?" Tonya asked.

"Home away from home." Amber glanced at me quickly.

I took the hint. "Well, I better get moving. Tonya, I'm going to try to meet your mom on my way back to the office."

"Can you tell her not to let the twins play with my dollhouse?"

"I can. I'll check in on you tomorrow, sweetie." I started down the steps.

She called out, "Hey, Ms. Trailor?"

"Yes?"

"Thank you."

The blue-collar area by the university was full of frame row houses once lived in by nineteenth-century ironworkers. Then their descendants. Eventually students discovered the neighborhood, and then developers noticed the mostly white, working-class enclave where river real estate curled up to the sprawling gardens of historic Hollywood Cemetery. I wondered what it felt like to have one's home constantly appraised.

Tonya's brother, Maurice, answered the door of the duplex. Built like a ballplayer, he wore his hair in long dreads that brushed his shoulders. He had the same great smile as his sister and was so soft-spoken I had to lean in to hear.

"Sorry, but my mom's at work."

"Can you give her my card?"

"Sure."

"And sign another one for my files?"

He looked at me as if I were crazy.

"It's kind of a UPS approach to record keeping." I'd learned this during my social work internship. Proof of contact attempts were no joke. "By the way, I promised Tonya I'd ask about her dollhouse."

"Do you think you can take it to her? The twins keep messing with it."

"Sure."

He disappeared into the apartment and came out holding a beautifully crafted miniature house, complete with rag rugs and wallpaper. I bent to examine the home. The nursery had little yellow ducks and the master bedroom had silver and blue stripes. The pantry was full of flour sacks and canned goods.

"This is incredible!"

"My dad made it for Tawny when she was little. She's been adding things to the rooms ever since. For birthdays and Christmas that's all she ever asks for."

I looked closer and saw a laundry hamper and an ironing board, even a toilet brush in the bathroom. The beds had frames and the couch was upholstered. "Wow. I want to move in. You sure it's okay for me to take it?"

"You mean with my mom?"

I nodded.

"She won't care." We started toward the car. "Less things around here to remind her of my dad, the better."

I took a deep breath. "So, I know your mother was really upset with Tonya. Is anything else going on?"

"What do you mean . . . *going on*?"

"Anything that you need any help with?"

"Naw. She was just upset about Tonya being pregnant and all. Plus she ain't a huge fan of Kelvin's. Anyway, we already got a social worker."

"You do?"

"Yeah. Mr. Dugid from Child Protective."

"When did he become involved with you all?"

"Last winter. After Tamara's teacher called the hotline and told them she wasn't dressed right."

"Oh."

"Mr. Dugid's okay. Mama likes him a whole lot."

As Maurice wedged the dollhouse onto the backseat, some of the furniture tipped out. I retrieved a tiny china cabinet, a wardrobe, and an old-fashioned cradle from the floor.

"Hey, where's the baby at?"

"What?" I asked.

"There was a baby in that crib!"

We scoured the weeds bordering the sidewalk and the street beneath the car, but it was gone. Maurice was seriously upset.

"Please tell Tonya I'll find it for her."

I headed back to the hospital, passing through a beautiful old neighborhood full of museums and elegant houses with well-tended gardens. The air held jasmine and magnolia. But it wasn't all rosy. Hanging back between two graceful homes was a low-slung, ocher building: the River City Women's Clinic. Right-to-lifers often heckled patients on the way in and out, an ongoing reenactment of the culture wars. I was stopped at a red light in front of the scrum, watching a teen hurry down the building's walkway. On cue, a man in a "Don't Tread on Me" hat and anti-choice shirt stepped from the group. He held up his phone. "Smile for the camera, little lady! So your friends and family will know where you were today."

Jesus.

When the girl tried to cover her face, she tripped off the curb and landed on her knees, narrowly missing my van. I threw it in park and got out to help. "Are you all right?"

"I think so."

"Too bad that didn't happen on your way in!" the man shouted.

"Yeah," squawked one of his confederates in a "Guns Save Lives" cap. "Might have saved you and your baby both."

"What's wrong with you people?" I demanded.

"I didn't even have an abortion," the teen whispered, taking my hand for help up. "I go there for my endometriosis."

"Smile, honey," the first man commanded again, holding up his phone as the girl hurried past.

"Shame on you," I said, so mad that my hands shook. "Do you honestly think you're helping anyone by being out here?"

"Say cheese!"

"You know what?" I said, glaring at him. "Fuck you."

Then I gave him the finger just in case he didn't hear.

CHAPTER FOUR

It was the unexpected autopsy results that alerted everyone to foul play. Before that, no one had suspected anything. According to the medical examiner, the presence of air in the heart could only reasonably be explained by a criminal act.

It's just been a few weeks since all this started, but already I'm finding it hard to remember happy times. Occasionally, little memories float by like dandelion down and remind me of sweeter days. Other times I'll grab hold of a recollection and find it booby-trapped, rigged with anguish over moments of past mistakes.

Being threatened with the loss of my children is brutal. The regret I feel about things I should or shouldn't have done is brutal, too. I pray that it's my weakened state that's causing me to be so harsh on myself, that's prompting me to remember every harsh word, every bedtime story cut short.

I understand why I'm allowed only supervised visits. My children are anchors. I would have packed us up and headed to Canada. Nothing is worth this separation—not even the financial decimation my parents would suffer if I jumped bail.

The last time I saw Poppy she sat on my lap the whole time, not speaking, just kneading the hem of my sweater with her little fingers as she rested her head against my breast. Nina started off the meeting with an air of breezy toughness that disappeared as soon as she finally agreed to give me a kiss hello. Simon asked me at least a half dozen times when I was coming home.

He's beginning to stammer.

Right before my mother-in-law came to collect them, Nina started to tell me about a confrontation she'd had in the school bathroom. Two older girls followed her in and asked if it was true that her mother was in jail.

"I told them no. Then I tried to leave, but they stood in front of the door so I couldn't open it."

"Then what happened?" I whispered.

"Then Adler, the meanest one, she said her father called you a murderer." Nina stopped speaking as a sob overtook her. I stroked her silky hair until her tears stopped. "Then Sadie went and put soap in her hands and rubbed it all over my face."

"Sweetie," I said, pulling her toward me. "I'm so, so sorry. What did you do then?"

"They let me go and I went to the nurse and told her I didn't feel good."

"Oh, Neens. My kind, sweet girl."

Soon Simon came over to us and we clung to one another until it was time for them to go. I watched them follow Mrs. Trailor out, three little refugees leaving the Department of Social Services' family room.

After they left, I saw that Poppy had worn smooth my sweater.

I leaned against Elliot's long, hard body, inhaling and exhaling with his slower sleep rhythm, aware that I was experiencing one of those rare moments when everything felt just right. I rose slowly to consciousness and thought about the night before. El had come home from work while it was still light and we took the kids to the park, walking behind them as they rode their bikes on the bumpy bricks all the way to Chimborazo Hill, where a Civil War hospital had once operated. We laughed together at how different the children were. Simon, ever vigilant, kept his eyes focused just past the handlebars, alert to anything that might cause him to lose his balance. Nina sat tall, frequently checking on Poppy, who rode behind her big sister while singing to the doll baby nestled in the pink basket of her tricycle.

The children were exhausted by the time we got home and went to bed without protest. El and I sat out on the porch swing and ate a whole quart of cookie dough ice cream straight out of the container. When the spoons scraped the cardboard, he leaned over and tucked my hair behind my ear and told me I looked beautiful. Later, we made love—the first time in weeks. The old and easy sweetness had come back when we climbed under the duvet, and we lost ourselves in the comfort of each other's bodies. A rare calm swam beneath the pleasure, and when it was over, Elliot held me tight. I fell asleep while I studied his beautiful face in the moonlight. I slept, just like I used to, safe in the tangle of his body. So it was no wonder that when I awoke it was with a desire to hold life still, to capture the flawless instant forever.

Right.

"She's up!" Poppy yelped, shocking my senses as violently as if she had doused me with a Slurpee. My eyes flew open and the fuzzy outline of the three children came into focus. They were staring down at me, standing so close to one another that they could have been attached. I was a little surprised by how disturbing they looked from this angle. I searched for something to put on.

"Poppy, hush," Nina reprimanded. "Daddy's sleeping."

"He's always sleeping," Simon remarked.

"Simon, you're revolting!" Nina stage-whispered as she watched her brother flake off a crusty scab from his elbow.

"You know," he responded, "you act like you're so mature, but you're still in your single digits." Then he turned his attention to me as I slipped on a shirt. "Boobs are so weird."

When Simon was five I'd discovered him prepping to perform an exam on Poppy. Like father, like son, I'd thought while escorting him to time-out for not respecting his sister's privacy. (I had also punished Poppy for not wanting any.) My only consolation was that little Charlie Kusik was heading down the deviancy trail first. My innocent-looking godchild had once tried to put his mother's hand down his pants. I gazed longingly at my place in bed. Elliot had already commandeered it.

"But Daddy has to get up vewy soon," Poppy said, sounding an awful lot like Elmer Fudd. "Today's Rides and Park Day!"

Elliot groaned, a signal for the kids to pounce. They crawled all over him. "Not an amusement park!" he said above their giggles. "Marti, say it isn't true!"

"I wish." The best feature of the annual excursion was its use as behavior management. We would threaten to withhold Rides and Park Day in the summer just like we'd remind the children of Santa-the-All-Seeing as soon as sweater weather hit. The second best thing about R&P Day was how brightly my parenting skills shone at the amusement park. Between the women in heavy metal T-shirts who cursed at their toddlers and the smug suburban ones who enunciated the consequences of every choice with exaggerated clarity, my self-esteem soared alongside the roller coaster. Otherwise, though, I pretty much thought of the place as Hell on the Highway.

"Today is going to be the best time yet," Simon announced. "I'm tall enough to ride everything now." His anticipation of the big-kid rides was actually a little surprising since danger was involved. He had basically come out of the womb a nervous intellectual. Simon liked assurances and contingencies. He preferred safety clusters to going anywhere alone. My son and I shared many of the same concerns.

"I was wondering," he said. "In heaven, how do you know where your family is?" Death was a recurrent theme.

"No one is ever lost up there, sweet boy," I said.

Elliot pulled him to his chest. "That's right, buddy. People are automatically reunited with family members. It's a law. Celestial gravity."

"Like magnets?" Simon asked.

"Precisely." Elliot nodded.

"Even the family members you avoid on earth?" I asked.

Elliot shot me a look but laughed. His mother, who ran a tight ship in everything she did, made me tense as hell. The idea that we might be sharing some sort of eternal compound didn't sound so heavenly.

"But," Poppy interjected, catching Simon's anxiety, "I don't want you to leave us alone here! I don't want you to die. Evah!"

With a tilt of my head, I lobbed the question over the net to Elliot.

"Guys, all living things die," he said. "So that's a promise we can't make."

"Will you promise you won't ever get divorced?" Nina asked.

"That we can promise," I said. "Come on, let's get breakfast!"

On the way to the kitchen I glanced into the never-used living room, where fat green velvet couches faced each other and where my favorite object in the whole house hung above the mantel. *Family in Blue* was a cobalt-and-sapphire study of three generations comfortably gathered around a table. The oil painting somehow captured love. I'd lusted after the piece every time I saw it in the window of an expensive Carytown gallery and was beside myself when Elliot surprised me with it. His Gibsons sat on either side of the fireplace beneath the gilt-framed canvas. The guitars, emissaries from a happy past, were gathering dust.

"Are Uncle William and Uncle Mikey coming to Rides and Park?"

"They wouldn't have done the countdown if they weren't coming, Poppy," Nina answered.

"The uncles always come," Simon added. "It's like their job."

It was true. William and Mikey took their duties toward my children very seriously. While the pretense was avuncular, I knew the real reason had more to do with arrested development. Despite being two very successful adults, they had both stopped maturing in their teens. Their very early teens. They were kids trapped in grown-up bodies. Their nieces and nephew were playdates.

My brothers had taken turns pumping everyone up for the trip, calling nightly with their twisted version of an Advent calendar, even conferencing everyone in to discuss rule revisions for Ass-Hat Bingo, R and P version. The scoring for the ten and unders was based on spotting things like high-tops, sibling disputes, and line butting. The adult version included categories of regrettable hairstyles, unfortunate wardrobe selections, hickeys, and most impressive cleavages. William rejected Mikey's entry one year, claiming that the neck-high cleft was caused by a too-tight bra and nothing else.

I followed the kids through the den, a space separated from the formal-ish living room by a pocket door that no longer slid all the way into the wall. Two navy couches draped with cozy cream blankets sat next to mismatched cases in which books lolled without order. *Gray's Anatomy* snuggled *Ramona the Pest,* and the nearly obsolete phone directory had migrated from the top of the refrigerator, passing itself off as literature. Simon's name was carved beneath the bay window (he'd claimed Nina had framed him), and stress-incontinent Batman had left dark stains that floated like lily pads on the old pine floorboards.

The lived-in house was as comfortable as a favorite sweatshirt.

After setting everyone up with cereal and cartoons, I headed back to dress, almost slipping on the community newsletter that had been slid under the front door. I skimmed notes about houses going on the market, a reminder to sign up for the progressive dinner ("This year's theme will be tapas and brews!"), and then a warning that caused my attention to screech to a complete stop. My neighbor, the impeccable Carter-Randolph Hayes, had discovered a rat in her laundry room and wanted to warn the rest of us. I don't know which I was more shocked by: the thing breaching the designer-decorated interior or Carter-Randolph copping to it.

Either way, I absolutely forbade myself from pondering the possibility of one coming in our place. The thought alone could send me into a phobic tizzy.

Elliot was still in bed, wrapped in the sheet like a cocktail hot dog. His pale ankles evoked a surge of pity. He'd barely been out of the hospital all summer. Just as he'd predicted after Clark Bane was whisked off to rehab, the department was understaffed and grumbly.

For weeks and weeks I'd been trying to smooth over as many things as I could in order to lessen his stress. I was self-conscious about my words and for the most part had (heroically) declined what I considered to be an open invitation to fight. I was wearing down, though, growing fatigued dancing around his shifting moods, weary from the work we required. Something had to give.

Sighing, I glanced at the bed to make sure Elliot was still asleep, then I pulled off my shirt. I had a theory that postchildbearing physical decline was an evolutionary response designed to keep women at home. One time I tried to share my hypothesis with Colby, but she said, "Stretch marks? What are these things of which you speak?"

"Come back to bed," Elliot said, reaching over to put his hand on the inside of my thigh, surprising me so much that I almost lost my balance.

"You're up?"

"Indeed I am," he answered with a lascivious grin, lifting the sheet to prove his point.

"Oh, Elliot. You know as soon as I lock the door all three of them will conspire to get in. It's Pavlovian."

He patted the mattress next to his hip. "C'mon. We can be fast."

Maybe a quickie will fuse the connection, I thought. Twice in twelve hours can't hurt. I was locking the door when an argument broke out and angry words carried down the hallway.

"Mom," Poppy cried. "Brian's being a badmean!"

"Just a minute, I'm coming." I smiled at Elliot. "Oh well, we've got to get moving anyway. William and Mikey are probably already there hitting on the ticket takers. You need to get up. Down, then up," I amended.

I entered the dark makeshift closet beneath the wide staircase. Having long suspected that things with tails might be lurking where the ceiling angled sharply to meet the floor, I hated the space. Elliot startled me as I reached for a jade sundress from a pile of clothes I had once intended to iron.

"God, Marti. This is an all-time low."

The walk-in came into focus. His side looked like a catalog, mine as if DEA agents had just left.

"Organizing in here is on my to-do list," I promised, placating.

"Right."

"Whoa, Elliot. What's with the tone?"

He used to get a kick out of my housekeeping challenges. One time in college he laughed so hard at the BLT that was stuck to the bottom of my art history text, he had to put his head down on the library table. I guess the cuteness factor had dimmed over the years.

"I'll work on it tomorrow. I promise. Come on, let's get ready."

"Marti, I don't know if I can go today. I don't know if I have it in me."

"What do you mean?"

"I'm just tired. I'm not up for the crowds. Your brothers. Any of it. . . ."

My brothers? I was speechless. The children would be crushed. Elliot read my expression and said quietly, "Thanks for understanding. I'll get ready."

He reached for his bathrobe and knocked his pants to the floor. His keys and wallet skittered by my feet. I bent down to gather everything up, grateful for a moment to compose myself. A piece of glossy paper had fallen from his billfold. It was a folded boat ad from a San Francisco travel guide.

"What's this?" I asked, confused by the nervous prickles down my spine. He'd gone to a medical conference the month before that was supposed to be so time-consuming that "it would be a waste of money" for me to go along. His words.

"Oh . . ." He squinted at the paper. "A group of us chartered a boat for a couple of hours."

"You did?"

"Yeah. Why? What's the matter?"

"Why didn't you tell me?"

"I didn't realize I needed to provide you with my calendar, Marti."

"What? I just thought you were too busy to do anything there. That's why I didn't go with you!"

"Well, excuse me for having some time off."

"Elliot—it's just—I don't know. Is it so crazy to be interested in what you're doing?"

He sighed. "Here it is. In a nutshell. It rained. We got wet. It was a shitty afternoon. How's that?"

"That's fine, Elliot. Thanks. I'm going to take a shower." And for one searing moment I hated him with every cell in my body.

I stood under the hot water for a long time. But I didn't cry.

I pulled myself together and went to the kitchen, where the kids were getting along again, the room humming with excitement. They were throwing out ideas about what goes on in heaven, theorizing about sleepovers and pony rides and shoe shopping. I rinsed the breakfast bowls.

"Mommy, what will you be doing at heaven?" Poppy asked.

"Probably the dishes."

The kids laughed.

I sat in the passenger seat, my de facto assigned spot whenever Elliot was with us for a car trip. The kids were behind us, playing their version of I Spy, making one another laugh with imaginary items flying past the windows. ("A dinosaur in a poopy diaper!" "A policeman with pimples and chicken pox!") I tried to enjoy the banter, but my eyes kept filling behind the sunglasses. When a rogue tear skied past the rim, I wiped it. Elliot took my hand in his own. "I'm sorry about before."

I pulled away, turned the radio on, and whisper-blurted, "Are you doing drugs?"

"What?"

"I never know which you is going to show up," I said urgently. "Your moods . . . El, they're out of control."

"I'm sorry." He glanced at me. "I really am. It's just so hard to do everything right, you know?"

His admission felt like the beginning of intimacy, and I felt a flutter of hope. "Maybe you need more downtime, El. To just chill."

"Some of the people from the department are thinking about playing golf together on Saturdays. Maybe I should join them."

I made myself smile. I'd meant downtime together.

"And, Mart, I think we ought to consider getting a housekeeper. We've got the money now. It would lighten your load." He was so quick with the suggestion, I wondered if the whole transaction had been preplanned.

I spent the morning holding sweaters and sticky cups and places in line. I waved as Mikey and Poppy went round and round on the miniature train. I cheered Simon on his first roller coaster and was comforted just by being in the presence of my brothers. They teased me mercilessly and loved me boundlessly. By lunchtime I was feeling better. On our way to the pizzeria, William walked with his arm around me, while Michael, who had just begun his fourth year in medical school, talked shop with Elliot. Within moments the two sets of adults separated and the kids were doing laps between us.

Will hugged me and pushed the hair out of my face, catching long strands in the joint of the sunglasses.

"Ouch!"

"That's for when you told Mom I was the one who broke the VCR."

"You *were* the one who broke the VCR."

"Beside the point. Don't forget how I defended you when that kid called you pubic-head."

"How could I forget? You bring it up every time I see you."

He laughed. "You doing okay, Martyr? You seem a tad taut."

"How's Dad?" I deflected. "Have you seen him lately?"

He lifted an eyebrow. "Yeah. He's crazy busy. I think he's heading to Pakistan soon. You know, Farti," he said, "you ought to consider accompanying him on one of his fact-finding tours to the Middle East."

"You want me to go to a war zone?"

"Okay, maybe not there. But somewhere. It'd be good for you."

"Maybe when the kids are older. I don't know how I could ever arrange that right now."

"What about Elliot? Couldn't he handle things for a week?" Will stopped walking and said in a serious voice, "Didn't he just come back from a big trip?"

"He was at a required meeting. Anyway, becoming an attending hasn't made a real big difference in his schedule. There's no way he could take any time off now to hold down the fort. Nothing's changed like I thought it was going to. Not yet, anyway." I faked a smile and changed subjects. "How's Mom?"

"Carolyn is doing amazingly well. She loves the new place."

"She said she set her studio up on the balcony overlooking the zoo."

"Yeah. It's pretty great. Must be weird for Dad, though. He really can't go home again."

"Just be patient." I laughed. My big brother had been waiting since childhood for our parents to reconcile.

"Hey, check this out—I was at one of the senior partners' for dinner and saw Mom had painted his two daughters. The portrait was hanging in the dining room in this big, fancy gold frame. I swear to God at first I wasn't going to lay any claim to it because both of the girls looked ugly as sin. Then they came down to say good night and I saw she'd actually cleaned them up."

I laughed. It had taken years for our mother to recover from the divorce. She'd been bereft—and angry—for a long time. The fact that she'd found success as an artist had been a gift she called her third-act surprise.

Will and I walked in silence. Squeals and shrieks came from a huge boat rocking faster and faster to turn upside down; the shouts grew louder the higher and higher it swayed and peaked when it finally swung over. I imagined bodies being tossed from their seats.

"Tell me about your job, Martyr. What kinds of cases are you getting?"

"They run the gamut from really basic—like helping women get the baby equipment they need—"

"Cribs and car seats?"

"Yeah. And diapers."

"Seriously?"

"They're stupid expensive. Someone even did a study linking maternal depression and child abuse to diaper rash."

"What?"

"Sitting in pee all day burns. Which causes nonstop crying. Which adds to family stress."

"Jesus."

"Poverty sucks. It affects everything. I have clients with more complicated problems, too. Last month I helped a developmentally disabled woman make the decision to surrender her baby."

"How?"

"Depends on who you ask. Maybe 'guided' is a better word. At first the mom wanted to keep it, but she's like a child herself. She can dress and use the bathroom on her own, but otherwise needs constant supervision."

"Does she live with her family?"

"No. A group home with six other developmentally disabled adults. Which I didn't think would be a great environment. One of the guys pounds the walls all day. It's a high-stress place. I struggled with it, though."

"Man."

"Yeah. In a perfect world there'd be enough programs out there that could offer all the accommodations and support the little family would ever need."

"Like what?"

"An apartment for the two of them. A full-time, permanent caretaker. Who grocery shops and does laundry. Homework too. Someone to be like a foster parent to both of them. The young woman can't really bathe herself. How can she be a safe mom? Get the child to the pediatrician for shots and earaches? She kept saying that she'd love her baby. It was really sad, Will. I had to explain that love is only the beginning. And then, after she started to understand, the caseworker at the home tried to get her to change her mind back. She even called Win—"

"Who?"

"My boss. To complain about me."

"What happened?"

"He backed me up. We haven't heard from them since."

We turned the corner and found the kids orbiting Mikey and Elliot in impatient circles. The guys were laughing with two very attractive young women, one teeny, cute, and bubbly; the other cool and beautiful in Lilly Pulitzer pink. Both of them were holding hands with a boy around Poppy's age.

"Will, Marti! Come meet some of my colleagues," Elliot said. He gestured to the small one. "Claudia's a rock-star delivery room nurse. This is her cousin Catherine, who is a member of our house staff. The big guy is her next-door neighbor."

I realized that Colby had pointed out the elegant resident before. We were grocery shopping together and the tall beauty whisked past us down the aisle, somehow making the basket over her arm look like a fashion accessory. Colby said John called her "Dr. Barbie" and was unimpressed by her style. He'd paged her to a C-section once and she'd been so slow in answering, he'd had to call for backup. Catherine compounded the original sin by bringing in suck-up cupcakes the next day. John, despite being a lover of all things caloric, had resolutely declined the baked apology and suggested she just be more responsive to her pager in the future.

"Hi," I said to the little group.

William, in hormonal overdrive, introduced himself.

Claudia bent to address Poppy, offering serious cleavage in the process. Both brothers took quick peeks. "Don't you just love the water rides?" she asked. "We brought Brock so we'd have an excuse to come."

"If Brock's ever busy, you're welcome to bring ours," I offered. My one-liner, which easily could have been a preamble to an entire repertoire about amusement parks, was cut short when I glanced at Elliot. His face had darkened. The nurse smiled compassionately.

The Anxieties shot to attention.

"Mom," Simon said, "I feel like we've been very patient. I'm starving."

I allowed myself to be led toward the eating area, where I ordered two large pizzas and pushed together two round tables. The rest of the family joined us just as the food was brought out. Michael was pumping Elliot for information about Catherine. "You're sure she's involved with someone?"

"Sorry, pal. I think they both are. Last I heard, Catherine was about to get engaged. Anyway—that'd be a hell of a commute, wouldn't it? Think globally, act locally." Elliot patted him on the shoulder. "So have you decided on a specialty yet?"

"Not yet."

"Well, I'd give OB a pass," Elliot offered, surprising everyone.

"I thought you really loved it," Mikey said.

"I used to, but thanks to people like William Maxwell, Esquire, here, I'm beginning to understand why some of my buddies are giving up obstetrics and just doing gynecology. Much fewer headaches."

"Gynecology without obstetrics is an appalling idea," I said. "The field's barely above suspicion when the delivery of babies is involved." My brothers laughed. My husband didn't.

"We don't just practice medicine," El went on. "We play twenty questions with invisible lawyers."

"What do you mean?" Mikey asked.

Elliot changed his voice and opened his eyes wide to imitate confounded doctors. "If I do this test, will I get sued? If I don't do the test, will I be sued? Factor in the malpractice premiums and the bad baby fund and our specialty pays out the wazoo."

"The bad what?" I asked.

William answered. "It was set up back when insurance companies were threatening to drop OBs. They were really getting slammed in court since they had twice the patients in the operating room."

"The mother and the baby," Mikey offered.

"Correct, grasshopper," William said. "Which translates to twice the number of patients obstetricians could be sued over. So the legislature came up with the Catastrophic Birth Program. Aka the 'bad baby fund.' Basically it's a no-fault trust for infants injured during birth. Doctors and hospitals pay into it as sort of an insurance against being sued for the cost of care. Neurological traumas are incredibly expensive. And endless."

"The fund covers the care?" I asked.

William nodded. "Yeah. But last I heard, there were issues. Some kids got covered, others didn't. One of the administrators embezzled like a million bucks. So no-fault or not, being associated with it isn't exactly a crowning professional achievement."

"Wait," I said. "Somebody stole from disabled children?"

"People forget that sometimes bad things just happen," Elliot said to William, ignoring my interruption. "Not everything can be laid at doctors' feet."

"Oh, c'mon, El," William interjected hotly. "Thousands of patients die every year because of medical fuckups. Things that are just chalked up to complications. Despite good intentions there are honest mistakes. And systemic ones. And just gross incompetence. Jesus, you can't even get hospital workers to wash their hands consistently."

"Easy, brother," Elliot said slowly, dangerously.

"Are you k-kidding?" Mikey laughed nervously. "He's just getting started."

"Seriously," Will said. "My firm's handling a malpractice case right now against a surgeon who screwed up dozens of procedures. Everyone knew. It was this whole silent conspiracy thing. No one was talking. The guy took out the wrong ovary. Left a sponge in someone else."

"That's like the quality improvement committee Elliot's on," I said. "Whenever something bad happens the risk management people hold meetings where they discuss it. But it always starts off with them reading a statement of confidentiality. Right, El?" He didn't say anything, so I continued. "That way the doctors talk without being afraid what they say will end up being used against them in a malpractice case. It's undiscoverable. Is that the right word? What I don't understand, though, is how that's even legal.

I mean it's not like these are priests in confessionals. They're doc—"

"The point is to make sure that the errors aren't repeated, Marti. To improve future outcomes," Elliot said quietly. "And frankly, I really don't feel like talking about this right now. On my day off."

My face felt singed.

William interjected, "R and P bingo!"

"Sorry," I apologized to Elliot, but he didn't say anything.

Simon stood. "Mom! I have to go to the bathroom. Immediately. I think I ate too much."

"Me too," Poppy announced, jumping up from her chair.

"I'll take them." Elliot stood. "Come on, Neens. You can go in with your sister. I might even be convinced to spring for a souvenir." The girls ran to their father, each grabbing a hand. Simon led the pack.

"What's up with El-Elliot? He seems really out of s-sorts." Mikey's words were coming out especially slow and deliberate, which meant that he was deeply upset.

"I don't know, Michael. It's been a long haul. He's burnt out. You know what it's like."

Don't you?

My brothers were unnaturally quiet. Their concern reverberated over the noisy crowd. I turned away, craving a cigarette. Of course, smoking wasn't allowed in the park. Also, everyone (with the exception of Colby and Win) thought I'd quit in college.

We stayed for the closing fireworks, but really, we were just going through the motions, a studio audience oohing and ahhing on command. By the time the finale shot patriotically into the air, I was hit with the bleak realization that we'd just had our last Rides and Park Day.

With Poppy nearly asleep in his arms, Elliot could barely mask his annoyance when the keys he'd given to me for safekeeping had seemingly disappeared inside my purse. My fingers groped the jumbled interior, getting more and more frantic as they repeatedly withdrew my own key ring, a dog bone, old pill containers, and my cell phone.

"Perfect," Elliot muttered.

I could have cried when his fob finally worked its way to the surface. Elliot didn't say anything, just held out his hand.

The sight of his outstretched fingers pulled out an old memory. We were in the bathroom bathing two-year-old Nina, together. She was playing with a washcloth, singing one of her half-confession/half-narco-corrido ditties. "Today I didn't wet my pants except on purpose when I was mad because Mommy said I had to take a nap," she warbled. "And I didn't waaaant to!"

El and I had bumped heads when we both ducked so she wouldn't see us crack up, making us laugh even harder. When we got it together, he took hold of my hand to help me stand.

That was then.

CHAPTER FIVE

At the Starbucks over in the West End, I sat near three women in tennis whites who were drinking skinny lattes, talking about Chappell Wycliff. They called the prosecutor by his nickname and speculated that Chap would "run statewide." (Which for them would mean a short election cycle or two before they'd be eating barbecue at the Governor's Mansion.)

Wycliff's route to prosecutor was very Richmond. Anointed behind the scenes by the old-boy network of city puppet masters, he'd recently been tapped to take over for the disgraced A. F. Conte. The hard-partying, outspoken former prosecutor had become an embarrassment to the municipal leaders. They were especially pissed about remarks he'd made about their pet project, RiverCity Rebirth. Conte had questioned some of the group's bulldozing ways and said the Rebirthers' motto, "A rising tide lifts all boats," should also mention that the wakes of their own yachts posed drowning hazards for people downstream. He went on to question how many of the city power brokers belonged to that country club, with "damn few minorities."

When he was subsequently surrounded on a deserted road for a broken taillight and a small packet of weed, there wasn't a lot of shock. Chappell Wycliff, undaunted by all the controversy surrounding his rise, had humbly accepted the role of prosecutor to "restore normalcy and the rule of law" in Richmond.

My stomach clutched when I heard my name. I listened to the women's appraisal in a kind of fascinated horror. A thin brunette told her companions how I never really fit in, how at the kids' school Simon's first-grade room mother made a point of including me, asking if I'd come and describe one of those Jewish holidays to the class. And that I said no. (Which was true—but only because I could never remember the particulars.) She then mentioned how someone else had overheard me mocking cotillion dances. (Also accurate.)

Just like I'm sure my father's liberal politics will make an appearance in the case, I assume the prosecutor will use my link to the city's ruling class against me. Depending on who's on the jury, I assume Wycliff will try to garner points for prosecuting a rich white doctor's wife. The truth, of course, is that it would be a cold day in hell before he indicted someone whose husband he golfed with. I used to secretly see myself as an ambassador between groups, crossing the divide. If I wasn't exactly graceful, at least I was trying.

But now I see I was less emissary than party crasher.

The drone of the overworked air conditioner was irritatingly loud. The dog days of the waning summer had set in with a vengeance, and the ancient window unit, severely disadvantaged by the heat wave, was barely functioning. I swiveled the chair around and rested my face on the cool glass. Then I made some calls.

"Andy Dugid here! What can I do for you?"

I was so startled by the deep baritone that the receiver fell from its cradle between my shoulder and ear, landing hard on my knee.

"Ouch! Sorry!" I giggled nervously. "Mr. Dugid—my name is

Marti Trailor. I'm a caseworker at the New Moms program. I've been working with Tonya Maines and I was wondering if I could just ask you a few questions?"

"I was just now combing my way through all my messages and saw yours. I was on vacation for a good little while and have been trying to triage. Anyway, let me just take a look at her mother's file to be sure she signed the confidentiality release forms. Is Tonya of age?"

"Yes."

"Okay. Hang on. This won't take but a New York minute." He came back to the phone. "We're set. Fire away."

"I haven't had any luck reaching Mrs. Maines. I was wondering if there was anything I should be aware of."

"Let me think for a minute."

Mr. Dugid sipped a drink. This was followed by a muffled sound that could only have been a burp. "Excuse me, Ms. Trailor. I had a chili dog for dinner and it's been coming back to haunt me ever since. Anyway, I've been checking in with Shirley for about eighteen months or so. I was assigned the case after one'a the twin's teachers called to complain about inappropriate winter attire." He leaned hard on the last phrase.

"You didn't think she was right?"

"I opened the case since it was borderline, but we're talking purely minor league. Shoot, Little League."

"What was the report?"

"The girl showed up to school without a coat a few times. Now, you want to hear about neglect—you shoulda been with me yesterday." I braced myself for the details. "I went with the cops into this place just filled up with syringes and trash and whatnot. There was rotten food all over the floor, and shoved up against the wall was a playpen with two babies in it. They weren't even crying. They weren't expecting anybody to pick them up."

"God."

"So that kinda puts things in perspective. Shirley's younger girls get bused over to one of the wealthier schools, so when the complaint came in I actually was wondering if the teacher meant wrong label." I laughed. "Anyway, Shirley wasn't paying as much attention as she mighta been, but she's a good egg. She and her kids have been staying with her brother and sister-in-law, who is a serious piece of work."

"Yeah, Tonya didn't make her sound like anyone I'd want to hang out with. If Mrs. Maines doesn't concern you, why have you kept the case open this long?"

"Actually, I closed it a long time ago. But I helped her find a nutritionist for the twins. They're both overweight and flirting with diabetes. Shirley and I also worked on a budget so they can eventually get out of her brother's place. Helped get some clothing vouchers. Things like that."

"A one-man wraparound agency."

"I wouldn't go that far. But I stop by the restaurant where she works to check in with her. I'm sure my elastic boundaries would be frowned on by more professional social workers. But she appreciates my interest and it doesn't cost me more than a few minutes a month. Is Tonya keeping the baby?"

"Yeah."

"Well, she ought to think long and hard about bringing it back over to her aunt and uncle's place. Look, Ms. . . . ?"

"Marti."

"Marti. Shirley Maines has been dealt a rough hand. But she loves those kids and would do anything for them. She called me up downright hysterical when she cut Tonya with that eyesore ring of hers."

"This has been so helpful. Now if I could only figure out how to get in touch with her."

"Well, I go down and meet with her at the restaurant. I'm sure she wouldn't mind if you drop by. Matter of fact, I'll give her a call and let her know to expect you. It's pretty slow in there right before the dinner rush."

"Could you set it up for today?"

"Sure."

"It's very nice of you to make the extra effort for your clients, Mr. Dugid."

"You ought to treat yourself to a number four."

"Sorry?"

"A strawberry waffle. Changes your view on the world. Order the whipped cream on the side. You get more that way. Let me know if I can be of any help later on. Where are you from, by the way, you sound like a lost Yankee."

"D.C. But my dad's from New York. I think the accent's in the genes. You ought to hear my youngest." He laughed. "Hey, could I ask your advice about something else?"

"Go right ahead."

"Another one of my clients just had a baby. She's said a couple of things that made my hair stand on end."

"Like what?"

"Like she mentioned her niece and said that even as a baby the girl had purposely gotten on her nerves. And in the inappropriate attire department, I was out there this morning and she had the infant dressed in a sweater suit even though it was so hot in her trailer I almost passed out. When I suggested she change him, she told me she knew if he was hot or not. Plus her attention span when feeding him was practically sadistic."

"Nothing like being in on the ground floor of upcoming attachment issues."

"Seriously."

"Well, I'd be real happy to take a referral."

"Actually, that's part of the problem. She lives out in the county."

The silence that followed contained the whole history of turf wars between the municipalities. "You're not satisfied with the intervention she's been getting?"

"Well, it's just that their approach is fairly . . . passive."

"Passive. That's diplomatic. You know, when the ink on my degree was still wet, Social Services used to go in like gangbusters and remove kids at the drop of a dime. Often, just for being poor. Now, the pendulum has swung so far the other way, it feels like we have to cool our heels until Junior actually gets his head fractured before we can do anything. At my last job, we'd mark cases 'JW.' For 'just waiting.' 'Course that didn't make it any easier."

That peculiar social worker noise, a blend of bewilderment and frustration, escaped my lips.

"You're singing the song of my people, Marti. We are a tired, overworked lot. What other services is this girl getting?"

"That would be JM."

"Pardon?"

"Just me. I better let you go. Thanks for everything, Mr. Dugid."

"Andy."

"Andy."

I leaned back in my chair and thought about my home visit with Larraine. I'd pounded on her door for a good five minutes while the baby screamed above the TV inside and frenzied pit bulls lunged from behind the jury-rigged patchwork of chain link, wire coat hangers, and leather belts. The stench made my eyes water. Finally, after I yelled that I was going to call the police to make sure everything was all right, Larraine grudgingly admitted me. The infant was draped over her arm, overdressed in a scratchy blue wool outfit, his baby face blotchy. I asked to hold him.

"You can take him while I go to the bathroom."

While she moved sluggishly down the short hallway, I stripped Harley, straightening his little arms to pull off the sleeves, leaning him forward to peel the material up over his lolling head, yanking the pants off. I chattered nervously to cover his whimpers, praying all the while that the bulky sweater suit was not hiding bruises or burns. A little cry of relief escaped my lips when I saw smooth skin.

"What do you think you're doing?" Larraine demanded, surprising me by her stealthy return.

"I thought he needed a new diaper," I lied. "But Larraine, it's too hot in here for these clothes. He'll get overheated, sick. You're just wearing shorts today. That's all he needs."

"I know how to dress my own kid." She grabbed the baby and plopped onto the couch. A dirty diaper folded into a softball bounced from the tight cushion. "So what do you want?"

"Nothing. It's just your basic run-of-the-mill visit to check on you all."

"I'm kind of busy, you know?" she said, retrieving a bottle from the floor. She held it to the baby's mouth in the same way Poppy fed her dolls: in spurts of attentiveness. Larraine was oblivious to his cries of frustration. I tried to show her how to hold his head up in the crook of her elbow, but she jerked away. "I know what I'm doing," she said.

I had to suppress the impulse to snatch the baby and race toward the car. "Larraine, I'm worried about you and Harley. I know how hard it is to be a new mom. How scary, sometimes. Even keeping up the house can be difficult."

"I'm not trying to be Martha Stewart."

"I'd be happy to help clean."

She shrugged. "I guess you could do the dishes."

"If you've got a big pot, I can sterilize the baby's bottles."

"In the cupboard," she said, reaching for the TV remote.

I went into the galley kitchen and started working, throwing little child-rearing snippets over my shoulder. "I know it doesn't seem possible now, but Harley's going to be crawling before you know it and you're going to need to childproof. I can bring out covers for the electrical sockets next time."

"Uh-huh."

I moved onto diaper rash and immunizations, while emptying the sink and wiping down the counters. Then I arranged the clean nipples and bottles on a paper towel. Feeling pretty good about things, I brought up her taking a parenting class. "It's so important to know what to expect," I said, drying my hands on my pants and walking into the other room. "I knew one mom who said there was something wrong with her one-year-old daughter because she wasn't getting potty trained. The mom just didn't know that a year's too young. But she attended this great program and—"

"Maybe that kid was hardheaded." Larraine glared. "I'm not trying to throw you out, but I got stuff to do."

"Can I come back out next week?"

"I'm probably going to be busy."

"I can help clean again?"

"That's okay," she said. "I'm good."

Basically, the morning had been an epic fail.

A knock on my office door brought me out of my mood. It was Tonya, who'd arrived for her OB appointment. The expression on her face made me laugh. "Oh, c'mon. It's not that bad. It could be worse."

"Nothing could be worse," Tonya grumbled.

"Sure it could—you could be seeing a dentist."

She smiled.

We walked out of the office and through the waiting room, where one of Win's clients was coloring in her little girl's coloring book. The child was looking on. I tried to figure out if it was a joint activity but couldn't tell.

The appointment was for eleven, which meant that we needed to sign in at a quarter of and then wait a good hour before being seen. As usual, I was dumbfounded by the sheer rudeness with which clinic patients were treated. Although one was white and the other black, the two receptionists were virtually indistinguishable. Both were named Christine. Both were equally masterful at using silence as a weapon. And as far as I could tell, the Christines' most notable administrative skill was a shared ability to process insurance information without ever shifting their gaze from the television set perched high in the reception area. But the attendings and residents loved the impenetrable barriers the gatekeepers erected and expressed appreciation with banal hugs, cursory queries about their private lives, and big boxes of chocolate on Secretary's Day.

"What's going on at Dan Whitcomb?" I asked Tonya, peeling the skirt off my sweaty leg.

"One of the house parents is getting ready to leave."

"New job?" Staff turnover at group homes often kept pace with that of the residents.

"I guess. She's getting married, though, moving up to Maryland. Amber and me got to go to her shower. It was over near Maymont Park at her friend's place. I've never been that way before. It's so pretty. I never knew there was a petting zoo in Richmond."

"It is a beautiful part of town." I shifted uncomfortably in my seat. The exposed skin on the back of my thigh had stuck to the pleather cushion.

"Where do you live at?"

"Church Hill."

"I love all those little shops and bakeries up there."

"I love them, too, but not the disruption they cause when they're being put in. Every time I see another permit taped to an old store-front, my blood pressure spikes."

"How come?"

"Well, for starters, whenever the construction workers pull up, rat colonies start scouting for new digs. Flips me out."

"Oooh, I hate those nasty things, too. Do you know they can swim up toilets?"

I clutched my chest.

Tonya laughed, then got serious again. "Anyway, that wedding shower made me sad. I mean I was happy for her. But sad about how I messed everything up. I always wanted bridesmaids and everything."

"Look, honey. Rituals are nice—but they don't guarantee anything. Life happens. We're in control of some things and not in control of others. And sometimes it's all about what comes after wrong turns. You can freak out because you missed your exit. Or you can enjoy the side trip. Having a baby doesn't mean your life is over. You get to write your own story." Which I knew wasn't completely accurate since poverty was a story all its own. But I said it anyway. And hoped really hard.

"What was your wedding like?"

I paused.

On my very first day in grad school, Dr. Light gave a lecture entitled "Social Work Is Not a Popularity Contest." He talked about the necessity of respecting institutional, professional, and interpersonal borders and the dangers of transgressing boundaries. When he was finished, I (stupidly) raised my hand and said I was having a problem understanding how to project empathy while keeping distance.

"There's one every year," he said condescendingly. "People who don't check their baggage before joining this field—shouldn't be in this field. There are clear injunctions against a clinician's self-disclosure. For good reason. Clients are not here for you to work out your own issues."

Which not only didn't answer my question, but scared the shit out of me.

Fortunately, my field placement adviser had softened both the injunction and the trauma by saying her own rule of thumb was to ask herself who was benefiting from making allowances.

"In real life, the proper distance between clinician and client is variable," she'd said during one of our weekly supervisions. "You're not going to have the same relationship with a violent sex offender as you do with an abandoned child. Providing comfort to that kid is very different than blurring the lines with the rapist. The important thing is to always practice mindfulness about whose needs are being met." Then, even though we were in her office with the door closed, she lowered her voice and told me the professor's nickname was Dr. Lighten Up. Which made me feel much better.

I made a quick calculation before turning to Tonya.

"It was in the backyard of the house I grew up in. My husband and his old band played music until breakfast." Elliot had even written a rollicking song about his proposal called "Streaks of Promise," commemorating the ask. He'd scripted "Marry me" in shaving lotion on the mirror, with an arrow pointing to the diamond ring in the soap dish. Only I'd overslept and the letters had run into the sink by the time I made it into the bathroom.

"Did you go on a honeymoon?"

"Yeah. We went to Amsterdam."

"Was it fun?"

"It really was."

We'd walked for miles, biked around canals, hit museums. We'd shared massive cones of fries that we'd dipped in mayo. We'd climbed into bed early and hadn't gotten up until late. I must have thought a thousand times that week: I married my best friend. . . . I married my best friend.

White Christine stood, emitted a long, wheezy sigh, and walked past us. Her arms rotated forward so that the fronts of her hands showed from behind. The other Christine called Tonya's name, repeating it twice in a low, resentful voice, as if she were paying by the word.

"Room five. Don't forget to give a urine," she snapped, buzzing us in.

Tonya ducked into the distinctly low-budget bathroom with its mysterious four-inch gap at the bottom of the door. She emerged a few moments later with a brown paper towel around a plastic container. I thought about my own gynecologist's office. It had a marble-floored restroom, soundproof stalls, makeup mirrors, and a revolving medicine cabinet that unobtrusively accepted samples.

We had just rounded the corner when a familiar laugh rang out from the other end of the hall. It was Elliot. He and the nurse from the amusement park were talking with an extremely pregnant woman in a wheelchair. El laid his hand on her shoulder, said he'd be by to check on her. I loved that he wasn't afflicted with patient-triggered attention deficit.

The nurse—

Caroline? Kelly?

—glanced up and waved.

Elliot walked over. "I didn't expect you over here today."

"I'm with a client." I gestured in the direction Tonya had gone. "Hey, want to have lunch?"

"When?"

"After this? Anytime between twelve and two. Depending on when the doctor-of-the-month shows up." I smiled.

He didn't.

"What's wrong?"

"Nothing. I was just waiting for a riff on uncaring clinic doctors."

"I didn't say they were *uncaring*, El. Jesus. I said they were late. Overworked."

"I'll try for lunch. I can't promise anything, though."

His Vocera went off, calling him to the nurses' station. I felt like crying, but I put on my social worker face and went into Tonya's exam room. She'd folded her jumper, shoes, and underpants in a neat stack on the windowsill so that I could sit in the chair. She'd set her urine specimen on the desk and put on a gown decorated with pink and blue kittens. I told her about my conversation with

Mr. Dugid and that I was planning on meeting her mother. She seemed pleased.

"Ms. Trailor, I'm going to need to find a place for after Dan Whitcomb. I can't go back to my aunt and uncle's. It wouldn't be right to anybody to bring a baby in there." She smiled. "Especially to the baby. My aunt is a freak the way she cleans all the time."

"Okay. We'll put that on our to-do list."

The appointment went smoothly. Richard Wood (the resident known as Dick Splinter) steered the Doppler across Tonya's belly. The baby's heart sounded like a bouncing tennis ball.

The three of us smiled.

"Could you be my doctor when it's my time?" she asked.

"It's more luck of the draw than that, I'm afraid," Richard said apologetically. "I might not even get a chance to see you in clinic again."

"Oh."

At the receptionist's desk, I shook my head and waited for one of the women to look up. When neither did, I realized then it was a dual power play. Them over us. Them between each other. White Christine lost. Sighing, she thrust out her arm for Tonya's clinic card. She ran it through the computer, made an appointment for the following month, slammed the piece of plastic back onto the counter.

"My mother would call them two bookends," Tonya said in the hallway.

"Yeah, they're a pair all right." I placed my hand on the hard swell beneath her maternity shirt and said, "I'm going to say good-bye to you two, here. I've got to go to the bathroom. I'm meeting my husband for lunch and I don't want to spend the whole time waiting in line to use the one down there."

She smiled at me. "Ms. Trailor, I'm so blessed to have you in my life."

A smile started somewhere in my chest. "Wow, other than your baby's heartbeat that's the nicest thing I've heard in a long, long time. Thank you, sweetie." I did a quick social work calculation and decided that in the professional scheme of things, being liked was better than the alternative.

Richard Wood and Dr. Barbie were walking down the hall when I left the bathroom. He was speaking in an insistent tone. "Seriously, Catherine. You do not want to be that resident."

"I get it, Rich," she said defensively.

I was dying to know what she did or didn't do, but they disappeared around the corner and took the story with them.

Along with greens and carrots, I mounded fruit and raisins and cottage cheese and sunflower seeds and watermelon in the Styrofoam container. I squeezed on extra ranch. When the register broadcast the weight in green neon, I felt my face get hot. I carried my pound of food to find Elliot. He was at the end of a long, crowded table, the perky Rides and Park nurse across from him. She helped herself to a chip from his plate.

"I'm Claudia." Her smile was white, white, white. "We met at the amusement park?"

"Right. Nice to see you again."

Just not in my seat. Or eating off my husband's dish.

The intimacy of the act flipped me out. I hated to admit it, even to myself, but jealousy was a founding member of the Anxieties. Ever since Elliot's earliest days as a med student, I'd been freaked out by the accelerated speed of simple flirtations maturing into full-blown hospital affairs. The long hours, shared rushes, and coed sleeping arrangements seemed to create the perfect conditions for hooking up.

"Hey," I said, stopping by Elliot. He shrugged slightly and opened his eyes wide in a look that meant *What could I have done? She just sat down.*

"I'm going to grab that chair." I nodded toward the other end of the table where I saw someone getting ready to leave, all the while hoping that I was approximating the attitude of Mature Professional Who Happens to Work in the Same Building as Her Spouse. I sat next to John Kusik, who unfortunately was sitting with Nigel Hill. I said hello, dug into my salad, and eavesdropped on the two young residents behind us. They were talking about the rule limiting the weekly hours house staff could work.

"Well," one said, "eighty is a nice round number."

"Yeah," the other replied. "And it's easy to remember since it's twice what other people work."

They laughed.

"But I'm grateful for those extra hours since we can learn so much when we're practically brain-dead."

That really cracked them up. They were seriously overtired. I smiled, then happened to glance at Nigel. A stain of anger was spreading across his face. The metal legs of his chair scraped the floor as he intruded into the women's conversation. He cleared his throat, resulting in a profusion of silence.

"House staff who cannot perform their duties while on call should be reported to their residency director. Which specialty are you in?"

"Neuro, sir," one answered.

"I see. And as for the purpose of twenty-four-hour shifts, Miss"— and here he paused to read her ID badge, allowing the fact to register that he did not call her Doctor—"Dancy, is to provide continuity of patient care."

Continuity of care!

Nigel continued browbeating the residents, providing an impromptu lecture about the training benefits of round-the-clock call. The young women remained silent. One of them looked as if she were about to pass out.

The mother in me woke up.

"Dr. Hill, don't you think it's the same thing as not allowing pilots to work on too little sleep?"

Nigel turned back to face me. "Pardon?"

"I mean, there are laws against pilots flying for more than something like nine hours in a row. For safety." My voice was semicalm, but my foot was racing back and forth between the chair legs like a chained dog.

"Hardly analogous, my dear. We are a training institution." He punctuated his words with a tight smile, quick and violent as a slammed door, dismissing me.

Fuck you, you pompous asshole. Fuck you, you short, pompous asshole.

I inhaled deeply. "It's funny that you're talking about continuity of care, because I was actually going to ask if there's any way my clients could see the same doctor—for at least some of their prenatal visits? I think it would mean a lot to them. Especially the really young ones."

Nigel stared at me. Hard. I forced myself to adopt what I hoped was a look of serenity.

"I don't think that would work in this hospital, Mrs. Trailor."

"Oh. Well, I guess I'm just unclear about what continuity of care means."

"Perhaps we should discuss definitions—as well as the merits of my teaching program—in a more appropriate setting?" Nigel asked rhetorically. He got ready to leave. "I'm sure Christine would be happy to set up an appointment for you."

"I'd enjoy that."

There was a mass exodus, and I watched Nigel stride out, followed by a group of interns and residents, bobbing like ducklings. The two young women he'd verbally assaulted looked like extras in a zombie movie. I kept eating, and eventually Elliot carried his coffee and came to sit with me. The two of us were alone at the foot of a long row of tables littered with detritus.

"Sorry about Claudia. She just sat down. I would have felt awkward asking her to move."

"That's all right. But she should have offered, don't you think?"

He shrugged, moving on. While I could dissect an exchange for hours, Elliot had no such tendencies. Subtext did not interest him. "What were you and Nigel talking about?"

"We sort of got into it," I admitted, pretending to concentrate on spearing a raisin.

"What does that mean?"

"We were talking about limiting call schedules. Continuity of patient care. His treatment of Natalie."

Elliot's head whipped around, checking for witnesses. "Marti! That's not funny. Christ!"

"No one can hear. It was just that he cremated two residents for having the temerity to question the schedule."

"When he trained, he was on every other night call," he said, as if that explained anything. "He has the 'I did it, you can too' attitude."

"And people let him get away with that?"

"I know you're going to take this wrong, Mart, but I'm beginning to understand that being on around the clock does teach you to handle just about anything."

"What? There is nothing redeeming about working conditions like that. Hello? Remember the accidental abortion?" I paused and then added, "Not to mention what the schedule does to families."

He was playing with his cup now, twirling his finger around the rim as if it could hum.

"Elliot—all I did was come to the defense of those girls, who were rightly questioning the policy of working people until they can't function properly."

He looked away.

So I started scrambling in my own defense. "Wasn't it you who told me Nigel said that if at least one of his residents a year didn't get divorced, he wasn't doing his job?"

"He was joking."

"Real funny."

"Marti—do me a favor while you're working here?"

"What?"

"Don't get me fired?"

Silence pulled up a seat.

"When will you be home?" I asked eventually.

"Hopefully around dinner. Tell Simon I'll get his bicycle seat raised tonight."

"Okay."

I made my way back upstairs, going by the nursery to try to improve my spirits. Standing in front of the glass was the couple chosen by one of my clients to adopt her baby. The woman was squeezing the back of her husband's arm. She lifted out of her shoes and squealed when the newborn yawned. They both hugged me when I stopped to congratulate them. I was gathering my things when Win popped into my office to show me a picture of his daughter. He was laughing. "Ari just learned about selfies. She sent like fifty."

"She's adorable."

"She looks like Lydia," Win said. "Only she's nicer. Usually. Everything okay? You seem sort of subdued."

"I have a little headache. I'm going to head home after I meet with Tonya's mom."

"Call me if you need anything."

I drove up Broad Street to the Grandy Ann's. I was pleased to discover the parking lot empty. As soon as I entered the building, it became clear why. The air conditioner was broken. Competing fans hummed, but the cheesy colonial-themed restaurant was humid, the air sticky with syrup and grease. I concentrated on not gagging.

"Ms. Trailor?" asked a waitress in a white bonnet and an apron-fronted, floor-dusting dress of robin's-egg blue.

"Hi." I smiled. We were roughly the same age, which was

disconcerting, as she was about to be a grandmother. She ushered us over to a corner table where two red plastic tumblers and iced tea sat waiting for us. "Even this thing's sweating," she said, flicking moisture off the pitcher.

I laughed.

"Andy called to say you'd be coming by."

"I just wanted to touch base. See if you had any questions for me about Tonya's living situation."

"Not really." Weariness seeped from her. "Look, I'm sorry, but I had a real bad night last night."

She went quiet, and I thought of those mysterious status updates from Facebook acquaintances—"God doesn't give you more than you can handle"; "Moments like this make the struggle worth it"; "I miss him so much already"—the kind you weren't sure if you were supposed to ask what was going on or not. I decided to ask. "Anything I can do?"

"I wish. My boy got caught up in that fight out in the county. At the football game."

"Is he okay?" There'd been a near race riot at an exhibition game between two high schools. "Was he arrested?"

"Him and about half his team."

"I'm so sorry. What happened?"

"The paper made it sound like it was 'cause Maurice's team was trash talking. But it was the other kids that started it up. They were doing a chant that went, 'It's all right, it's okay, you're going to work for us one day.'"

"Wow."

"Then they pretended to recognize our team's equipment, saying their school had donated it. And a lot of our boys were freshmen and hadn't ever been out there before. Never saw a separate science building. Or a student parking lot."

I thought of the project I'd been involved with at my own kids' school. Children were bused in from a housing project on Saturdays, and we'd tutor them in the state-of-the-art multimedia center. Davien, the little boy I partnered with, said, "Ms. Trailor, how come your kids get these things every day? Not just on special ones?" I'd been at a loss trying to explain unfairness to a second-grader.

"So," Mrs. Maines said while erecting structures out of sugar packets, "our boys lost their tempers."

"I can't say I blame them."

Which seemed to surprise her. "Anyways, about Tonya. I didn't mean for her to up and leave like that. But if my sister-in-law thought we were about to bring a new baby in there she'd put us all out. She can't stand noise or mess. She never lets me forget we're guests. Even though I pay half the rent." She reached for some more packets. "That's what I'll never be able to forgive my husband for. He left and took our home with him."

"I'm sorry." When she didn't respond, I said, "Your daughter makes the same little houses."

"Yeah—we have contests. Sometimes I can get them four levels high. Big deal, huh? They'll be able to put that on my tombstone. That and being able to pay for everything in coins. I can add change up faster in my head than most people can count dollars."

"You've also raised a lovely girl, Mrs. Maines. I look forward to the time I spend with Tonya."

"Thank you."

She pulled out a pack of Salems from her apron pocket, holding out the leather cigarette case. "Since nobody's in here."

"I'm trying to quit," I said, taking one.

"Not all that successfully." She laughed. "So do you need something from me? Some forms signed?"

"No. I just wanted to meet you. I'm going to help Tonya find an apartment."

"I appreciate all you've been doing, Ms. Trailor."

"It's my pleasure," I said. "It really is."

I went to retrieve the children, a task that consisted of a

ninety-minute rush-hour crawl through three of Richmond's distinct quadrants. I drove to the nouveau riche Far West End, where I picked up Nina from an enormous new house hidden behind fast-growing, builder-planted Bradford pear trees. Then we went back past Church Hill to a funky artists' community on the East Side, full of bungalow stepping-stones between once grand estates. Poppy had gone for the first time to visit with Cece, whose sculptor-father was working on a bust of Einstein in the open-sided studio next to the bohemian mansion. He walked Poppy over to the car.

"Anytime I can return the favor," I promised. "Or a kidney—if you need one."

"How about a liver?" He grinned. "Having one on ice would be reassuring."

"Mama," Poppy said as we pulled out of the driveway, "I don't like it over there."

"Why?"

"Too many big scary masks. Like that one in the garage."

"That's a sculpture, not a mask," I corrected.

"Well, they don't have good eyes. And they will probably come in my dreams tonight."

"We'll keep your light on."

"Or you can sleep in my room," Nina offered. I smiled at her in the rearview mirror. She was one of the most maternal people I knew.

We made our way south over the James River to retrieve Simon from Colby's. I climbed out of the car to hug her and waved at the boys, who were playing a card game on the porch. "You look tired, Cole."

"Thanks."

"Is everything okay?"

"Yeah. My source on the Stocker thing is running me ragged, though. He's making me drive all over creation to meet him because he doesn't trust the phones or e-mail."

"How Deep Throat."

"Seriously. The story does have ugly written all over it, though. Big Pharma is a freaking cartel. My one little article about the horn-dog conference at the end of the summer has morphed into a five-part series about drug companies."

"What else are you focusing on?"

"The heroin epidemic and the connection to physicians and legal narcotics."

"I didn't know there was one."

"Yeah. Docs prescribe painkillers for all sorts of things. From wisdom tooth extraction to amputations. Then stop the refills. Heroin is a cheap substitute and you don't need an appointment."

"Hello, Pulitzer."

"It's not an original investigation, but I am bringing it home. So, from your lips . . ." She smiled and pointed heavenward, then bent down and waved at the girls in the backseat. Nina waved and Poppy blew a loud kiss. Colby stood and put her hand up to block the still-blazing sun. "I've started cross-checking RSVPs to Stocker's event so I can see which of the doctors who are attending are also getting sleazy money."

"How?"

"There's a Web site that tracks compensation between drug companies and prescribers."

"Seriously?"

"Yeah. And check this out. One drug company apparently uses personality tests as part of their screening process for new hires. And, big surprise, candidates who don't have problems with rule breaking are ever so attractive."

I was struck by a scary thought. "Cole—is this safe?"

"Safe as exposing all-comped debauchery and kickbacks can be. Okay. Gotta go. My Pulitzer awaits."

Simon came over, hugged Colby around the hips, and climbed in. "Did Dad raise my bike seat?" he asked.

"He told me this morning that he was going to."

"Good." He smoothed flat his seat belt. Then he checked to make sure the car door was locked. Nina caught his nervous gestures and smiled sweetly at me in the mirror. It was the first time I realized she was aware of her brother's anxiousness.

When we got home we found that Elliot had indeed adjusted the bike. Only its handlebar skewered a note that read: "Scheduled doc at Free Clinic had a family emergency. No one else to take her place. Home by 11:00. XO."

CHAPTER SIX

Wycliff is poised to ride the trial in to the attorney general's office. He made some coy announcement about meeting with friends and supporters over the weekend. At his side was his boxy wife in requisite West End red wool sweater with gold buttons, black skirt, and practical pumps. She didn't say much, but she smiled appropriately, offered the occasional look of consternation, and nodded while her spouse outlined his vision for law and order.

The bastard has combed through my life, my job, and my family. During the short press conference that was held in his chintz-covered living room, he intimated that the search warrants had yielded significant discoveries. "While I obviously can't say more about an ongoing investigation, allow me to reiterate my commitment to justice for all citizens of our great commonwealth—white, black, rich, poor, old, young. Born and unborn. Everyone."

Except me.

I awoke to find my foot tapping to Bonnie Raitt. The Brices' annual Summer's-End Party was on the calendar, and apparently I was excited even in my sleep. Though Bob and Paige were around a decade older than El and me (and always seemed that much more grown up), they were both really welcoming. Department-related events often required a dose of vodka, Xanax, or a light combination of the two, but this annual celebration was always loose and fun. Plus it was raining, which meant no golf. Which meant I'd have company on the bleachers at Little League, gymnastics, and swimming. For once.

Over the past few weeks, Elliot and I had reached an unspoken détente, avoiding the nuclear buttons, trying to chill things out. It seemed to be working. I was beginning to think that we were cycling out of the darkness. Elliot had even taken the kids out for breakfast and to a nursery, returning with pots of late-blooming roses that the five of us planted together.

I tried to extricate myself from the tangled web of bodies without waking anyone. (There had been a total migration into our bed over the night.) Nina, wearing an old hospital scrub shirt as a gown, had thrown one of her muscular legs across Simon's bare ankle. He was topless, but in Christmassy flannel pajama bottoms that had obviously gotten too short. His narrow little chest was slowly rising and falling in deep sleep. I looked over at Poppy, who was watching me. We smiled at each other and her pale hand appeared on my olive wrist.

We headed into the kitchen together. I loved the unexpected moments I was able to snatch with individual kids. It fit my requirements for quality time: a period when my children were not intent on killing one another or trying to provoke me into doing it for them. I watched Poppy inventory the artwork on the walls, appliances, and cupboards. The cataloging compulsion had been born when she witnessed me fold the hundredth nursery school potato print and put it in the trash. It had been a maternal faux pas of the highest order. Her little shoulders relaxed when she saw that all of her rainbow period portraits were where they belonged. I sat down and patted my lap, onto which she dutifully climbed. "Tell me a story about a little girl who has to go to school and has to bring a lunch box and eat at school even though she doesn't want to," Poppy commanded.

I laughed and hugged my five-year-old tightly. "What a unique plotline, Poppy-flower. How did you ever come up with that?"

She shrugged modestly.

"Once upon a time, there was a little girl who was old enough to go to school but hated the idea of eating there. Every day during the summer she woke up thinking, Oh no, it's one day closer to school and the cafeteria. And soon there were no days left. There was only one evening left, so it was time to go shopping for school supplies. Her mommy said, 'Little girl, you and I will go out and get the things you need.' So they went and bought new shoes and under-pants and a backpack and a pencil box for markers and crayons. And a lunch box. It was the greatest-looking lunch box in the whole store, with a matching thermos that never leaked and a special place to keep quarters for ice cream. The little girl fell in love with it. And she hugged and hugged the wonderful, beautiful mommy who bought it for her. On the way home they talked about what she would bring to eat: peanut butter and jelly, a bright shiny apple, cookies, and juice. The little girl decided eating at school was going to be so fun she even slept with her lunch box that night. The end."

"Next tell a story about car pools."

"That's too scary."

Her body tensed.

"I'm joking, Poppyseed!"

I wish.

Car pools were a nightmare. A veritable Rorschach test for parents. Who was I kidding—for mothers. I never would have dreamed I'd be an active participant in heated discussions about equitable distribution of shifts based on numbers in sibling groups. Or consequences of driver tardiness. Or the moral bankruptcy of installing a child with a contagious malady (like head lice) in somebody else's SUV.

Poppy climbed down. "I'm going to get dressed now."

Simon came in and said, "I've been thinking about it and I'm going to take up chess."

"Really? Who do you know who plays?"

"Charlie. And the uncles, too."

"That's great, sweetie! Let's order you a book about it. I've never been able to figure out the whole strategy thing."

"Good idea."

"Thanks. Why don't you go wash up?"

"Okay."

He and Nina passed each other in the doorway without comment.

"Hello, firstborn," I said, kissing her head.

"Morning," she said sleepily.

"Do you want to eat before dressing?"

"I don't know."

"What's wrong, honey?"

"Nothing. I don't know. It's just that one of the new coaches said the judges at competitions look at things like that."

"Like what?"

"Being too fat. So I'm going to start watching what I eat."

"Nina!" I slowed down, tried to modulate my alarm. "You absolutely don't need to be concerned about things like that. You are nine years old. You have to eat to grow."

"Okay, but—"

"No buts. If that gym is handing out eating disorders, I will yank you out of there so fast they won't know what hit them. Got it?"

"Yes," she said. Her science class had (shockingly) done a unit on anorexia the year before. "I'll get dressed and then come down and have cereal."

"Good plan."

"Fine."

I started shoving things into the dishwasher, cramming silver-ware into the undersized tray, stacking bowls on top of plates like caps. "Seriously," I muttered. "What the hell?"

"I don't think always room for one more includes appliances," Elliot said from the kitchen threshold.

Which made me laugh.

"You okay?" he asked, concerned.

I told him about Nina. "I'm going to call the gym next week. Nip this shit in the bud."

"Go get 'em, Mama Bear."

I smiled before I noticed he was wearing khakis and a button-down. Work clothes.

My question came out angry. "Where are you going?"

"I've got to go in. I have a ton of paperwork."

"But Elliot, this is supposed to be your day off. I told the kids that you'd watch them do their sports."

He stared at me for an interminable beat. I had the sudden urge to stab him with a crusty fork. We stared at each other, and when we spoke again, our terse sentences could be measured out in tea-spoons. "Do what you want, Elliot."

"Which means?"

"Do what you want."

Or (alternative translation): Fuck. You.

His shoulders dropped, the visual to the weight of my demands. "Let's back up a little here, Marti, all right?" he said quietly. "I won't be gone all day. I have some things that need to be cleared up be-fore Monday. I'll get it all done in a few hours. And be home for the day tomorrow. Okay?"

"Fine." I wanted to suggest that he go in on Sunday instead, but at that moment it seemed like too much effort.

"I'll see you later."

I watched him leave, the height of passive aggression.

No wonder people get shot in the back.

I struggled to force closed the dishwasher with my hip and went to take a shower, stepping over the toys, shoes, and dog bones that littered the path, ignoring them as if they were supposed to be there after all.

This will pass, I told myself, willing the steam to erase my tensions. I had recaptured a fraction of my earlier spirits until I went back to the kitchen and noticed a note stuck behind the wall phone next to the window. It was waving in a gust of wind as though eager to deliver its bad news. In his pristine print Elliot had written, "Forgot to tell you—Katie called late last night and can't sit tonite. xo."

I stared at the little Post-it in disbelief. This party had been the only grown-up activity on my calendar all summer, and I wanted to go. I was mad. Not so much at Katie for standing us up (shit happens), but at Elliot for leaving the note. Where was it decreed that all child care complications belonged to me? I took a deep breath and with dogged determination arranged sleepovers for each of the children by the time they had donned their proper athletic attire. Elliot and I were going to have cocktails and crab cakes after all.

Three sporting events and sixty miles later, I finally deposited the kids at their friends' houses, an accomplishment nearly torpedoed by a frantic search for Poppy's doll, Poppy, who was finally found beneath the driver's seat.

Letting myself into the house, I was immediately suspicious of the quiet that had settled in the family's absence. Elliot wasn't home. Still. So I showered, applied my makeup the way I had been taught to do at the remedial sessions at my hair salon, and put on my sexy black silk dress. I picked up the clothes on the floor and used Magic Marker to cover the scuffs on my high heels. I gave Batman clean water, changed earrings twice, and made the bed. I checked to see if my cell phone was working and saw the battery was so dead that it wouldn't light up at all. "Shit."

I plugged it in and read my texts. The first was from Win: "My hooptie's in shop. Can I hitch ride to party? Xmas bonus in play."

The next was from Elliot: "Leslie Hill in labor. Baby breach so prob be here 4while. See you @home."

I pushed aside breakfast leftovers and gave in to the tears that had been building for a long, long time. I exhausted myself and almost fell asleep at the table. The phone rang.

It was Win.

"Marti?"

My voice was squeaky and he asked if I was all right.

"Yeah," I said, sniffing. There was a pause because it was clear that this wasn't true. I used a napkin to wipe the muddy mascara tears from my cheeks.

"Well, did you get my text?"

"Mm-hmm. But I don't think I'm going to the party. Stupid Leslie Hill has gone into labor. So Elliot has to stay at the hospital."

"I see. Well . . . can you come out to play anyway?"

"What?"

"I'd be honored to escort you."

I hadn't even thought of going without Elliot.

"You just want a ride," I said accusingly.

"Woman, you wound me to the quick."

"All right. I'll go."

When I got off the phone, I experienced an unexpected lightness. Spending the night alone would have been too much. I went to the bathroom and washed up. The crying had left my eyes greener than usual. My hair was behaving and my skin was tanned from the day outside. Looking good fed the exhilaration.

I drove quickly with the windows down. The wind tangled my curls and loosened my mood. I tapped against the steering wheel, keeping time with Coldplay. For a moment I was transported back to high school and on my way to celebrate Senior Beach Week, with nothing holding me down. It hadn't gotten dark yet and Richmond was still bustling. On warm nights, parts of the city turned their pockets inside out. Doors and windows were wide-open, loud music played, and cooking smells floated from front-stoop grills. As soon as I crossed the threshold of Monument Avenue, the tone changed. The festivities shut down as square footage went up. The mansions by the bronze Confederate heroes atop their anatomically correct horses were intent on keeping up appearances. Outdoor entertaining took place on private terraces in the back.

The wide, tree-filled boulevard was deserted except for a smattering of sightseers having their pictures taken in front of the Arthur Ashe monument. The likeness of the tennis player was the only one I'd ever seen visited. Probably because of the struggle to have it put up in the first place. While it was before our time in town, I knew firsthand that the fight to integrate the Dixie memorials had been ugly. My dad had lent his support to the people working to desegregate the statuary, managing to seriously piss off the strange coalition of country clubbers and bikers who'd joined forces to keep the bronzes white. He even got death threats over it.

I turned onto Grove Avenue. Win was sitting on his apartment steps, looking particularly handsome. His tanned skin had gotten even darker and the laugh lines were radiating toward his black eyes.

"Hello, favorite employee."

"Only employee," I corrected as he climbed in.

We drove for a while in comfortable silence. "Any news on Leslie?" he eventually asked.

"No, but I'm sure that as long as she's got half the hospital hovering she's going to drag it out."

"Meow." He laughed.

"My allegiance is to Mrs. Hill-the-First."

"Did you know VIP syndrome is an actual thing? I just heard about some prince who came over from Saudi, or someplace, for chemo. He demanded his health care team stop wearing gloves."

"Why?"

"He said it was rude. So they broke infection protocol. Huge mistake."

We'd left the Fan and its cramped vertical architecture to enter the Near West End, where so many of the brick homes had been expanded with asymmetrical wooden additions that the streets seemed to be lined with one-armed amputees. I turned onto Cary Street Road, pointing out particularly lavish mansions surrounded by acres of tremendously lush and wildly expensive land located within the city limits.

"We are approaching Windsor Farms on the left," I told Win in a tour guide voice. "This is where old money lives and breeds. Think of it as an aristocratic ecosystem behind slow-growing boxwoods. Up on Libby and Grove are boutiques, sidewalk cafés, private schools, a university, and a country club. Members of the First Families of Virginia are born, marry, and die within the same mile and a half. Forays outside of the neighborhood or limited gene pool are rare. Integration generally occurs between eight and five. See that house?" I pointed to a sprawling one-story stucco English cottage.

"Yeah?"

"Elliot and I went to a wedding reception for one of the other residents there. It was unbelievable. Southern *Twilight Zone.* The groom's mother answered the door with her butler." I switched into my near perfect imitation of aristocratic Virginia matrons, laying on the first syllables just long enough to imply Money with History. "Y'all come in! Come in! I'm Poonie. Sawyah's mother. And this here's Linley. He's like family, aren't you, Linley?" My voice returned to normal. "Like she makes her family stand around in white coats saying, Yes, ma'am, yes, ma'am."

"Is Poonie short for poontang?"

I snorted. "I like the Near West End names that sound like corporations, too."

"Like?"

"Maclain Valentine Hollins. Who shouldn't be confused with her cousin Hollins Valentine Maclain." I looked over and smiled at Win. "Another bizarre custom I got introduced to at that reception was the Gift Room, where all the wedding presents were laid out for public inspection."

"No way! How did yours rate?"

"The one I switched cards with was very well received."

"I think we ought to do a research project on southern aristocracy. Turn the spotlight on the other end of the spectrum for a change." He put his arm up so his hand rested on the back of my seat. I could feel him looking at me. "What about you, Mrs. Doctor's Wife? Aren't these people your playmates?"

I felt the stirrings of discomfort. "No, not really. I mean, even though I see them, I'm not really of them. I've never quite meshed."

Win had unexpectedly touched upon one of my self-truths. I often felt that I didn't belong. It was like being life's scholarship student. Despite having the same trappings as the other congressional offspring, mine were always mixed with a heightened sense of social responsibility. I could never just enjoy them. My father made sure of it. Which was good—just not easy.

"My parents are comfortable, but divorced. Elliot's family has boatloads and plan on taking it with them."

Win laughed. "What does Elliot say?"

"Yeah, we generally avoid this topic."

"Hey, you'll appreciate this. Ariana called before you picked me up. Her hamsters, Ballerina and Jessica, had babies and she wanted to know if that meant they were gay."

"Oh God, that always happens! Whenever you buy a pair of female hamsters, sooner or later one of them grows a penis."

I blushed almost immediately after saying penis. Even connected to rodents, it didn't seem appropriate.

"Hey, you're a pretty fun date," Win said. "Saucy."

I blushed harder.

"Marti. I'm just kidding." He ruffled the back of my head the way my brothers did. "By the way, you look very pretty tonight."

His fingers burned my scalp.

I gripped the wheel a little tighter and resumed the guided tour of the Far West End. The farther we traveled, the newer the homes. Enormous houses, newly sprung from the fertile earth between Richmond and Charlottesville, had erupted into whole executive communities. While expensive, they lacked the acreage of their counterparts a little farther east. The yards were so disproportionately small, the houses looked like rows of cartoon hippos balancing on teeny shoes. I parked in the Brices' driveway; Win whistled at the size of the house. "They're all the same out here, you know," I whispered, while trying to brush little orange pebbles from inside my sandals. "Every house in every cul-de-sac follows the same Richmond decorating formula. No deviations."

"Which is?"

"Season-appropriate flags hanging above the front door. Things like snowmen, seagulls, dogwood sprigs. Inside you'll find the requisite antique flower prints, chintz upholstery, reproduction furniture, and family portraits in ornate gold frames." Which made me think of my mom. I wondered if she ever advertised in Richmond. It was a huge market.

Win pointed to the banner of autumn leaves waving from its pole in the night breeze. "Good call."

Paige came to the front door herself. Mother of two well-mannered sons who always said please, thank you, and ma'am, she was the unofficial department hostess. She was also Hospital Volunteer of the Year three years running. And the worst thing about her was that she was genuinely sweet.

"Oh, Marti! I'm so glad you made it! I read that great article in the *Times* about your dad. I'm so glad he's going over there. He is so wise. I saved the clipping for you—in case you wanted another original. Of course with the Internet, that's probably an obsolete exercise."

"Not at all! I'm trying to make scrapbooks for the kids—so that's lovely!" I introduced Win.

After telling us to go get drinks, Paige excused herself and Win said, "What was that all about?"

"The stuff about my dad? Um, have you ever heard of Stewart Maxwell?"

"The congressman?"

I nodded.

"Seriously?" He winced a little. "Wow. I can't believe you never told me."

"Sorry. I tried to figure out how to work it into my résumé but couldn't quite pull it off."

Being the daughter of Someone Famous was a mixed bag. I was never quite sure where my identity started and my father's ended. In some cases it was clear: like when Daddy, who couldn't stand the possibility of his children failing, would say things like "I'll just make a few calls and see what kind of an internship I can scare up for you on the Hill, Marti." Other times it was murkier. In high school I suspected a few friendships were founded on name-dropping.

We made our way to the living room, where a bar had been set up. Shimmering pieces of shiny aqua material had been tacked to the walls to create the illusion of being underwater.

"That reminds me," Win cracked. "I need to find the bathroom."

He briefly put his hand on my bare arm. The sensation of his fingers took a long time to fade. I wondered if he had left some sort of an imprint. Colby was across the room, extending a glass to the bartender for a refill. I made my way to her.

"Hey, girly-girl. So little Miss Second Chance is in labor? Bless her heart," she said with all the sincerity the phrase usually contained. "Last time I saw her, her belly button was pushed out so far I thought she had a hard-on."

I laughed. "Hey, Mikey's been trying to pump me for information about Dr. Barbie. What do you have on her?"

"How on earth does he know Catherine Stamp?"

"Met her at Rides and Park."

"Lord, your brothers are incorrigible. Tell him that she is one of the Stamps. Stands to inherit beaucoup tobacco dollars."

"Anything else?"

"Let's see . . ." She tapped her cheek in mock concentration.

I smiled and waited.

Colby endorsed Liz Smith's theory that gossip was just news in a red dress.

"Catherine Stamp. Catherine Stamp. She had a weeklong coming-out party at the Rivah following the Bal du Fille at the club; she was the first Stamp girl to become a doctor instead of marry one; and her mother was Carlyboo, the high-test grande dame who overdosed on tranquilizers and mint juleps."

I knew about Carlyboo. The unexpected passing of the socialite commanded serious ink.

"That's sad," I said. "Did they ever figure out if it was an accident?"

"I don't think so."

"Cat or dog?"

"Definitely dog."

Inferred pet preference was social shorthand. Colby and I believed that self-sufficient felines and their single aficionados were more likely to remain that way. Dog owners, on the other hand, were at least forced out to the curb, where it was possible to run into other dog people. Choosing a cat over even the most obnoxious yippy little poodle could seal one's marital status.

"Hm," I said. "Breed?"

"Something prissy. An Afghan, maybe. With a fourteen-karat-gold collar."

I always thought it was funny that Colby used this classification system, as she hated all variety of pets. She claimed they were just vehicles for germs and even called poor Batman "Bacteriaman" to his face.

"Any other info for me to pass on?"

"Did you tell Mikey that John isn't a fan of Dr. Barbie? I mean that's pretty much the only intel he really needs."

Paige appeared in the doorway. "Excuse me, everyone! I just got a call from Bob. Little Tara Corelle was born a few minutes ago. All is well with new mama and baby. Hopefully our significant others will be arriving soon."

A smattering of polite clapping broke out and I whispered, "Tara Corelle! Sounds like Confederate dinnerware."

Colby smiled, adopted full-on southern. "The hostess pattern, hearkening back to simpler times, comes in lily white."

"Which looks lovely atop a tablecloth with a stars-and-bars motif."

"Hey, your cute boss is looking pretty forlorn over there all by his lonesome. You should rescue him while I give the sitter a call. See if the boys have done her wrong yet."

Win and I walked outside to sit in wicker chairs by the pool.

"It's pretty out here, isn't it?" he asked. "Kind of like being in a watercolor."

Bach was wafting across the patio, reminding me of garden parties I attended as a child. Holiday get-togethers and fund-raising pet shows at McLean estates inevitably included powerful congressmen, judges, lobbyists, and journalists getting drunk in a group, while the progeny carried on illicit activities in elaborate tree houses and professionally decorated bedrooms. The air had cooled, providing a faint glimpse of fall. Leaves were turning over in winds from a distant storm, their undersides shining silver in the moonlight. A crisp smell made me think of being little and the anticipation that accompanied the fading summer. Autumn always meant new teachers, clean notebooks, fresh TV shows. Like still-wrapped gifts, the days seemed full of potential. It was my favorite season.

Win cleared his throat. "So is there anything else you'd care to impart, Mrs. Maxwell-Trailor?"

"Hey, I don't know anything about your lineage!"

"True, dat. Let's see. I come from a long line of autoworkers, union organizers, and very angry housewives. Purely local folk." He looked over at me. "What was it like growing up on Capitol Hill?"

"Pretty weird. The tabloids would have killed to hear the conversations that took place between all the politicians' kids. You ever want good dirt, hang out with the offspring."

"Thanks for the tip." His fingers encircled my wrist; my breath caught. I tried to cover it with a little cough. "Marti, I didn't mean to make you uncomfortable before. I think I was a little hurt. Which is stupid and I'm sorry."

He took back his hand and I pretended not to have noticed any of it.

"Me too. It wasn't like I was keeping it secret. It just never came up. It's not easy dropping it into a conversation. Here are those case files. By the way, my dad is one of the most powerful men in the country."

"Does Elliot know?"

I laughed and settled back into the chair. "Win, how did you end up here?"

"Without Ariana, you mean? I have Lydia and Bart to thank for that. They told me he was going to be transferring to D.C. He's a lawyer for a firm that has offices in both cities. So I heard of this job, applied for it, got it, and moved down, knowing that I'd be able to pick Ari up for the weekends." His voice took on an unfamiliar bitterness. "Then Bart changed his mind. Decided not to take the job after all. Joke was on me. I shouldn't be surprised, though. Sleeping with another man's wife is probably a pretty good predictor of all sorts of things."

"You could always go back."

"It's not out of the question."

Which whispered a chill over my shoulders.

He leaned back in his chair. "Marti, I've been meaning to thank you for how much you've done at work. I don't think I could have gotten the program anywhere near where it's at if it hadn't been for you." He smiled broadly. "You've been a gift. I'm glad you forced me into hiring you."

"That is an outrageous statement." We grinned at each other. "Truthfully, Win, the job has been a gift to me."

We were comfortable in the quiet until a merry roar announced the arrival of the late guests.

"I'm going to run to the bathroom," I said.

In the kitchen I overheard the hosts in a heated exchange. I was about to back out when I noticed Colby listening intently to the fight going on around the corner. Paige's whispered voice carried.

"Seriously, Bob? Two and a half hours? I spent a month getting ready for this party for your department and you show up when it's almost over?"

"Honey, these were extenuating circumstances. She's Nigel's wife."

"Oh, don't get me started on that man." She blew her nose. "You want to know what the worst part of this whole godforsaken day was?"

"Do I?"

"Natalie came over this morning while I was putting the flowers out."

"Oh no! Was she drunk?"

"She was sad, Bob. She's been disappeared. Her whole life has been upended. And I'll tell you something else. You may like Nigel, but I'd drink, too, if I'd been married to that son of a bitch.

He's a narcissist and he's mean. Natalie told me one of their girls blew off a couple of dinners with him last month—so he pulled her out of class and yelled at her in the hall. He humiliated a fifteen-year-old at her school because he felt disrespected. This day has just sucked, and all I can think about is going to bed. I'm so mad, I could just spit."

Colby and I made our way to the powder room, which was occupied. Paige appeared, all signs of distress erased, and offered the master bath. It was enormous, with marble fixtures, a fancy exercise bike, and a television above the sink.

"Taj Mah toilet," Colby said with a whistle after our hostess retreated. "That was some scene out there."

"Really." But I was aware of this guilty relief that had accompanied the eavesdropping. If the Brices had fights like that, maybe what Elliot and I were going through was just par for the course. I opened the window and helped myself to one of Colby's cigarettes while she peed. "That was a terrible story about Natalie. Did I tell you I bumped into her at the grocery store?"

"No," Colby answered, unrolling a few squares.

"She had all this peanut butter and tuna in her basket and I was like, Uh-oh, she's hoarding now. But then she told me she volunteers at the food bank and always brings in extra stuff to donate during her shift. She was stone-cold sober. Maybe she'll be able to get it together."

"I hope so. Did I tell you I'm doing an article about divorce?" Colby said, washing her hands.

"Wow, your assignments are all over the map."

"Half the staff's being squeezed out. Pretty soon I'll be covering the classifieds and delivering papers from my bike."

"You ever consider setting up a reporters' relief fund?"

Colby laughed, opened the medicine cabinet, and began twisting pill bottles to read labels. "You know who John Gottman is? The psychologist?"

"No."

"He watches couples talk to each other and can predict which ones are going to make it."

I took a last drag and flushed the butt. This was not the conversation I felt like having. "How?"

"He looks for things like eye rolling."

"What?"

"Yeah. It's a sign of contempt, which is one of the 'Four Horsemen of the Apocalypse.' Another one is defensiveness." She turned. Little tucks of pain had appeared around her mouth and eyes. My breath caught.

"What's the matter, Cole?"

"Tomorrow's New York."

"What? I thought the appointment wasn't until next month!"

"The doctor's going to some sort of conference and his secretary called yesterday to move it up. It was either go tomorrow or wait until November."

"How are you doing?"

"I'm trying real hard not to think about it. But Charlie seems really okay. He's growing like nobody's business. I think he even passed Simon. That's gotta mean something." Her brown eyes held mine. "This is the big one, you know."

I nodded, reaching for calm, but was taken totally off guard. I looked at my best friend and felt the old sense of paralysis return. When Charlie was little and so sick, when he'd vomit and vomit from the chemo and never even cry because he didn't know any different, I would stand by feeling helpless. Everyone's suffering had raged on and on.

"Five years of remission is considered a cure."

"I know," I whispered, squeezing Colby's hand. "How's John?"

"Making a lot of dumb jokes. And eating like a horse. He's put on close to fifteen pounds. He'll be better once we get through this."

"Do you want me to come with you?" I'd gone up with Colby

and Charlie a couple times when John couldn't go. Ever since Charlie's oncologist had left Virginia to join the faculty of Sloan Kettering, the Kusiks had been commuting to New York for care.

"John's fixed it so he can come. Thank you, though."

We left the bathroom together. And then, because I had forgotten to pee, I went back in, praying silently all the while for my godson's health. I took a deep breath and made my way toward the chair where I'd stashed my purse.

John and Colby were standing with Peter Hayden and his date. Peter was talking, gesturing with his beer can. "It's a great idea. You could convert your garage into John's House of Sleep. People would check in and you'd put them under for a few weeks and when they woke up they'd have lost weight totally painlessly! It's a natural!"

"Definitely has potential," John said. "I could see about partnering with a plastics guy. We could throw in some liposuction, a little rhinoplasty . . ."

"Sign me up!" I laughed.

John whipped around. Colby wasn't kidding. His jowls were jiggling with the movement. "Marti! What are you doing here, sweetheart? I didn't expect to see you tonight. Elliot said something about the babysitter canceling."

"Well, I got industrious and doled out the children," I said. "Matter of fact, one of them is terrorizing your babysitter right now. I'm going to go give El a call. He must be frantic thinking we've all been kidnapped. I forgot to text him that I was here."

But John was wearing an odd expression, and when he opened his mouth a beat passed, as if he'd momentarily forgotten his lines. "Um, actually, honey, I think I saw him go toward the pool."

Humiliation rushed to my face. "Oh! Well, I guess I'll hook up with him out there."

I walked around the house, slogging through dread.

He was sitting at the deep end. With Claudia. Their shoes were off and they were making slow, blue circles with their feet. I was unable to move. Weeks passed between each breath. And then Elliot threw back his head and roared at something Claudia said. I was edging away from the scene, and had almost made it, when Win called out my name. "Marti! . . . Marti! . . . Paging Marti Maxwell-Trailor." His body followed his voice and he came up short as the total scene presented itself. Both Elliot and Claudia stood and faced me.

I want to die. I want to die. I want to die.

"Hi, Elliot," I rasped. I needed a hit off my inhaler. "Our wires must have gotten crossed. I'm not feeling well and I'm heading out, though."

"I'll come with you, Marti. I just stopped in with a group of people celebrating the new Hill," Elliot said brightly. "Claudia was kind enough to offer me a ride."

"How very generous." I smiled my very best.

Elliot started toward me. "So I can go home with you."

"You're welcome to stay, Elliot. Keep up the celebration."

"No, I just wanted to make an appearance."

I was conscious of every breath.

Elliot picked up his shoes and walked around the pool, away from Claudia and toward me. Win hung back. Out of the corner of my eye, I noticed Claudia's cousin standing on the brick walkway. She was holding two drinks and looking extremely uncomfortable. I pretended not to see her.

"Win, if you don't mind, would you catch a ride home with Colby?" I was on autopilot, arranging car pools as my marriage fell apart. "I hope you all will excuse me, but I really need to leave now. I have a terrible headache." Which wasn't a lie. With no dull ache of warning, my brain suddenly felt as though it were being squeezed through my right eye. I tried to take long, dignified strides around the house, but my exit was hampered by my spike heels, which kept sinking, cleatlike, into the lawn.

I bent down and snatched the sandals off my feet.

Waiting for Elliot to match cars with the drivers who'd deep parked the van, I could no longer hold back the tears. When he climbed in, he repositioned the seat so that his knees wouldn't bump against the steering wheel. "Marti, what the hell are you so upset about?"

"You said you couldn't go to the party. And then you came without me! So you could play water footsy with that nurse!" I cried, furiously kicking at the coffee mugs and car toys that kept bumping my ankles.

"For Christ's sakes, Marti! We had to section Leslie so we got out early. I thought I'd just come by to say hi. It wasn't a big deal and it wasn't planned—if that's what you're getting at. We were just sitting there."

"Are you sleeping with her, Elliot? Are you having an affair? Is that why everything I do is wrong?"

He made an unexpected sharp left turn, then pulled up behind a parked BMW.

"How dare you ask me that, Marti? Haven't I proven my faithfulness? Haven't I proven it yet?" His voice, so full of hurt, confused my thinking. I knew what I saw, but I also knew it was possible to misread things.

"Marti. Look, I'm sorry that I didn't go home first. But think about it—you wouldn't have even been there if I had. It just didn't seem like such a big deal." He tilted his head. "You came with Win and I'm not accusing you of anything."

Which stopped me. And I was suddenly overwhelmed with relief. At the obviousness of what he was saying and the fact that I didn't make a real scene. I shuddered at how close I'd come to Natalie Hill's behavior.

"I'm sorry, Elliot. It was a shitty thing to say. Really shitty. But it's the tension between us—I don't know what it is and I don't know where it's from. Sometimes things seem better and then they seem worse. I don't know what's going on."

I waited for him to reassure me. When he spoke it was in a whisper. "I don't know either. I'm worn out. From work and . . ."

But his words ambled off.

"And what?"

"You want the truth?"

"What?" I whispered, frozen.

"I can't live with the anger anymore."

Blindsided, I said, "I'm not angry, El. I'm sad. The only thing I've ever been upset about is wanting to be with you more—wanting you to be more of a presence in the family. You're the one who is always blowing up."

"Do you have any idea what it's like being guilt-tripped about work, or volunteering, or even trying to catch up on sleep? You bitch at me as if I were responsible for the whole goddamn system. Nobody at the hospital has complaints about me like you do. No one else accuses me of shirking responsibilities." He looked out of his window and rubbed his eyes. His next words came out in a murmur. "I just need a little peace. A little space."

"Elliot, I've been alone—for the past decade—while you've gone about your career. Which was supposed to be your space. And I've missed you and waited for you. And now, when things are supposed to be improving, they're getting worse."

Our breath was causing the windows to fog. He opened his and then turned back to me. "You sure have a funny way of showing you miss me."

"So you're saying that if I were nicer you'd be home more? It's not schedules or being short staffed? Or drug-addict doctors? It's me?"

"Forget it, Marti. I knew you wouldn't understand."

"You're right." My hands were shaking. I clasped them together to still their trembling.

"All I'm saying is that I work hard."

"I do too."

"Well, that's a choice you made. You didn't have to. Especially now—when I'm finally earning a decent living!"

"Seriously? Are you suggesting that I shouldn't have a career?"

He cleared his throat. "I just think we need to reevaluate some things. I'm not sure this is what I want."

Whoosh. "'This' being what, Elliot?"

"I don't know. I just need some time. To figure things out."

"What does that mean, you need some time? You're putting me on probation?"

"Quit blowing this out of proportion, Marti."

"Are we having the same conversation?" To which he would respond only with another disappointed head movement. If we had been in a room, he would have walked out. "Elliot, do you know how hard it's been for us—your children, too—to be around your shitty moods, your self-centered behavior?"

"If I'm that bad, maybe you ought to think about doing something."

We drove through the city in silence, and when we reached home we were as awkward together as strangers. In the bedroom, he turned his back as I undressed. But sometime in the dark hours of early morning, Elliot reached for me. And with hungry relief I responded, covering his neck and stomach with kisses, my hands frantically groping the familiar terrain of his body, desperate for reassurance.

Which never came.

"I can't," he whispered. And pulled away.

As I tried to will myself back to sleep, I thought I heard him whispering, "I'm sorry, I'm sorry."

But it might have only been the rustling of the sheets.

CHAPTER SEVEN

My lawyer is sitting at his desk, scowling. "What's wrong?" I whisper.

He swivels his computer around to reveal a picture of me standing in the street giving someone the finger.

"Wait. What is that?" I'm totally confused. "Is that Photoshopped?" Then I remember. "A girl was being harassed coming out of the women's clinic in the Fan. She tripped. They wouldn't leave her alone."

"Flipping off a group of pro-lifers is hardly going to help your case. Virginia's commitment to choice is thinner than shaved ice."

"I didn't know all this was going to happen," I said defensively.

"Fox has been running it every half hour or so," he continued. "Alongside a picture of your father. Just to drive home your bloodline."

Huge, chest-aching sobs suddenly bubble up from my core.

Leland opens his arms. He smells of starch and aftershave. There's a small splatter of mud on the top of his right shoe. The HVAC system switches on. His stomach gurgles. I never want him to let me go.

"You can let it out, Marti. For a few more minutes. And then we need to get back to work."

I got ahold of myself. "You watch Fox?"

Elliot and I managed to keep things civil following the Brices' party, but the atmosphere was so tense that I felt as if I were breathing smoke. It was like my childhood home before my parents finally threw in the towel.

Outwardly, Elliot and I were careful with each other. Our interactions were brief, cauterized with surgical precision. We were polite and spoke in tones usually reserved for discussions of terminal illness. The most casual of touches chafed; accidental eye contact burned. Finally, I realized what all of the extra hours that he spent at the hospital were: a de facto separation.

Something had to give, but I wasn't ready yet. Delaying the confrontation was like postponing a doctor's appointment for unmistakably dire symptoms. I could wait. Elliot may have denied involvement with Claudia, but I knew that the whole story had yet to unfold. I just didn't feel ready to handle it. I didn't have the emotional provisions I would need for the news. Work provided me with the truest relief. The more difficult my clients' problems, the less space my own could occupy.

On the way back from a home visit I took a detour and drove down the Kusiks' street. The neighborhood may have offered million-dollar views of the river, but it wasn't quite as tony as the adjoining area a little farther west. A crime-ridden community jostled its other hip. Colby's Victorian came into view. I looked with longing at their lovely home. They weren't due back for another couple days. She and John had surprised Charlie with a trip to Disney World. A celebration.

I thought of the e-mail Colby had sent from New York.

"IT'S A CURE."

I had read the words again and again, then printed out the note and placed it in the strongbox that held all our birth certificates. I barely had time to smile, to once more consider the good news, when Colby's black SUV appeared. For a terrible moment I feared I had crossed some mental health divide and was hallucinating. But she honked like a northerner and motioned for me to park.

"My goodness, it's a friendly visitor," she drawled, bending down to talk through my window. "What brings you into the area? Surely none of *my* neighbors are in need of your professional services?"

"Cole. Charlie . . . that was the best news." We held each other's eyes, then both looked away before dissolving into tears. "When did you get back?"

"Yesterday. Everything about that place vexed me. What could you possibly have been thinking, letting me go there?"

"I didn't know you were going," I argued. "How did you escape the happiest place on earth, anyway?"

"We had to cut a deal that Charlie could plan our next vacation if we didn't have to stay out the week. And it's a good thing, because boy, do I have news about my article. Do you have time?"

"Yeah."

I have time for anything but thinking about my life.

I turned the ignition off and leaned my elbows on the open window. "What's going on?"

"So, remember how I told you the Stocker piece morphed into a multipart series?"

"Yeah."

"I interviewed this guy at Help Now. The walk-in treatment center?"

I nodded.

"He had chronic pain that was originally treated with prescription narcotics. But then his doc tried to wean him off and he ended up on heroin. He had a family, coached his daughter's softball, worked at a garage. And lost it all. He has this incredibly sad what-the-fuck-happened aura. When I asked what was the original medical issue, all he'd say was plumbing problems. I thought it was just because he was embarrassed. But he called this morning and told me everything started after he had an impotency device put in. He had to have it removed after scar tissue formed around it. Some days he can barely walk."

"And the doctor cut him off his pain pills?"

"Yep. He didn't want to get in trouble for overprescribing."

"So, hello, street drugs."

"Right. Welcome to the world of unintended consequences. I asked the name of the implant, and guess who made it?"

"Holy shit."

"Yup. Well, actually it's a company Stocker bought. But yeah. They gave him one hundred thousand dollars and a nondisclosure agreement. They could sue him for talking, but he said he thought about it last night and decided he's got nothing left anyway, so they can have at it. The company ruined his life."

"Wow."

"I'm going to figure out if this was a one-off or a common complication. How would that be for a scoop?"

I didn't say anything.

"This would be a perfect time for you to mention my brilliant reportage." She pushed up her sunglasses and studied me. "Marti—are you okay?"

"More or less."

"Come inside." She ushered me into her house. "All right. Now tell me what the hell is going on."

"Elliot and I are falling apart, Cole," I said, weeping. "He says he needs to reevaluate things. And he's having some kind of thing with Claudia."

"Claudia? Claudia who?"

"Claudia Slut Home-Wrecker. I don't know. A cheerleader nurse after my husband," I moaned. "She's related to Catherine Stamp."

"Are they having an affair?"

"He said no. We didn't really talk about it, though. John didn't say anything?"

"About what?"

"Claudia and Elliot!"

"Marti, you know me better than that. Do you honestly think I wouldn't have said anything? Called you if I knew you were hurting? Used it as an excuse not to go to Disney?"

I gave her a look. "Elliot says I'm always bitching at him. But it's about wanting to be with him. And be connected. He's basically just stopped talking to me, Cole. I can't even remember the last conversation he initiated."

"Marti, you know expressiveness has never been his strong suit."

"What if we're doing to our kids what my parents did to us?"

"What do you mean?"

"Me, Mikey, and William were like radios. Attuned to every danger. It's happening to my own kids. They keep showing up to draw attention away from us. What am I going to do?"

"Well, what are your options?" she asked, opening cabinets, measuring coffee, and putting out the cream and sweeteners.

"What do you mean?"

"You know—choices. Alternatives." She placed the cups on the table and pulled a box of prematurely decorated Halloween Oreos out of the cabinet. "I'm not sure I can think of another synonym. Here . . ." She smiled, offering the package of orange-filled cookies.

"What choices do I have?"

"For God's sake, Ms. Hull House, you social workers spend right much of your time making lists of choices."

"Not for ourselves."

"All right, then let me facilitate the process. One: You keep going the way things are going. Two: Have a full-fledged confrontation and see what happens. Three: Do marriage counseling." She paused. "Or four: Just bag it."

I stared at her.

"Marti, come on now. Pull your head out of the sand, girl. You have to think about what you need. I don't think you've been happy for a long time. And I'm not just talking about whether or not Elliot's getting a piece at the hospital. I'm talking about how he makes you feel. You've been tiptoeing around his moods like a mongrel on hot pavement for a long, long time."

I was so startled, I didn't know how to respond. I didn't realize how bad things had appeared. "Colby, don't you like Elliot?"

"I don't like how you're always appeasing him."

"I just want him to plug back in, so I've been cutting him slack. Work has been shitty since Clark Bane got put away. Nigel's been on a tear."

"If you want my opinion—"

"I don't think I do."

"Bullshit, darlin'. If you didn't, you wouldn't have shown up in the first place."

"I didn't plan on coming here, Colby. I didn't even think you were in town!"

"Be that as it may, you're here and you're stuck. My opinion is that you are pathologically afraid of confrontation. Beyond a little sarcasm, you'd rather strip naked and walk down Broad Street than stand up to people."

"That's not true," I protested. "I advocate for my clients all day long."

"I mean for yourself. Look, I'm sorry that Elliot's having a rough time at work, but come on, that does not entitle him to treat you this way. And in terms of plugging in, the man's cordless."

"What does that mean? Colby—"

"We're not only talking a hard day at the office here, okay? This has been a long time coming." She put her hand on my arm. "I think you should think about how things have changed. It's not all you, honey. I can guarantee that."

Her back was to the huge window and I looked over her shoulder past the trees, across the raging James, to the Richmond skyline, where tobacco warehouses, glass office buildings, and church steeples crowded together like a clutch of flowers with uneven stems. "This isn't who he always was."

"I know. But at a certain point, you hanging around waiting for him to change back doesn't make a lick of sense. You all need to get some counseling. The important thing here is that just because Elliot doesn't like you bitching at him doesn't mean what you're saying is wrong. You might need help saying it better, but that doesn't take away the validity of what you feel. John and I went to counseling. You know—after Charlie."

"You did?"

"Yeah. I was falling apart." She stopped talking and tipped the mission oak chair away from the table. "Not publicly, of course. I did it the right way, the southern way. But nothing was working out the way I had planned." She interrupted herself with a harsh laugh. "Obviously."

She rarely talked about the emotions that accompanied a child with cancer. We'd talk mechanics of treatment protocols or shopping lists for when she couldn't get out. But never pain. It had been a dismal time.

Charlie had a fever and an earache shortly before his third birthday. And then a sore throat he called a hurt neck, followed by such violent diarrhea that he went from training pants back to diapers because he couldn't get to the bathroom in time. And then, appearing like an unexpected snowstorm in the middle of the night, bruises covered his back and stomach. The pediatrician went from benign reassurance to an emergency referral to the pediatric oncologist. "Anyway, first I went to the shrink alone. It was after we had sort of gotten into the routine of everything. And, uh . . ." She wiped away a tear. "Sorry. I was carting Charlie to all of his appointments while John was in another part of the hospital doing his residency. And I was cleaning up after the poor baby. Sweeping up his hair. Trying to get him to eat. Remember?"

I nodded, tears dropping straight down onto my lap.

"I went back to work because we couldn't survive on John's salary, and I'd be on deadline and would have to pick Charlie up by five because the sitter's husband didn't like a house full of kids when he got home. Even sick little bald ones. The shit. And Charlie would always be cranky by that time of the day and I'd never know if he was just tired or getting worse."

Colby's words were melting into each other. "And then we had that horrible winter and Charlie had that idiot snowsuit that he loved because he thought it made him look like Superman. But the hood kept covering his face and I'd drive with one eye on him so he wouldn't suffocate by the time we got to the tollbooth. And we had that goddamn car seat that kept hitting him in the head when I tried to buckle him in." I laughed at the memory of the guillotine harness. Colby had ended up abandoning it in the Trader Joe's parking lot.

"With every day that passed, the further I sank. And the less I could reach out to John. Because the only way he could keep himself sane was by working. And eating. And all I knew was that I was losing it. I was terrified all of the time. Charlie would scratch himself or get a bump, I'd think *relapse*. And John was afraid to come home. I was so overwhelmed that I kept wishing I was dead."

Colby blew her nose in a napkin and took a deep breath. She seemed to be motionless, held still by the light coming in from the window behind her. She spoke deliberately, her accent even stronger. "So that was when I went to the therapist. I was so sure he was going to commit me, I packed a little suitcase and left it in the trunk of the car. But he told me I wasn't crazy. He said that John needed to be involved in the counseling. It was a vindication I didn't even know I needed. But I was taut to the popping point. John and I had to learn how to cope with Charlie's illness—together." She stopped to smile. "The doctor told us he was going to give us waltzing lessons."

"What's that mean?"

"He said having a child with a serious illness is like dancing on the roof. You have to look down sometimes, but the goal is to dance whenever you can. This is the one shot we have, Marti."

"And you really think it was this therapist that helped?"

"You know what I normally think of mental health specialists. All the morons out there I've interviewed for articles . . . but he saved me. Honestly, Marti. After a few appointments I realized that if John couldn't be my partner, I'd have to learn how to dance alone. For Charlie. For me. I'd been reaching out for John but just grabbing air."

"Jesus, Colby, I can't believe I didn't know any of this. I'm sorry I wasn't there for you."

"Are you kidding? All those nights you came over and sat with me? It's what I needed. I'll never forget that time that I was making that special formula for Charlie, remember?"

I shook my head.

"It was when he went back to a bottle for a while and I was so exhausted. He couldn't tolerate milk real well so we had to use that other stuff. I was at the end of the can, trying to scoop out the last of the expensive powder—it probably cost more than cocaine—and somehow I just dropped it and all that formula spilled onto the floor. It was too late to get more and I lost it, boohooing all over the place. And you said, 'Come on, Colby. No use crying over spilt you-know-what.' And for the first time in forever I laughed. That was like a gift of sunshine."

We smiled together.

"Marti, please get some help."

My smile faded. "I know it's ridiculous with me being in the business, but it never occurred to me."

I started to feel a little uncomfortable and wondered if the Anxieties were rousing. Then I realized that what I was experiencing was an unfamiliar sensation of hope. The possibility of someone guiding Elliot and me away from the marital abyss, where we had been teetering for so long, was a tremendous relief.

"The shoemaker's son goes barefoot." Colby grinned. "Or, in your case, in ugly footwear. Look, it sure as hell can't hurt. I'll write down his name and number. Pass me some paper." I bent over to open the kitchen drawer that held a neat stack of menus, sharpened pencils, and virgin scratch paper while she continued to talk. "But Marti, if it doesn't help, you've still got to take care of yourself. You've got to be strong enough to be on your own. Pray for the best, prepare for the worst."

"And pirouette whenever possible?" I cleared my throat.

"Exactly."

"I feel like we just slept together."

"Was it good for you?" She glanced at her watch. "Shit. I've got to go. I have a meeting with my inbred editor in fifteen minutes. Chanly, remember him? The one who used to be fun when he was a reporter?"

"Is he the guy who'd hit redial five times in a row and then write, 'Repeated attempts to reach Mr. Smith for comment were unsuccessful'?"

"One and the same. Of course he'd deny it with his dying breath. Hey, I almost forgot. I've got some gossip. Natalie Hill checked into Betty Ford. The children are with Nigel, Leslie, and little Tara Pyrex. The second family has had to contend with a group of very unhappy offspring from the first."

"How'd you hear about that at the Magic Kingdom?"

"Snow White. The other thing she told me is that Dr. Barbie is having a fling with a married attending. All the money's on Bob Brice."

Which stunned me.

We walked out together in silence. Next to the van I heard a weak mewing from under a boxwood bush. It was a tiny black kitten, covered in mulch and twigs. I picked it up and ran back to Colby, who was getting in her car.

"Do not think, for a red-hot second, of handing me that germ-on-feet. You take it."

"Batman would eat it," I implored.

"Hm." She locked the car door with a flourish.

"Okay, okay." I Siri'd the address of the no-kill shelter and kept the trembling baby on my lap for the whole ride across town. The girl at the desk immediately started cooing when she reached for it. She reassured me that someone would adopt it but still I felt a little teary saying good-bye to the helpless thing. I don't know why.

CHAPTER EIGHT

For weeks at a time, I am able to direct my mind straight ahead. But every once in a while the thought of ending up in prison catches me unaware. Then, with no warning whatsoever, I am careening wildly across black ice, desperate and terrified.

I know the Wellard Facility for Women. It's a hellhole, a holding facility for the wretched. Soon after I started working, I went there to visit a client who had been arrested on a loitering charge. Twice I made the hour drive into the country, watching the neighborhoods thin out, and then the trees, too, as they became more and more sparse, until the sentry towers announced the imminent rise from the earth of the brown brick campus. The building design was sadistic, octagonal, and sharp edged, without a window in the entire structure. Rounded skylights were supposed to provide light, but they were blind cataracts staring out from the roof, orbs encrusted with decades of filth. It's a tomb for the living. Hopelessness courses through the bleak halls thick as sewage. But it was the hostility that got me most. It would ignite from a low drone to a screaming roar. And it never went away.

———————

Elliot was cooking with the kids.

"What are you doing here?" I asked, still putting on mascara as I walked into the kitchen.

"He lives here!" Poppy laughed.

"My meeting got canceled so I thought I'd whip up a little breakfast for my favorite customers." He'd made pancakes in the shape of initials. An M wearing sliced strawberry berets was waiting for me.

"It looks delicious. Thanks."

He took hold of my hand when I reached for the plate. I hoped my smile looked more natural than it felt.

The doorbell rang just as I finished my last syrup-drenched bite. "That's Katie. I'll let her in. I actually have to zip out for a home visit." I kissed the tops of everyone's heads. Elliot's, too.

"Hey, Neens, don't forget to let Batman out," I called over my shoulder.

I opened the car windows and tried to push away all thoughts except those about my client. Gina Loftin had given birth to a premature, crack-addicted four-pounder, whom she named Malcolm and then promptly abandoned. Some kind of permanent placement had to be arranged.

The farther south I drove, the more the racial landscape changed. From black to white to really white. When I stopped at a red light, a couple of guys working on a car read my "Proud Democrat" bumper sticker. "Hey, lady!" I looked over. "Proud Democrat this," one shouted, grabbing his crotch. *Nice.*

I pulled onto a side street with identical ranchers and well-tended lawns. The Loftin name appeared on a mailbox sprouting both American and Confederate flags. I rolled my eyes. No contradiction there. Pale blue Priscilla curtains in pigtails revealed a living room with furniture pushed up against the walls. Even the coffee table hugged the perimeter. I was looking in, thinking a dance might break out at any moment, when someone came to the door.

"Can I help you?" She was in a wheelchair.

I introduced myself.

"Here, honey. I'll unlock the screen, but you have to wait until I back my chair up a ways. It opens in, you see." I followed her, appreciative as she clicked off the television. A lot of clients didn't even bother to lower the volume.

Then I realized it was because she didn't want any competition. Words shoved their way out of her mouth as though her throat were on fire. She didn't stop. Gina's sassiness. The failing public schools. Rap music. Genital warts and Armageddon's approach. The coming race war. Which church I attended. She barely breathed. My ears got tired. Every time I tried to disengage, she plowed on. When something triggered a detour about godless Democrats, I began to wonder what exactly constituted legal self-defense.

I decided to give her a few more minutes to unload and used the time to organize my mental purse. Make appointments for back-to-school physicals. Call exterminator before annual mouse pilgrimage under stove. Oil change. I hoped I'd be able to remember everything to add to my Google calendar.

"Mrs. Trailor? Like I was saying, I hate to impose, but you seem like such a nice woman. And I really do hate to ask, but could you do me a favor, honey? Would you mind running to the drugstore for me? I'm almost out of insulin needles."

"Not at all!" I sprang up.

"Now that Gina's gone off and Pastor Gus is on vacation and some undesirables—"

"Really, Mrs. Loftin, it's fine!"

"They changed brands on me, messed my insurance all up," she said, handing me a hypodermic to check against the new ones. "Take this to make sure they give you the right kind. I wish I could use those pen things, but I can't. Still have to draw up the medicine the old-fashioned way."

The throwback pharmacy was one of the last holdouts against the drugstore chains that stared each other down every few blocks. I bought a limeade at the soda fountain, listened to country music coming from a speaker on the counter, and eventually started to chill.

When I dropped the box off, Mrs. Loftin asked if I wanted to come back in.

I declined graciously and went back across the river.

I was logging the visit in Gina's case record when Win appeared in the doorway, a suit bag over his shoulder. He'd spent the last week in Michigan. I was so happy to see him that I just barely stopped myself from jumping up and hugging him.

"Win! How was your trip?"

"Fair. Actually, that's an overstatement. Want to have lunch? I'm starved. The bag of seven pretzels and thimble of soda were oddly insufficient."

"Gluttony is not very appealing," I said primly. My spirits were rapidly improving. I often replayed our conversations, remembering his one-liners, smiling to myself. Our friendship had taken on its own life, put to bed at five, then revived each weekday morning with the coffee he brought in for us both.

"Care for a change of scenery?" he asked. "I'm not up for the hospital's Monday menu."

"You bet." I wondered if he knew I'd been avoiding the cafeteria. In the days since the Brices' party, Win had tactfully withheld comment about the swimming pool incident. For which I was infinitely grateful. We walked to a busy sandwich shop. I told him that I had met with Mrs. Loftin.

"What were your impressions?"

"Clinically?"

"Yeah."

"Is 'fucking lunatic' a diagnosis?"

"Yes, ma'am." Win gave our identical orders to a waitress with hair dyed so black, her skin looked like computer paper. "What about Tonya, what's up with her?"

"I told you she decided to keep the baby, didn't I?"

"I can't remember. The southern air affects my brain. Makes me logy. Is she going to move home?"

"God, no. We're looking for an apartment. This afternoon, actually."

Win leaned forward to grab the tray. His brows were knit together and his bottom lip was pursed, dimpling his chin. When I looked at him questioningly, he tried to erase all signs of sadness and smiled. "C'mon, kiddo. Let's go."

We found a round table near the bathrooms, unoccupied because of an overturned drink. I grabbed a wad of napkins and cleaned the mess while Win held the food. Pinches of distress dimpled his brows as he set down the tray, took a seat.

"Why so glum, chum?" I asked.

"Ariana's having a real hard time adjusting to the divorce."

Without thinking, I put my hand over his. After a few seconds he gently slid his out from under and rubbed his eyes. I felt embarrassed. I had only meant the gesture to be one of concern.

Win seemed unaware. "Lydia and Bart broke up. Actually, that's not right. He broke up with her. She's crushed. The prick swept her off her feet and she basically gambled everything on him. But it was just sport fucking. He ruined a marriage en passant, and it turns out this wasn't the first time either. He gets some kind of a thrill, I guess. Lydia was devastated, she cried all weekend. We both did, actually. She screwed up and is realizing it. Finally."

"Boy." I could barely imagine the sea of remorse Lydia was flailing in.

How do you take something like that back?

"She, we, uh, talked about the possibility of reconciling."

The way he said it, I was sure that they had slept together. I was so mortified by a surge of jealousy that I overcompensated, clothing my words in much more enthusiasm than called for. "Well, that's great! Just great! Will they move down here? Or . . ." *Please say no, please say no!* "Would you go back up there?"

But he didn't say anything at all, just continued to massage his eyes, kneading his lids in a slow, soothing motion.

"Win?"

Finally aware of his own level of distraction, he looked up. "I'm sorry. I don't know. I really don't know what to do. Did you ask if I would go back up to Detroit?"

"Yeah."

"No. Not now, anyway. I signed a contract. I made a commitment. Another one. I don't think she has a whole lot of room to ask me to do that." He lifted his eyes. "Do you?"

"I'm hardly the person to be approached for marital advice." I jerked my shoulders and eyebrows into a goofy shrug. "Want an ice cream?"

He laughed. "You know what—that might be just the therapeutic intervention I need. I'll tell you what, Marti Maxwell-Trailor, I'll let you off the hook, excuse you from my marital morass, if you'll treat me to a chocolate cone with Snickers pieces."

I blushed at my transparency. "I'm sorry, it's just—"

"I know. And you're right. We'll both leave our marriages outside the office. Park 'em, as your pal Colby might say, like wet umbrellas. Deal?"

This, too, felt a little dangerous. "Deal."

I went to buy the cones. We walked back to the hospital together, occasionally being bumped into each other by people in greater hurries than we were. Tonya met us when we got off the elevator. "Hey, Ms. Trailor."

"Hi there. You all ready for some apartment hunting?"

"I was scared you were going to forget."

I smiled. "No way. I love looking for apartments. I think I may have been a Realtor in another life."

We trudged through five, each horrid; the second to last set off a bout of near hysteria. The only light in the basement studio came from the iridescent eyes of an electric portrait of Jesus. On my way out, I tripped over the cord, interrupting the incessant library-like hum of the picture, blackening the orbs.

"You done blinded him!" Tonya squealed. We both tried not to laugh in front of the landlord, but it was useless.

The last place on the list was perfect. While it was only one room with a low-pitched ceiling over a single bed, it was bright and well furnished and had room for a crib. It was also within walking distance of the high school.

"It reminds me of my dollhouse!" Tonya exclaimed, looking at the little green-and-blue-plaid love seat and rocking chair with matching cushion. "I don't think I've ever wanted something bad as I want this," she whispered on the way down to talk to the landlady, who lived in the two floors beneath the converted attic.

"You think I should take it, Ms. Trailor?" she asked, turning toward me.

"Yep," I answered, throwing nondirective counseling to the wind. "I really do."

Rather than being reluctant to rent to a single mother, the landlady was thrilled at the prospect of having a baby in the house. On the way back to the group home, Tonya turned to me.

"Um, I got a favor. And you can say no if you're too busy 'cause I know it's an imposition and all. And it might even not be allowed . . ."

"What is it?"

"See, um, Dr. Stamp—do you know her? A lady doctor down to the clinic?"

"Yeah, I've met her."

"Anyways, last time I had my appointment she told me to sign up for that Lamaze class. She said it helps a whole lot. I, uh, I was kind of hoping you could be my coach?"

"I'm really honored that you asked me. I just don't know if I can figure it out logistically. How about I talk with my husband and see what I can work out?"

"I know there ain't no way my mother'd do it. I thought about asking Amber, but she falls out just thinking about blood."

On my way home, I thought about how exciting it would be to witness the birth and decided to work hard to arrange it. The kids and I spent the evening sorting socks, the benchmark activity of an approaching school season. I dumped out the large cardboard box labeled "Sole Searching" and the four of us classified, by size, color, and loss of elasticity, the lone stockings.

Long after the kids went to bed, Batman barked, announcing Elliot's return from the quality improvement meeting.

"Hey," he said, putting the folder he was carrying onto the coffee table. Batman jumped up and knocked it down.

"Get down, damn it!" He brushed the air in front of the dog as if he were slapping him. I bent to retrieve a sheet that had landed by my feet. It was a chart redundantly labeled "Confidential Settlements, Departmental. CONFIDENTIAL." "Here," he said, opening his hand. I gave it to him. "Thanks."

He left the room. I heard him slide open his desk drawer, then go into the bedroom closet. When he came back he was in jeans and a sweatshirt. He perched rigidly on the couch, reached for the television control, didn't speak. Remote Man, I thought to myself. Screw it. I went straight for the punch line.

"Elliot, one of my clients asked me to be her birthing coach. I'd like to do it. The class is just for a month of Friday evenings. I'll try to find a sitter, but do you think you could arrange to be at home if I can't?"

"You're kidding, right?" I felt my back stiffen. Tension filled the space between us. We might as well have been rival gang members coming upon each other in an alley. "You know I can't guarantee that, Marti."

"Why can't you have one night off a week on a regular basis?"

"Because that's the way Nigel has it set up. It's a rotating call schedule." He used the supremely patronizing tone of voice of his father, slowly enunciating his words as if language comprehension were my problem.

"I understand that, but since this is for one of his clinic patients, maybe he'd make an exception?"

"I doubt it."

He began channel surfing. Bright images flashed at a dizzying speed. Some of the colors spilled onto the walls. The accompanying sound was loud and disjointed. The activity seemed violent.

"I would really appreciate your help, El."

He turned, his handsome face an unreadable mask. "Well, fine. If you can find a sitter, I'll let her go if I'm off."

"Okay."

"Actually, I'm a little surprised that you would want to take this on, Marti. It's not like the kids are grown. Do you really think it's a good idea to start working at night, too?"

"It's four ninety-minute sessions, Elliot. Jesus, you sound like a character on *Mad Men*."

"C'mon, Mart—"

And for some reason that was what did it. "Elliot, we can't keep going like this. The hostility is so awful. Colby—she gave me the name of a therapist, one that she—"

"You've been talking about us?" His voice was low, menacing. "About *me*?"

"To Colby, Elliot! About what things have been like. The doctor sounds really good. She and John went to him—"

"Good for them. I have less than zero interest in talking to anyone about us. And I would really appreciate it if you would stop. Maybe what you ought to be thinking about is how you've changed." Before walking out, he looked at me with such disgust that I barely recognized myself in his eyes. I sat there feeling as though I'd been deposited in somebody else's life.

How did this happen?

CHAPTER NINE

"I know you don't like press, Marti, but this is a very good piece."

Leland is fanning the air with a magazine. I've already seen the article. It's about my dad. Of course, my indictment for murder was discussed in the second paragraph. But unlike other accounts, this one stressed the circumstantial nature of most of the evidence. A little slant of sunlight between the blinds.

I had a terrifying epiphany during discovery. Leland was given access to the state's case and was filling me in on what he'd found in their files. All of a sudden it came to me. A good prosecutor can twist the most innocent event into a noose. Chappell Wycliff will do that and will then use the leftover cord for a rope line outside the Governor's Mansion.

A second syringe was found in my possession, this one in the top drawer of my office desk. I knew where the other came from, but this was a mystery. Midway through discovery, I had a full-blown asthma attack and was taken to the ER for a shot of adrenaline before I could resume the session. That was before we were informed that there was a recording of me leaving the crime scene. When Leland asked to see it, Wycliff's assistant informed him that he'd have a copy delivered shortly. Leland furiously objected to this and came close to accusing the prosecution of evidence tampering. It ended up that Leland would view the original film as soon as it came back from the lab, which was trying to remove static from the images.

"Look, Marti . . ." He is still waving the magazine. "Information like this will get to the jury. You'll see. Controlling the spin is imperative. This is worth weeks of PR."

He points at the picture framed by the columns of text. It is a decades-old photo of my very young father marching with his father. And Martin Luther King. Leland doesn't spell out what he means, but I know. Since I'm going to be tried in the city, much of the jury will be black.

"Now, if this case was out in one of the counties, I'd venture that we'd have to do a little rehabilitation," he says heartily, removing his expensive sport coat to reveal a crisp white shirt tucked into Saturday afternoon khakis.

"Like what? Releasing a picture of my mom at a Tea Party rally?"

He laughs.

Sometimes Leland reminds me of every lawyer joke I have ever heard. I wonder if he's ever given a moment's worth of thought to whether or not I am innocent. He's not really interested in that. It's all about winning. There is something so disheartening about this, I'm afraid I may weep. I am reminded of Elliot and his friends talking about impressive diagnoses they made—the patient, the *person,* absent from all of the self-congratulatory discussions.

Leland misreads my face and says, "I know you're wearing down now. But it's too early for that, girl! Buck up. Look alive! The fight is just getting started!"

I half expect him to slap me on the back. He waits for a response, but I am momentarily incapable of providing one. He says nothing, just studies me, something approaching alarm beginning to tighten his brow.

Finally I whisper, "Okay."

He is relieved. "Good girl. I want you to practice speaking up. You need to be definite in the courtroom, Marti. Jurors get suspicious of people who mumble."

The morning after our fight about the prenatal class, I awoke confused by the breakfast sounds coming from so close. I stood and felt as though I had been given an anesthetic, the effects slow to wear off.

"Are you sick?" Nina asked suspiciously when I made my way into the kitchen. "Is that why you slept on the couch?"

"No. I just fell asleep out there." I smiled, assuming a reassuring tone of voice. I filled a mug with water and stuck it in the microwave.

"It's because you and Daddy were fighting last night," she declared.

I tried to remember what she may have heard—what was just internal artillery and what I actually said.

"We were talking about schedules, sweetie."

"Right." Tween sarcasm achieved in one syllable.

"Nina, don't push my buttons this morning. I'm not in the mood. Go get ready to meet your new teacher. And try to find something to wear that doesn't look like it escaped from the hamper."

I showered and had just finished putting on a blue tank top and white capris when all three of the kids burst in.

"Mom?" Simon asked. "If I'm really nice all day, would you consider rewarding my behavior with some of those soldiers from that toy store?"

He was talking about the shop outside of Colonial Williamsburg, where we'd gone for a surprisingly pleasant outing in the beginning of the summer. Amid overheated actors decked out in wool costumes and tourists stunned by the humidity, we saw milk churned into butter, herbs ground into medicines. After that we all had lunch in an authentic tavern, where we were served by a sadistic waiter who brought out the order one item at a time. But we had laughed a lot and Elliot had been present, really present, the whole day. He led the kids in a discussion about totems during which Poppy claimed me as her spirit animal (which made Elliot howl with delight), and then he taught them the words to "Crash into Me" while we waited for our sandwiches. The four of them sang together, Nina's sweet, clear voice carrying above the restaurant din. When they finished the last line, the people behind us clapped and El got the kids to stand and bow. An older woman stopped by and put her hand on my arm. "What an exceptional family. You are very lucky indeed."

On our way home, we stopped at a toy store. A display case of little iron militia wearing blue and gray mesmerized Simon. While I indignantly pointed to the museum card that read, "The War of Northern Aggression," Simon nursed the birth of a new fixation. Those soldiers had fought their way into daily discussions.

"We'll see," I said. "All right, let's get going! Poppy-flower, go find your shoes so we can get to the open house to meet your new teacher. I know you're going to love kindergarten. I can't believe how mature you are."

Uninspired by my motivational speech, she inched out of the bedroom dragging her baby doll, Poppy, behind her.

"How come Daddy's not going?" Nina asked from the hall, where she was doing a gymnastic stretch.

"He's got work, honey."

"So do you," she pointed out.

"Well—it's easier for me to take the time off." I studied my daughter, but she was unreadable. Had she heard the whole fight last night? Without fanfare, she had prematurely crossed a developmental threshold and was now able to banish her emotions from her face. "What's wrong, honey?"

"It doesn't feel like you like each other that much."

"That's not true. Of course we like each other—we love each

other." I took a deep breath. "Anytime people live together there are differences and disagreements. People fight sometimes."

"How come he hardly ever does things with us?"

"Sweetie, Daddy's a doctor. Doctors always have to be available to their patients. He does really important work. He saves lives and brings babies into the world."

And therefore, whatever you're doing or need is secondary.

I had just allowed Doctor's Spouse Syndrome to spawn Doctor's Child Syndrome, and I was furious with myself. When Nina left I put my hand on the corner of the dresser. The sharp edge dug into my palm and I thought about maybe going alone to the therapist Colby recommended. I needed help.

Right then, as if she knew I was thinking of her, Colby called.

"Martha Helen, I'm so glad I caught you!" She was using her finger-bowl-and-charm-school voice, which made me smile.

"Hi."

"You doing all right, Marti? You sound vexed."

"Fair."

Simon appeared in the doorway, so I put on my bright voice. "I only have a sec. It's meet and greet day at school."

"Shake and fake. Poor you. Just wanted to let you know that I went out for dinner last night and when I went into the bathroom this ill-mannered creature answered her cell phone while I was sitting on the toilet. I almost climbed over the stall and snatched her bald-headed."

I laughed.

Colby had a list of restroom rules a mile long.

"Call when you can talk," she instructed. "I'm worried about you."

I piled everyone in the car and headed to the school.

Mr. Brandt, Nina's new teacher, was so cute that both of us were momentarily tongue-tied when we met him. A Jussie Smollett doppelgänger, he smilingly described the upcoming year. He complimented Nina's posture and asked if she was a gymnast. She responded by standing even straighter, saying yes, and falling in love. I saw it happen.

Poppy's classroom was a happy jumble of primary colors and livestock. Along one wall were two rabbits, an aquarium of neon fish, and a canary named Spot. Mrs. Tomasowki, fresh out of an education program, was as perky as her room. She gave Poppy a handheld tour and then knelt to ask all sorts of respectful questions about her doll, further endearing herself to her newest pupil. Because I had been having horrible fantasies of having to home-school my baby, I almost kissed the woman as we said good-bye.

Relief swept me down the hallway.

And then we reached Simon's class. It was bare and oppressive, with a deafening buzz from the fluorescent light. Except for the names of the students printed on halfhearted paper telescopes stapled on the wall, there were no decorations. After an impersonal smile, Mrs. Meridy made no effort at conversation, suggesting instead that we look around and feel free to ask questions. She stood in front of her immaculate desk with her arms crossed, guarding it from any ill-mannered children who might try to lay claim.

The teacher's silence resulted in me entering the Babble Zone, where whole sentences acted like kids on an Easter egg hunt. I gushed about Simon's summer, his sports, his recent interest in chess and the Civil War. How he often was the most mature person in gatherings of any age.

The more the teacher acted like a polite but bored seatmate on a train, the faster I danced.

"Okay, Mom," Simon eventually said. "Let's go."

I looked at my middle child, who had completely deflated. I couldn't believe that I'd made the annual tuition appeal to his grandparents for this.

Great.

Just fucking great.

At O'Malley's Buffet, where we could make return trips to the loosely defined salad bar, Simon ate only a roll. I reached across the table, pushed his surfer-boy bangs off his forehead, pinched a fallen eyelash off of his cheek, and instructed him to make a wish.

"I wish I didn't have to go to school," he whispered.

I was sure I had read in some parenting magazine advice about just such a problem. Children need to be taught coping methods was the gist. So against my better judgment, I said, "Come on, Simon. Let's give her a fair chance. And anyway, I think you're tough enough to handle her even if she's not the greatest." Then I actually said, "Life isn't always fair."

Which triggered tears.

Simon never cried.

"It'll be okay," Nina said.

I left a tip and led everyone outside to the parking lot. I was overcome with confusion. Parenting dilemmas were so varied, so complicated, that I often envied my young clients' reflexive responses. Instead of obsessing about the right course, the one that would be approved by current child-rearing masters, the teenage mothers followed their instincts, then moved on.

We were heading back to the van, weaving our way through parked cars, when Poppy let out a shriek. "I forgot Poppy! I forgot my baby at the table and I need her vewy much!"

As I turned to go back, Simon said, "I'll get her."

He jogged toward the restaurant, and just as I started to warn him of a van that had appeared in the corner of my eye, the cranberry-colored vehicle sped up to reach the mouth of the parking lot while the light was still green.

The world spun as I watched my child become airborne.

"*Simon!*" I screamed. "*Simon! Simon! Simon!*"

And then he landed.

I had never experienced true terror until I heard the silence. Simon was on the ground, one of his arms bent crazily. He was totally still. Behind me, Nina brayed like a wounded animal and Poppy dropped down between two cars, rocking back and forth, patting her chest. The woman driving the car was screaming, hysterical. "I didn't see him! Oh, my God! Oh, my God! I didn't see him!"

"Ambulance." I was using an unfamiliar voice. It belonged to someone in control, someone present. "Get an ambulance."

Simon's eyes were closed, his hair beaded with gravel. His little name tag from school was still on his shirt. One of his untied high-tops had been knocked from a sockless foot.

"Wake up! . . . Simon! Wake up!" I instructed, as if I could command him into consciousness.

He lay still.

"All right, that's all right, baby. It's okay. It's okay. You can stay sleeping. You're going to be fine, my love. And I'm going to get you out of that horrible woman's class right away. I should have done it when we were still at school. I just got confused, is all," I said, sobbing. "Give me another chance. I promise to do better. . . ." I began stroking his head, praying with all of my might. "Simon, please get up, honey. Wake up and give me another chance." He didn't move. "Please let him be all right. Please let him be all right," I kept repeating, not stopping until the aborted wail of an ambulance turned off midcry, shocking me into focusing on my surroundings. I looked up and realized I didn't see Poppy. Panic escalated into hysteria.

"Poppy! . . . Poppy!"

Nina found her. She'd wet her pants. They approached as though walking toward a fire. They couldn't look at their brother. The rescue workers gently moved me out of the way, and one of them began to examine Simon. I was aware of disjointed phrases spoken into his shoulder microphone. "Unconscious. . . . Correct. Obvious compound fracture right radius. Still unresponsive." The man turned toward me. "Okay, ma'am. We're going to hustle him down to the hospital. You can ride with us."

My chest was getting tighter and tighter, rationing my air supply. "Can my other two?" I was watching myself, surprised that I could form words. The squad drivers exchanged a brief look and then agreed to let Nina and Poppy ride up front.

At the hospital, Simon's stretcher was raced past the hordes of faceless people in the emergency room, providing a momentary diversion, briefly silencing their own misery. My girls followed behind in stunned procession. After we had been parked in an examining room and a brusque triage nurse barked her questions at me, I called the OB-GYN Department.

The Christine who answered said that Elliot wasn't available. Which seemed to be the final trigger for an all-out asthma attack. "I . . . need . . . to speak . . . with . . . him. This is . . . his wife," I panted, my fingers searching violently for the inhaler in my purse.

"He doesn't have any clinic patients scheduled this morning. But I'll see if anyone knows where he's at." And then, before I could say anything else, I was put on hold. Tighter and tighter squeezed my bronchial tubes as I turned the purse upside down on the desk, sifting through its contents until the L-shaped inhaler finally tumbled out. Without swiping the opening free of debris, I cradled the receiver under my chin and sucked in the medicine. Little pieces of tobacco and dirt clung to my lip and tongue. Tears streamed down my cheeks as I watched the backs of the doctors working on Simon.

Christine came back on the line, a little smirk in her voice. "I'm sure sorry, Ms. Trailor, but no one—"

I interrupted, forcing the words out with a puff of medicine.

"Get . . . him . . . to . . . the . . . emergency . . . room." I stopped and tried to breathe in. "His son has been hit by a car." I hung up and sucked in another dose of medicine, holding it in my lungs until they burned, leaning forward to catch my breath. Black spots danced before my eyes.

"Momma!" Nina screamed from the corner. Poppy whimpered.

"I'm okay," I huffed, opening my arms to the girls to hug them, conserving my breath by not speaking. One of the residents saw my distress and came over, her stethoscope already in hand. She listened quickly to my chest, went to the drug cabinet, and drew up an injection.

"Here, Mrs. Trailor. This is epinephrine. Have you had it before?" She spoke softly, obviously breaking protocol and trying not to call attention to herself.

I nodded.

"Good. It ought to help. Your little guy is going to want his mother upright."

I was unaware of the needle's sting and only vaguely aware of my heart racing from the medicine. I took hold of a hand from each daughter, and the three of us clutched one another, a silent chain of stiff paper dolls.

"Marti!" John Kusik came running through the door, looking half-crazed, his lab coat open over his big belly and flapping out and behind like fins on an old car. "Oh, Marti, sweetheart, what happened!"

"Where's Elliot?" I whispered.

"I'm not sure. They're looking for him, though. We'll find him. He must be somewhere."

"Somewhere?" My whispered question climaxed hysterically.

"Slow down, hon," John said. He put his fleshy hand to my cheek, and the move had a surprisingly calming effect. He spoke in a low voice. "One of the nurses thought he signed out after rounds. Nigel's got someone trying your house. He's probably at home sleeping."

"He's here, John! He had a meeting."

"Okay, then, we'll find him. And in the meantime, I'm here." His right eye twitched a little. "I'm an old pro at this."

I nodded and allowed myself to be pulled into a hug. His girth encompassed me and I relaxed into him. For a moment I felt tamed.

"Have you taken your asthma medication, Marti?"

"Yes."

"Excuse me, please."

We both looked at the young resident, who spoke with a French accent. He was holding his small, compact body in the upright posture of a well-mannered schoolboy. He actually waited for an invitation to speak.

I tried to smile encouragement, but my lips didn't respond.

"What is your plan?" John asked.

"We're going to proceed down to Radiology now, Dr. Kusik. I feel a CT scan is in order. We also want to get his arm examined by the orthopedist right away. With your permission, Mrs. Trailor, one of the nurses will show you to the doctors' waiting room. I'm sure you'll be far more comfortable in there. You may adjust the air-conditioning, which should help with your breathing."

I nodded, but my fear, which had been dormant for a few moments, returned.

Please, God, let Simon be getting special treatment because of John and not because he's dying.

The tiny Haitian resident looked up at John. "I'm sure the attending will appreciate the opportunity to check on young Simon himself."

John nodded and looked back at me. "Now, I can either stay with the girls or go with Simon down to Radiology. It's up to you."

The choice almost undid me. I looked at the girls. Both of them seemed to be teetering on the edge of catatonic trances, rocking on their heels, their eyes glazed. A screaming silence was coming from Simon. Where the hell is Elliot, I thought wildly, trying to decide who would be most damaged by abandonment. All of the doctors were looking toward me, waiting.

John stepped in.

"Look, Marti. I think I'd like to be with Simon. Since I work here. You know? Okay?" He squeezed me one last time and accompanied the group as they guided the wheeled table into the hall. The back end hit the doorframe, but still Simon didn't move.

"Hold his hand for me, John. Please don't leave him alone. Don't let go of him!"

"Take the girls down the hall, Marti. I'll catch up to you soon."

We stayed in the lounge a long, long time. We sat on the vinyl couch, where I was bookended by my daughters, my arms around their quivering shoulders. Eventually the girls slept, but fitful twitches jerked their thin limbs like sudden gusts of wind. Poppy smelled of pee.

I stopped myself from replaying the moment of impact by staring out of the window. I studied the groups of people walking toward the hospital. I counted strollers and sweaters, car horns and radios. I refused to let my mind idle because I knew that terror would fill the vacuum and consume me.

I jumped when the door finally opened. I had been expecting to see John's large body and for a brief moment I looked blankly at my husband, not recognizing him.

"Where is he?"

"X-ray," I whispered, my voice clouded by tears.

Elliot spun around to get to his son, slamming into John, who had just appeared behind him. His face was lit by a huge smile. "He's going to be all right, guys. He's going to be just fine. He's got a broken arm and a concussion. But no internal injuries. His brain is fine. The chief of radiology just finished reading the CT scan. Neuro was up there, too. That's what took so long."

Elliot and I wept together in each other's arms.

He offered his hand to John. "Thank you."

"Take me to him," I begged.

"They're getting him set up. We had a long conversation. He told me all about his new teacher. She sounds fairly heinous. I had one just like her in fourth grade."

"Wait!" The significance of his words took a moment to register. "You mean he's awake? Oh, take us to him, please—"

"We'll go up in a second. They're going to keep him here for a couple of days. But we couldn't have asked for anything better. He'll be up on Peeds in a regular room. He's been given a pretty hefty dose of painkillers. I waited until he fell asleep to come back to get you. When I couldn't find . . . While Simon was having the scan, I called Colby. She was going to call William. I hope that's okay?"

"Of course it is!"

But I saw annoyance flash in Elliot's eyes, gone as quickly as it came. In that one instant, I realized that the two men weren't real friends. They were merely husbands of best friends, tied together like relatives at obligatory family events.

I reached out and grabbed John's hand and kissed it. "Thank you, John. For everything."

"You know better than that. Colby'll be here soon to get the girls."

"Thanks," I whispered again. For the first time since we had left the restaurant, I took an unobstructed deep breath. It inflated my lungs and filled my chest.

"You okay?" Elliot asked.

"Now, I am. Can the girls see Simon before they go?"

"Sure."

A medley of Disney princesses and superheroes greeted us from the walls on the Peeds floor. When a bald nursery schooler rounded the corner, both Nina and Poppy gasped. The little boy, whose eyes stared dully from sunken sockets, was making a halfhearted attempt to produce engine sounds while pushing a racecar along the chair rail with one hand and pulling an IV pole with the other.

Nina yanked my shirt, making me lean close so I could hear her whisper. "That's what Charlie used to look like."

The observation startled me. I never would have guessed that she'd remember his appearance after chemo. It had been so long ago and she had been so young. The sponginess of childhood memories was unnerving.

"You're right, sweetie. It's the medicine to make him better that made his hair fall out. It'll grow back." I nodded toward the little boy. I knew it was the baldness that was frightening, not the cancer.

Simon was in a private room, lying in the bed. His arm, in a cast with green-and-brown camouflage design, was elevated on a pillow that rested on his stomach. He turned toward us, eyes soft and out of focus. I was crying again before even reaching the bed. I knelt to kiss him, and our tears merged on his cheeks.

"I'm sorry," Poppy whispered.

"For what, Poppy?" Elliot asked, bending to her.

"She forgot her doll in the restaurant and he was running back to get it when he got hit," Nina answered.

"Poppy," El said, "this wasn't your fault. I promise."

Simon made a funny sound and opened his mouth to speak, but his words were nonsensical. "That teacher took my soldiers. I wanted to play with my soldiers. She took them from the window. Mommy, I want them."

"Oh, honey," I soothed, stroking his hair. I was freaked by how snowed he was.

"What's wrong with him?" Nina asked, backing up.

"It's the pain medicine, honey. It's like being asleep and dreaming," Elliot answered calmly. "He'll be better tomorrow. But I think you both should give him a quick kiss and we'll wait for Colby in the lobby. You brother needs to get his rest so he can heal."

In a flurry they were gone and Simon was asleep again. Simon's dinner tray sat next to his bed untouched. The evening sky, peeking through the orange drapes, was turning eggplant. The traffic noises outside of the window were slowing down. Elliot had gone home to pack bags for us, and I was sitting beside Simon, systematically turning the tattered pages of a large-print *Reader's Digest* someone left behind. I had just finished "Amazing Survival Story" and was about to start on organizing tips when a familiar voice came from the doorway.

"Martha. Dear. How is he?"

No.

I clutched the magazine to my chest and braced. Elliot's mother was standing in the doorway, poised to spew forth an entire conversation in barbed italics, nodding her disproportionately large head, up and down, up and down, as though agreeing with something. "Mrs. Trailor!" I said. "Elliot didn't tell me you were coming—"

"How could we not? Admiral Trailor is parking the car. If he can find a place." She folded her arms across her nearly flat chest.

I relayed the neurologist's prognosis, standing to feel less at a disadvantage.

"What a relief! We were scared to death. But what I can't understand is how it happened. How on earth does a child get hit in a parking lot, holding his mother's hand?"

Zap. There it was. The first shot. Usually Mrs. Trailor's assaults were subtler, her disapproval wrapped in aggressive silence. In normal circumstances, a visit from the in-laws required a trip to the medicine cupboard for a prophylactic tranquilizer. Just to take her edge off. Ironically, there I was in a hospital, world's largest drug cabinet, with no relief in sight.

The presence of Elliot's father was announced by his trademark hissing. It was a high-pitched *whish* he made by blowing air over his tongue, like a kid practicing the *S* sound. He stood in the doorway, erect and overbearing. His oval-shaped head was bald and blotchy pink, an Easter egg impatiently removed from the red dye. "Martha, how is the boy? You're not being too hard on yourself, I hope."

In fairly short order, my own mother and brothers were also in the cramped room, all offering reassurance over Simon's sleeping form. Had my father not been in the Middle East, he too would have been in there, comforting and joking.

The room was closing in with all of the hovering bodies. For some reason clear only to William, he began juggling three balled-up tissues, adding to the chaos. Everyone was there except for Elliot, who I was beginning to think might never reappear.

Barring a Xanax, a drink would have been good. Ever since the first Trailor-Maxwell barbecue years before, alcohol had effectively blurred the sharp-edged differences between the families. For everyone. Liberal Jewish intellectual and rigid WASP military run out of common ground real quick. I always felt as if I were straddling a fault line when both families got together. The quake was definitely going to come; the question was just what kind of damage it would bring and where the divide would end up. In the meantime, cocktails all around helped. I longed for a minibar.

While Simon lay like a centerpiece, out cold and totally oblivious to the emotional meteors streaking through the room, I played hostess for another hour, dancing faster and faster, trying to defuse potentially explosive interactions before they detonated. My sense of claustrophobia intensified.

When Elliot finally returned, suitcases in hand, he assessed the volatile situation and smoothly escorted everyone out, making suggestions for sleeping arrangements on the way to the elevator. I heard their final good-byes and dropped the curtain of composure. When he returned, he switched the light off as he entered. The room seemed quieter in the dark; someone's beeping IV down the hall grew louder. I began to whisper through the tears.

"When he didn't make any noise, I almost couldn't go to him, El. I actually thought about just running the other way. So I wouldn't have to see him. That quiet was the worst sound I ever heard. There was nothing. Nothing. I know I wouldn't survive if he—"

"It's okay, Mart. He's going to be okay."

"There was a moment . . . more than one, when I thought—"

"How did it happen?"

"One second we were almost at the car and . . . Oh God. I think I'll always see that van—"

"When I got the call, my first thought was of his fear of dying—that maybe he'd had some sort of premonition."

I shuddered and Elliot held open his arms. I fell into them and we both cried for a long time. Tears of terror. Tears of relief. We eventually released each other and I went to grab toilet paper for us to blow our noses with. When I returned he said, "Couldn't you have grabbed him, Marti?"

If he had sucker punched me, I would have been less stunned. I stumbled back into the bathroom, sank onto the low lip of the walk-in shower, put my head on my knees. He eventually opened the door. "What I said came out wrong."

Which wasn't an apology.

I looked past him. Reflected in the mirror were two people who'd just survived a terrifying ordeal together. Alone.

"I need to get some sleep," he said.

By the time I followed, he was lying back in the hospital recliner and his breathing was as even as Simon's. I returned to my own stubbornly upright chair and picked up the magazine again. In the glow of the streetlight, I struggled through an article about C-sections and gluten intolerance. I tried to make sense of the over-size words until they tripped off the page, one after the other.

In the way dreams work, I surfaced not to the accident, but to a wonderful memory. It was back when Nina was a baby. The three of us went to a bluegrass festival out in Southwest Virginia.

I'd laughed when El packed his twelve-string. "Like a kid bring-ing a mitt to watch a baseball game?" I asked as he stood it next to the diaper bag in the back of the Toyota.

"You'll see." He smiled.

We wandered the crowd of coal miners and hippies, and he stopped to jam with pickup bands far from the stage. Nina was in a backpack. She blissfully kicked my sides with her little feet, keep-ing time with the Appalachian rhythm. Elliot kept reaching over to kiss her fat ankles. It was a day of perfect moments.

Remembering them hurt.

I went into the bathroom, turned on the light-slash-noisy fan, washed my face with the stuff from the soap dispenser, and pulled back my hair. When I emerged Elliot was peppering Simon with math problems to reassure himself. When he found no deficits, he hugged him carefully, said good-bye to me, and went down to the clinic to check on some of his patients.

"I was thinking," the seven-year-old angled after we were alone, "that since I got hurt maybe Mrs. Meridy wouldn't be the best teacher for me."

I laughed and felt huge relief that his craftiness was intact. "I'll see what I can do."

The various relatives staggered their visits. It was easier for me to deal with my mother-in-law one-on-one than with an audience. Before leaving, Mrs. Trailor asked for directions to a mall because both girls had outgrown not only their coats, but their shoes as well. In a burst of retaliatory passive aggression, I thanked her and gave directions to a distant shopping center, the path to which I knew would be plagued by traffic jams and road construction.

William and Michael stopped by on their way back to Washington. Michael glanced at Simon to verify the depth of his slumber and then spoke quietly.

"You should have seen Mom last night, Mart. Mrs. Jailor was taking things out of the cupboard and putting them in the dishwasher. Making little snippy comments about your spring cleaning being two seasons late. And all of a sudden Mom went ballistic."

I braced myself. "What did she say?"

"Have you," Mikey impersonated, "considered medication for your cleaning compulsions?"

I groaned.

"She's right, though, Mart. That is a biblically fucked-up family."

The dysfunction in the Old Testament used to give him

nightmares. Then I realized he had said family. Not couple. He had included Elliot.

Simon whimpered and his eyelids fluttered as though he were struggling to wake up. I gently pushed the hair from his face and bent down to kiss his forehead, where rusty abrasions had formed during the night.

"Hey, W-Will? Do you want me to g-go down and get the c-car? Meet you out front?" Michael asked.

"By yourself? Are you kidding? The only thing you can do single-handedly is sex."

I saw surprise flash across my younger brother's face. William had just changed plans on him. All of us were going to talk about something whether Mikey wanted to or not.

"What?" I whispered, bracing myself. "What's the matter?"

"We just want to know what's going on with you and Elliot."

I shrugged slightly.

"W-we're here for you," Michael offered.

"I know." I allowed him to pull me into a hug and nodded into his chest. "I can't talk about anything now."

William cleared his throat. "Tell Simon his favorite uncle says to look both ways from now on."

At dinner I was picking at fries when a dozen Mylar balloons were delivered, each weighted down by a heavy Civil War soldier. Simon let out an uncharacteristic squeal when he saw the blue and gray warriors and my heart leapt at his excitement. It was the first time all day he had smiled.

I was untying the little men from their strings when Elliot came by to say good night.

"Home run in the gift department," I said, smiling.

"What?"

I pointed.

"Wasn't me." He shrugged, kissing the top of Simon's head.

"Really? Who could it have been?"

"Just about anybody who's spent more than ten minutes with him this summer."

"That's true." But it tugged at me. And when I asked Elliot again who he thought might have sent them, he snapped, "What difference does it make?"

By the third and last morning in the hospital, I was ready to jump out of my skin. My mother had ridden the train back up to D.C. and the Trailors had dug in for the duration, making morning and afternoon visits, taking turns in the lobby with the girls, and driving me crazy in Simon's room.

It was discharge time, and I was maneuvering a metal belongings cart down the hall, the task hindered by a rogue wheel, when I saw a familiar shade of orange hair. Larraine. She was bending over the water fountain, her snug shirt creeping up to reveal a tramp stamp of a sun interrupted by red stretch marks.

I would have backed down the hallway if she hadn't caught me and glared.

"Larraine, what are you doing here?"

"Like you don't know." Her nostrils flared, shrinking her eyes.

"I'm sorry . . ." I smiled a little, trying to deflect some of the hostility. "I haven't been at work this week. If you left me a message, I mean. I'm a little behind."

"Harley's got something wrong with his blood. Septi-something."

"Oh, I'm sorry to hear that."

"The doctor says it's my fault 'cause he got it from a ear infection."

"Was he sick for a while?"

"How am I supposed to know? All that kid ever does is scream. The doctor told me he was going to call Social Services—so I don't appreciate you acting like you don't know nothing about this!"

Her pale finger poked through the air at me. She was commanding a lot of attention from the lounge at the end of the hallway, and I felt embarrassed blood rush to my cheeks. If I had been in my official capacity, holding a clipboard, maybe, it wouldn't have been so bad. But I wasn't. The professional shield offered no protection during off-hours. She approached and I flinched. It wouldn't be the first time a social worker bought it at the hands of a disgruntled client.

"Larraine, I don't work for Child Protective. Remember?"

She seemed to consider this. "Well, can you call them off of me, then?"

"I can't. But I'd be happy to come out and help you with Harley."

Which didn't go over well. Larraine's overgenerous bottom lip deepened to an unsavory shade of purple. "I never asked you to come poking around in the first place. Looking down your nose, telling me to clean my house."

"Okay, Larraine, okay. I hope Harley gets better soon. And I'd be more than happy to talk with you. But right now, I need to go. You have my number if you want to call me at the office."

"Fuck you, you stuck-up bitch! And anyways I'm pregnant again. And ain't none of y'all going to come near this one!"

Perfect.

Which was when I saw Nigel standing next to my mother-in-law outside of Simon's room. They were both watching the scene with identical expressions of disdain.

"Goodness. I've never seen anyone so angry," Elliot's mother oozed as I approached. Only because you don't have eyes in the back of your head, I thought. "Anyway, dear, Dr. Hill stopped by to check on Simon's progress. Wasn't that lovely?"

It was standard colleague etiquette.

"Mrs. Trailor," Nigel said to me, "is everything all right?"

"Unhappy customer," I responded, trying to smile. The last thing I wanted was to get into a conversation about my job with either of them.

"Have you ever wondered, young lady, if you were in the wrong business?" Nigel asked.

"Excuse me?"

"Sometimes people misfire when choosing careers."

It was a body slam. He wasn't saying that social work was a hard job. He was saying I wasn't good at it.

Mrs. Trailor drove us all home, where she had dinner waiting with water glasses, bread plates, and unnecessary silverware. She commented on the fact that nothing matched and that she'd found only two salad forks. "What happened to the service you got when you married?"

"For fuck's sake," I thought I uttered just in my head.

When a screaming silence of shock broke out, I realized my mistake. The children looked from one of us to the other, three little weather vanes in distress. "I'm sorry," I said quietly. "I'm grateful for all of your help. Truly. I'm pretty frayed, though. Obviously. And not having matching dinnerware isn't that important. To *me*, I mean. Especially right now. Okay?"

It wasn't.

Less than an hour later, they climbed into their gleaming white Escalade and headed back to Annapolis. I was so relieved that I could have danced.

CHAPTER TEN

It's interesting to see how relationships peel away. The first to go are the most superficial ones, of course, the people you chat with only in car-pool lines or the checkout aisles. They get busy when they see me coming now, studying shopping lists or searching their purses. Then there are the women I've actually spent time with, have gotten to know—and even liked. Most of them have scattered like dropped coins.

Paige Brice is an exception. She wrote me a beautiful note and offered her home for my parents to stay in. It made me cry. Someday I'll know what to say to thank her. I got a card from Natalie Hill, too. In a shaky hand, she declared confidence in my innocence and asked me to call. I was touched by the gesture, but I can barely speak with my own family, let alone peripheral people. From the children's school I received a letter in which outside counseling was recommended for the kids during "this trying period."

Wycliff's universe is growing alongside his political aspirations. His candidacy has conferred star quality upon him. It's the kind I recognize from childhood, the importance of the politician measured by the posturing of those around him. The buzz. I saw it in the hallways of the courthouse before voir dire: people waiting to be acknowledged and momentarily exalted through the attentions of the next attorney general.

Win called. It was the first time we've spoken since this whole thing started. He has phoned every day, but I can't bear to speak with him. Colby tricked me into it last night by telling me it was my father on the line. As soon as I heard Win's voice, I burst into tears. So did he.

"I wish I could hold you," he said again and again. To which I could only nod, unseen. Before he called I had been looking in the medicine cabinet, searching for the right cocktail of drugs. Just in case.

Somehow Win seemed to understand what I was contemplating. "This will go away, Marti. And I'll be here," he said. "Waiting for you."

And then he extracted a guarantee that I wouldn't do anything to harm myself.

I gave it to him. In the grand scheme of things, what's a broken promise?

The long weekend was finally over. It had been a rough couple of days, full of nightmares about the accident and temper tantrums born of anxiety. Elliot had been present, but only barely.

Simon climbed into my lap. "I don't want to go to school. My arm hurts."

"I'll give you a Tylenol, sweetie." I tousled his hair. "At least Mrs. Meridy's not your teacher. Then you'd have a pain in your butt, too."

"You'll get to show everyone your cool cast," Nina said.

Just as he seemed ready to capitulate, Poppy announced that she hated kindergarten and wasn't going.

Please give me strength, God.

"Poppy, you have to go to school. It's the law," Nina warned, employing one of my more effective parenting tricks. The penal code appealed to the younger children's fascination with jail, the quintessential Time-Out.

But Poppy remained stoic, arms crossed. "I don't want to go. Not evah! Mrs. Harder is as mean as a witch."

"Who's that?" I asked.

"My teacher!" She slammed down her Tigger cup so hard that milk splashed all over her outfit. Fast, angry tears followed.

"That's okay, Poppyseed. I'll get you something else to wear. Anyway, your teacher seems lovely. But her name is Mrs. Tomasowki. Why do you call her Mrs. Harder?"

"She said to call her Mrs. T 'cause her real name is Harder." Both Nina and Simon burst out laughing. One look at my youngest warned me that if I so much as smiled, there'd be no way in hell I'd be able to force her to go to school. Ever.

"Knock it off, you guys. Poppy, you finish your cereal. I'll get you a different shirt."

She just nodded and fished for the dull-colored marshmallow star in her bowl. Going through her bureau was the epitome of a brink activity. Poppy's drawers were crammed so full of outgrown clothes she wasn't ready to part with that they were virtually impossible to open. I pulled a new dress from the closet. She allowed me to change her whole outfit, but then her face clouded with an all-too-familiar expression. My shoulders retracted immediately.

"These socks don't feel nice!"

I took a really deep breath. "Poppy, I will readjust the seams. Once. Then that's all. Understand?" Her eyes filled, but she nodded. Fortunately the car pool honked. After waving them off, I realized that I didn't ask why she'd said her teacher was mean. I sighed, hoped it had been just a passing sentiment, because I knew the uptight headmaster would never allow two Trailor children to play musical classrooms.

For the first time in weeks, I was alone in the house. Alone with my thoughts. I called Win and told him that I'd be late and then called Colby and asked her to come over. She heard my distress, didn't hesitate.

We sat on the old wicker swing on the front porch, taking turns with our feet to rock back and forth. The soothing motion was accompanied by a rhythmic squeaking. Her gardenia perfume floated toward me.

"He blamed me for Simon's accident, Colby."

"Jesus, Marti."

"He says I've changed. Kind of like an emotional bait and switch. I was one way when we got married and now I'm not. I wish you knew how much he used to love me."

"I do, sugar. Did you talk to him about counseling?"

"He's not interested."

"You could still go."

"Maybe." I smiled. "Or you could be my proxy."

"You mean say something like, uh, I have this friend . . ."

"Exactly."

Her voice dropped a little and she looked into my face. "What about a trial separation? So you can figure out what you want? It's not only up to him."

The swing's glide was so comforting, her words just floated by. Somehow the conversation was softened and the harsh reality of divorce took on an almost peaceful aura.

I had begun testing the idea of separation, trying to imagine life without Elliot. I knew that when I finally surrendered to its inevitability, it would be like letting go.

"I've been reading about divorce and kids," I admitted.

She reached over and took my hand. "What have you learned?"

"Basically, everything boils down to two theories. Splitting up is better than a toxic marriage. And short of an abusive household, children don't want to come from broken homes."

"Jesus. That's helpful."

"I know, and what if the answer is different for each child?"

"You're going to have to just help them through it. Seriously, what's going on now can't be good for anyone."

I nodded. "I can't take the unpredictability anymore. I just wish I knew how we got here."

"Shit happens. But Marti? Do me a favor? Get all your financial affairs together. Just in case. Stop being such an airhead about money. Find out where Elliot keeps the important stuff. Bank papers, insurance policies, his 401(k). The 409."

"The 409?"

"It's a cleaning supply."

"Ha. Ha."

We hugged in the driveway and I tried to hold on to the calm as I drove into work.

Win's angry voice carried from his office.

"Look, Lydia. Damn it! I'm doing everything I can. I didn't exactly plan this, you know. My being down here was a result of Bart's handiwork." Pause. "I *told* you I forgive you. But I can't fly up there every time something happens. We're talking five hundred dollars a pop." There was another pause. "Why do we keep going over the same territory?"

When he slammed the phone down, I considered retracing my steps, but he came out before I could make a move.

"Marti! Welcome back. How's Simon? How are you?"

"Everyone's at school, which is a step in the right direction. Are you doing okay?"

"Ariana's been acting out. Lydia's ready for the gas pipe." The expression on his face was pure misery. "I guess I'll just rack up some more frequent-flier miles. Pretty soon I should have enough for a round-trip to the moon. It's getting old."

"What's going on?"

"School started a few weeks ago up there and Ariana's been acting out. Lydia has to force her out of the car every morning. She refuses to ride the bus. I believe we're looking at an elementary school dropout."

"I'm sorry."

"I guess it's time to find a kiddie shrink. Before things escalate."

"There's nothing wrong with that, Win."

"I know. I just thought it wouldn't be until adolescence. But we could clearly use a little guidance."

I spent most of the day trying to catch up on my case files, using it as a way to keep my dying marriage in its box. Both Win and I needed to stay late after work—I wanted to pick Tonya up for the Lamaze class, and Win had to catch up on some work. There was something cozy about being in the suite in the quiet of the evening. I called home for the second time to check on the kids. All three of them were giddy with excitement, brimming with grade-school gossip. Sonya, the new grandmotherly sitter Colby had recommended after Katie returned to school herself, was preparing dinner and had already initiated baths. I thought it must be something like having a wife. I blew kisses into the receiver and hung up.

When the sun dropped beyond the expressway, I tapped the papers on my desk into neat stacks of totally unrelated piles and got my stuff together. I went to say good night.

"Hey." I smiled.

Win looked up from the newspaper he was reading. "Getting ready for an evening of heavy panting?"

"How very rude. What are you doing?"

He held out the obituary page that ran tributes, poems, and letters addressed to the deceased.

"Catching up on my favorite section. Here's a good one." He cleared his throat and read in a southern singsong.

Waylon Rennie,
Though we had our trials and tribulations
Our ups and our downs
I learned you were the only one for me
Now that you're gone.

Win's eyes twinkled. "Whoever put that in must have a paper-
boy with a hell of an arm."

We smiled at each other. I perched on the chair across from him.
"My favorite section is the Sunday wedding announcements. I put
my hand over the captions and guess which girls had their recep-
tions at the country club."

"You can tell by the head shots?"

"Yeah. It's not that hard. Right off, you eliminate the minorities. The Jewish girls. And, of course, girls with bad teeth—lack of
orthodontia is a dead giveaway."

"An instant disqualification."

"Right. Then you're left with a smaller pool of candidates." I
could feel my eyes widen. "And here's where the skill comes in. The
single strand of pearls is a given, so you have to identify the look. It
holds cotillion, riding lessons, and a semester or two of unrestrained
behavior. All in the tilt of the head."

"What's your record?"

"I generally bat a thousand," I said proudly.

"Versatile *and* modest." He held my eyes with his for a moment.
My face got hot. Then he cleared his throat and stood. "Speaking
of the newspaper, how's that wild woman doing?"

"Cole's good. She's working on a big undercover piece about
Stocker Pharmaceuticals." Instantly I realized my slip. "Oh, Win!
Please don't repeat that! I wasn't supposed to tell anybody!" And
then to my horror I burst into tears.

"Hey. It's okay, it's okay. I won't tell anybody. I promise." He
came over and pulled me into him. "It's not just that, though, is it?"

"No."

"Do you want to talk about it?"

"Not yet. Okay?"

"I'm here." And then just like my brothers, he kissed the top of my head.

"Sorry," I whispered.

"Don't be."

"It's getting late. I've got to pick up Tonya."

"I'm ready to go, too. Wait a second and I'll walk you to your car."

I began to suspect that he had stayed late so I wouldn't have to walk to the dimly lit parking lot alone. We said good-bye on the highest level of the garage with the yellow glow of streetlights and the steady sounds of traffic reaching us from far below.

"Take care, little Marti."

My attraction to him was so strong at that moment, I couldn't look up.

"Bye, Win," I whispered.

I felt as though I had somehow ended up in someone else's life. My marriage was falling apart and I had to avoid eye contact with my boss. What brought me here?

Tonya was waiting on the front steps, holding a pad of paper, pen, and the requisite pillow. After strapping herself into the car, adjusting the belt below her stomach, she told me that her mother had bought her a portable crib. "But she won't bring it over 'cause it's bad luck."

"I guess she's warming up to the idea of being a grandmother." When Tonya didn't respond, I asked, "Is something wrong, honey?"

"Well—no, not really. At least I hope it . . ."

"What is it?"

"It's just that the nurse asked me who my coach was and I didn't want to say my social worker. So I told her a friend. Is that okay?"

"Sure it is."

"Thank you. Again. Know what else my mama brought me?"

"What?"

"A new dining room suite for my house. On account of me breaking the table a whiles back."

I was confused for a moment until I realized that Tonya was talking about dollhouse furniture. "That was thoughtful. Where are you keeping that—in your room?"

"Yeah. When it's only me and Amber on the girls' side, I keep it out so we can use it. But when other girls are staying there I get one of the caseworkers to lock it up in the office. I don't want no one messing with it, you know?"

"Definitely. It's a work of art."

"For Christmas one year I got a whole family to put inside. But the little girl doll, she came out of the box missing her arms. My daddy, he went to try and return the set, but they wouldn't let him. They said he didn't have no proof that it came that way. I told him it was all right. But it wasn't. I didn't like her as well as the boy. I'd make myself hold her, though. But I could put her down after I counted to twenty."

I imagined her forcing herself to be kind to the little plastic doll.

"Ms. Trailor? What if there's something wrong with my real baby?"

"Oh, sweetie. You heard the doctors tell you everything is fine. I know it won't help for me to say don't worry—but try, okay? All new moms are scared."

We entered the public library and sat in a double circle on the floor of the community room, coaches behind expectant moms. The last time I'd done this, I'd been on the inside, resting against Elliot's bent knees. He'd tortured me by leaning forward and repeating our instructor's words. Words that had no business being uttered aloud. "Rectal pressure," he'd crooned.

"Stop!" I'd begged.

"Enema, enema," he'd chanted under his breath. I had laughed so hard that I'd snorted.

The memory filled me with almost unbearable grief.

"Okay, people, let's get started," the current instructor said.

I forced myself to refocus. She was wearing a flowing skirt and a sleeveless shirt that revealed the loose skin on her arms. Her gray hair was long and proud. "Take a cube from the bucket," she said, passing around a stainless-steel container. "It's cold, but it won't be for long. Hold it in your hand. Next, fill your lungs with air. Concentrate on moving your breath in and out, even though you are experiencing discomfort. Do it with your partner. Iiiin. Ouuut. If you have a thought, let it go. No judgment, no criticism. It's just a visitor, a little bird perching for a moment on the porch of your conscious mind. Let it fly away. Breathe with your partner." I stopped myself from giggling.

Tonya and I were clumsy at first.

"Iiiin," the instructor intoned. "Ouuut."

We finally got it. Our pattern fused. When paper towels were passed around, I realized I hadn't even been aware of the ice melting.

"If I do my job right," the teacher said, "you moms will be able to let go of labor discomfort by breathing and mindfulness shared with and modeled by your coach."

We went through a series of exercises and the time disappeared. On the way back to Dan Whitcomb, Tonya said, "Ms. Trailor, I don't know how I'll ever thank you for doing this with me."

"You just did."

As I watched her go inside, Win called to ask how the class went.

"Crunchy, but good."

The conversation meandered and I smiled in the dark. The boundaries of our relationship had been inching into new terrain, triggering confusion whenever I allowed myself to think about it. Like the afternoon Win had gone to pick up sandwiches and I'd answered his insistent office phone. I told the disembodied nasal accent on the other end that he'd be back in a few minutes.

"Oh, this must be Marti. I'm Win's wife, Lydia. I've heard so much about you."

I refrained from asking how, after a divorce, Lydia could still refer to herself as Win's wife. Instead, I chose to say, "I've heard a lot about you, too." The implication that Win and I spent a lot of time together discussing his marriage was so nasty, so catty, so untrue, that as soon as I delivered it, I entered the Zone, babbling incoherently to compensate. I don't know which one of us wanted to get off the phone more.

CHAPTER ELEVEN

I ask Leland's receptionist for water. She brings me a heavy glass. I take a big sip in a futile attempt to get rid of the cotton-mouth I am constantly plagued with. I lean back into the waiting room couch and squeeze my eyes shut, refusing to allow my mind to swim toward the fading possibility of acquittal. Instead I think about how many people I hate. It's a full roster. As if she can see the darkness of my heart, the receptionist says, "I've been praying for you, Mrs. Trailor."

I never know what to say to that. I open my eyes. "Thank you."

"I had your name added to our prayer chain. We've got a lot of members."

I thank her again.

"You know," she says kindly, "when God closes a door, He opens a window."

"Do you think I'm supposed to jump?" I ask.

When Charlie was sick, I went with Colby to see a priest. He was a hippie type who ran a drop-in center for street people. She'd interviewed him once for a story and said he was the only minister she trusted. She kept asking him how God could hurt her baby. Patiently, again and again, he said, "God didn't make Charlie sick."

"Then why do we pray to Him to make him better?" she demanded.

"We don't. We pray for strength, Colby. And the love and support of our friends." Then he took both of our hands and said, "God is in the lawns mowed and pot roasts brought over."

"Not in any of the ones that have been left at my house," Colby retorted. But she seemed calmer when we left his church.

I wonder if he's still in town.

Leland ushers me into his office and says that the prosecutor took the death penalty off the table. But he's going for twenty years to life. It's like trading side dishes at a restaurant.

"I don't care, Leland!" I practically scream. "I didn't do it! Remember?"

"Bear with me now, Marti. It's my fiduciary responsibility to present everything to you. Okay? It's my job. You wouldn't want me to get in trouble with the bar, now, would you?" He chuckles like a patient uncle and glides his wheeled armchair up to the conference room table.

We have moved in here so that the three of us can look at the papers together. The carpet has just been cleaned and gives off a sweet smell. My eyes water.

Leland has brought on a young assistant to do some investigating. Shane O'Shaunessy looks like a little boy. Thin, reddish-brown strands fall straight across his forehead, and he has a smattering of childish freckles across his nose. His face gets really red when he talks. The color starts with scarlet patches on his cheekbones and spreads to his ears and neck like fruit punch on a paper towel. When he gets really nervous, he rocks in place. I find it hard to believe that he is as good as Leland says.

First, Shane has me tell him the story of that night, describing everything from the moment I parked the car until the day after. I go through it all again, even the part about Win and seeing Carter-Randolph. Leland does not wince this time. Then Shane asks me to talk with him about the evidence that was found in my possession. I tell the truth—that I don't know where the syringe in my desk came from, but the other one belonged to Mrs. Loftin. I get a little hysterical when I realize that just because I know where it came from doesn't mean it won't be used against me.

"Calm down now, Marti," Leland says. "Getting upset is not going to help anything. I had another long discussion with Mr. Phillips last night. He's going to make a fine witness. He's completely on board about painting a picture of the alternate suspect."

My attorney doesn't say that it would have been a hell of a lot better for my credibility if I hadn't spent the night at Win's.

He doesn't need to.

I was warming my hands on a coffee mug, rubbing my bare foot on Batman's back. My heart was pounding and I was struggling not to lose my shit. Elliot and the kids were on their way to Annapolis for his parents' anniversary party. Right before they took off, he and I stood on the front porch. We talked about separating.

Poppy, Simon, and Nina were in the car, unknowing witnesses to the demise of life as they knew it. Elliot had come back to grab the gift, a portrait he'd commissioned my mother to paint of the three kids. He tapped his fingers on the frame. "Are you sure you won't come?" he dared.

"I can't, Elliot. Tonya's counting on me. She doesn't have any backup."

He shook his head in disgust.

"I'm sorry. Really. I'll drive up early tomorr—"

"Don't worry about it."

"Elliot, come on! You've missed an occasion or two over the years."

"I'm done, Marti."

Time froze.

"What?"

"I'm done. Finished. Checking out. Enjoy the childbirth class. I hope it's worth it."

How can words, conveyed on nothing but a puff of air, stop the world?

"Elliot. Wait. Please. Let's talk about—"

"There's nothing to talk about. I'll come for my things when we get back. I'd like to pack, though, when the kids aren't here."

So this is how it ends. Not with a bang or even a whimper, but with logistics.

"Okay . . ." I leaned against the newel post for support. "I suppose the truth of the matter is that I don't have it in me to try and make you love me anymore. I can't live with the heartache."

"Marti, I never meant for this to happen."

"And what, Elliot? That's supposed to make it better?"

He tried to put his hand on my arm.

"Don't touch me," I said quietly. Then I made the leap. "What's so great about her, Elliot, that you're so ready to throw everything else away?"

"Marti, it would have happened any— You and I have grown apart."

"Oh, that's cute, Elliot. Grown apart. I was stationary, raising the family. *You* did the growing. When was it, though? When exactly did you stop loving me?"

"Understanding that you're not happy doesn't come in an envelope. And it's not that I don't love you. You're the mother of my—"

"Bla bla bla. Don't say anything to them. I want to be there when they're told."

"Sure. Of course. I'm sad, too, Marti."

"Having someone waiting in the wings has to be some kind of comfort."

"Are you going to be all right?" he asked.

I turned from him and went inside, closing the past behind me.

The silence made me dizzy. The house seemed emptier than I thought was possible—more cavernous, even, than the day we moved in, when our apartment's meager belongings barely outfitted the first floor. Back then, before giving way to couches and clutter, the hollow space had been furnished with promise. Now, disappointment seeped out of every crevice, and unwanted but impending change echoed in the hall.

I made coffee and sat at the kitchen table, trying to collect my thoughts.

I need to call William for the name of a lawyer. I wish I had taken Colby's advice about getting my finances in order. I should meet with the school counselor and—

The phone rang and interrupted my list making. It was the ward clerk from Labor and Delivery. Tonya had been admitted, almost a month ahead of schedule. I put fresh water and food out for Batman and drove down to the hospital, where, while comforting the mother-to-be, I tried not to fall inside the sinkholes of desolation that kept opening up.

And in the sick way the universe operates, the resident assigned to Tonya was Catherine Stamp. Every time she pushed open the door, I was confronted with the specter of Claudia Cantrell. I was able to maintain my professionalism, but Catherine was cool bordering on rude. She came in without knocking and left without warning. At one point she brusquely reached around me for the stethoscope hanging from a hook, and her sleeve brushed my eye. I began thinking about what I'd say to Elliot about her bedside manner.

Then I remembered.

I told Tonya I needed to stretch my legs and ducked into the hallway to pull myself together. Visiting hours had ended and the corridor was steeped in a melancholy light. I had my head down and was trying to regulate my breathing when I heard my name.

"Hey, Marti! How're ya?" cocky Peter Hayden asked, striding toward me wearing blue scrubs, a Dallas Cowboys surgical hat, and his ever-present leather boots. He was also wearing the grin that accompanied his incorrigible flirting.

I tried to smile. "Hi, Peter. How are you?"

"The consensus is not bad. Not bad at all." I didn't bite, so he asked, "What brings you to my neck of the woods?"

"I've got a client in labor."

"Well, you picked a hell of a night for it. It's a goddamn madhouse."

"What's going on?"

"We've got a private patient in with complications. Of course the chief complication is that her husband is vice president of South Banks and they're pretty sure they're the only people who've ever had a baby. They're requiring serious hand-holding. And the frigging computer system has been acting up. Oh yeah, and Dr. Hill's ex has been roaming around again like some half-crazed coyote, looking for him. Plus Trauma just pulled the anesthesiologist upstairs."

"Ouch."

Right then, someone called his name and he loped down the hall. I was relieved; I had no reserves. I tried to call Elliot to check on the kids, but he didn't answer and I felt sick imagining him glancing at the caller ID, switching it off. I didn't trust my voice to leave a message. I texted: "I'm at the hospital with my client. She's in labor. Please tell the children that I love them."

The air inside Tonya's room had fouled.

"Hi," I said.

"What time is it, Ms. Trailor?" I could barely hear her over the fast pant of the fetal heart monitor beat. I started to look at my watch when Tonya grabbed my hand and groaned. Pain propelled her shoulders straight off the pillows, ending in a tight crush of my fingers that pressed my wedding band deep. Then she retched violently. I grabbed the kidney-shaped basin and caught the watery brown liquid.

When everything calmed down, she turned to me.

"Nine ten," I said, which got a little smile. But tears were welling, clouding the brown of her eyes. In a husky whisper she said, "It's taking so long. And it hurts so bad."

"First babies always take longer, honey," I soothed. "Where are we in the name department? Or are you still going through your top two hundred?"

"Camron if it's a boy. Camra if it's a girl."

"I think I detect a theme."

"Ms. Trailor—I've been wanting to ask you something. Do you think you could be the baby's godmother?"

The old professional distance problem.

Another labor pain saved me from having to answer. Tonya threw up again.

"I'm getting pretty good at this," I said, handing over a tissue. But I was surprised by the appearance of pinpricks at the base of my head—a nervous symptom I associated only with the pediatrician's waiting room.

"Can't I have a little something to drink?"

"Remember? The nurse said if your labor doesn't progress soon, we might be looking at a C-section. So you can't have anything in your stomach just in case. Except the ice chips," I added.

"Will it hurt? A C-section?"

"No—it's not bad at all. I had one. The anesthesiologist will give you a shot in your back so you can't feel anything. Then before you know it you'll feel a little tugging and you'll be holding your new baby!"

Tonya slowly smiled while I tried to ignore the memory of the temporary paralysis that had made me stark, raving crazy on the operating table. Elliot said the anesthesiologist gave me the biggest injection of Valium he'd ever seen.

"You drained the hospital supply," he reported, mock proud, when I finally got feeling back in the lower half of my body.

The door opened and Catherine Stamp appeared, large shiners of exhaustion beneath her eyes, lank strands of blond hair escaping from a once glamorous French braid. I had been charting her deteriorating appearance over the hours and thought she now resembled a mug shot of her former self. On her way around the bed to the computer on the retractable arm, Catherine didn't say anything when she kicked my foot. I felt like kicking her back.

"Crap." She was having trouble signing on to the machine and reached for the chart clipped to the bed and began jotting notes. Her purple-inked words curled in private school formation.

A new nurse knocked and came in, heralding the night shift. "I'm Barbara Harris," the grandmotherly woman said with a smile.

I introduced Tonya and myself. Catherine didn't look up from her note. "Poor Tonya has been in labor since early this morning," I said.

"This child on his own timetable?"

Tonya nodded and began to sniffle.

"I've been in on more births than I can keep track of, and I swear the longer the labor, the sweeter the baby. Don't worry about a thing, sugar. You're going to be just fine."

She went over to the whiteboard and wiped off the day nurse's name with the side of her hand, then wrote her own in a cheerful flourish. She was so warm and nurturing, I felt like bounding into her plush chest for comfort. Next to her, Catherine Stamp seemed even cooler and more WASPy. Without preamble, the doctor laid her hands on Tonya's belly, trying to reposition the baby.

"Owww," Tonya moaned.

"Sorry about that," Catherine said unconvincingly. "So, the plan is to get this baby out so we can all get some sleep tonight."

"They work these residents to the bone," Mrs. Harris said, clucking. Tonya suddenly vomited again and this time was barely able to lift her head. Mrs. Harris said something comforting as she nonchalantly wiped Tonya's mouth and then stripped off the messy top sheet, all in a fluid motion. She replaced the foul linen and said she'd be back in a few.

Nigel was standing in the doorway.

"Goodness. You're working late, Mrs. Trailor," he said. "Is Elliot babysitting?"

"They're up in Annapolis."

"Oh, that's right. It's his parents' anniversary. May I see the chart, please, Dr. Stamp?"

"I've had trouble signing on," Catherine said, trying to hand him the clipboard.

"Let me," he ordered. She squared her shoulders and moved out of the way of the computer. Nigel tapped aggressively on the keyboard and was almost immediately successful. He toggled between screens and then said, "Everything is looking fine. So how are we feeling, Miss Maines?"

"All right, I guess." In relation to his self-importance, Tonya had assumed the grateful demeanor of a neglected child. "Just tired, mostly, sir."

"Well, it's called labor for a reason, my dear. It's hard work. But you're in good hands. Dr. Stamp is one of our most promising residents."

"Yes, sir."

"By the way, Mrs. Trailor, I noticed that Dr. Stamp here has seen your client in clinic before. You must be quite pleased. Continuity of care and all."

Now it was my turn to square my shoulders.

He turned to Catherine. "I'm going to be leaving in a few moments, Dr. Stamp. You may reach me on my cell if necessary. Of course, I don't need to remind you that Dr. Hayden is your first line of defense."

"Big plans, Dr. Hill?" she asked with an ingratiating smile.

"I'm going to be stopping in at the Stocker event downtown. Then off for the weekend."

"Have fun." I smiled innocently.

The sound of the machines refilled the room. Mrs. Harris came in, Peter behind her. "Catherine, I'm going to go ahead and section room two," he said, not advancing over the threshold. "I'd wait for you to assist, but Anesthesia's only got one warm body down here so I want to get it done before anything else comes up. The heavy Trauma load is screwing everything up. I need you to check three, seven, and twelve. Okay?"

"Sure, Pete. I was going to rupture the membranes in here. She hasn't progressed at all in hours. I'll add a Pit drip if that doesn't do the trick."

He stuck his head back in. "Well, don't do it too soon or you could end up without a dance partner."

He flicked me a grin and left.

Catherine looked at Tonya and smiled faintly. "I'll be back in a little while. You'll be a mommy before long."

It was the warmest thing she'd said.

We sat quietly, no music or TV, listening instead to the steady beat of the machine. Tonya's labor stalled, the violence of the contractions diminishing to the point that she dozed between them.

Catherine returned, impatient and brusque. I couldn't imagine what kind of shape she'd be in at the end of her shift. She was the poster child for reforming the on-call system.

"Would you mind moving," she snapped, acting as if I were man spreading on a New York subway. Before I had the chance to scoot my chair out of the way, she pushed past.

She pulled gloves from the box on the counter and put them on, releasing a sweet cloud of powder into the air. She rubbed Tonya's thigh with her knuckles. "You awake?"

Tonya nodded.

"What I'm going to do now is rupture your membranes in order to speed up delivery. I'm going to need you to let your legs fall open and relax."

She sat down on the stool at the foot of the bed. When the door opened again a chilling scream from across the hall filled the room. I glanced up and saw Mrs. Harris, her mouth yawning in alarm. She was staring at Catherine, who was ripping the wrapper off a long plastic instrument.

"Dr. Stamp?" the nurse said. "Dr. Hayden is doing that C-section. I got the impression he's going to be tied up for a while."

Catherine nodded absently and said to Tonya, "Get ready to feel wet."

"I thought he wanted you to wait—"

Catherine looked over after she had inserted the instrument inside of Tonya.

Within seconds an urgent rush of liquid splashed out of Tonya.

The look on Mrs. Harris's face paralyzed me. She was standing next to Catherine and her mouth was open. I could see her tongue. Her eyes were wide in horror. And then I realized that the steady, rapid-fire rhythm of the fetal heart monitor had slowed to an inconsistent, halting beat. A high-pitched alarm went off.

Catherine screamed, "Get Hayden. Hurry! Hurry!"

The nurse was already gone.

"What is it?" I asked, my voice shrill and hysterical.

"Oh no, no. Oh goddammit," Catherine kept whispering, holding both of her hands inside of Tonya, trying to stop something from happening.

"What's going on? Please tell me, Ms. Trailor," Tonya said, turning toward me. Tears were puddling at the base of her nostril and then dropping onto the bed. "Oh, it hurts! It hurts! Is my baby all right? Oh, please somebody tell me my baby's all right!"

I said nothing. I knew better than to make any promises.

"Here! Help get her head down and legs up!" Catherine yelled at me.

We struggled together for an eternity until the door was thrust open and Peter Hayden, dressed in used surgical scrubs, came running in with two nurses barking orders to each other.

Mrs. Harris touched my shoulder and said, "You need to wait outside, honey."

"Noooo," Tonya wailed as I forced myself away.

"I'll be right outside the door. I promise I won't move," I said, drifting away in slow motion from the frenzy. Out in the hall, I leaned against the wall near the door. Frantic words could be heard above Tonya's cries.

Unfamiliar voice: "I'll get Anesthesia!"

Hayden: "You'll have to call up to Main Eight! The only one we have down here is still in with a section. And he can't leave her—she's still under!"

Mrs. Harris: "I'll prep!"

Catherine: "I can't push the head off the cord! It's totally jammed!"

Hayden: "Keep trying, dammit! Is it still pulsating?"

Catherine: "Barely. Oh shit!"

Tonya: "Ms. Trailor! . . . Ms. Trailor!"

Hayden: "How long has she been NPO?"

Catherine: "Except for ice—she hasn't had anything in over six hours."

Hayden: "Congratulations."

Tonya was being wheeled out on her bed. All the covers were off, her naked, swollen body was thrashing, huge dark brown stretch marks clawing her hips. She was rolled away quickly and I was left alone in the hallway to stare in at the empty room.

I stood lost for a moment, trying to decide what to do. I knew I needed to call Tonya's mother, but I didn't have any information. Finally, I just left a voice mail saying that there were complications and she should try to come to the hospital as soon as she could. I went back to the room and sat on the chair where the teddy bear I had picked up in the gift shop hours ago was perched. I watched the hallway.

Time passed so slowly, I almost stopped waiting. I crouched low against the wall and just gave in to a dull sense of being. At one point I thought I heard Nigel's voice around the corner but never saw him. Finally, Peter came down the corridor. I stood. His whole body screamed bad news. My heart began racing in my throat as he drew nearer. I had to fight the urge to inch against the wall toward the exit.

"You're Miss Maines's social worker, Marti?"

"Yes."

"Why don't we go into the family lounge," he said, guiding me into a little chamber at the end of the hallway.

He turned on the light, illuminating two tacky prints in cheap rose frames. The room was decorated in 1980s mauves and gold, ringed by a wall border of autumnal flowers that ran the perimeter at eye level. It was a fitting environment for the delivery of bad news.

"Boy—it's not too often that we have a social worker right on the floor when we need one," Peter said as he went to the conference table in the middle of the room.

"What do you mean?"

He sat on the edge of the table and pulled his Cowboys cap from his head. "I'm afraid there were problems. The baby's alive—but there was trouble with the cord, which caused hypoxia."

"What's that?" I asked quietly.

"Lack of oxygen to the brain. The damage appears to be global, devastating. Her Apgar scores were as low as they get. Her color and muscle tone are way off. She's on a ventilator. I'd say we're looking at a probable prognosis of a chronic vegetative state."

"Oh God." I sighed, trying hard not to cry.

He looked at me with concern. "Are you all right?"

I'd seen two children in chronic vegetative states at the hospital. They'd been attached to life support machines that whirred and sucked and pumped every minute of every day. For years their little faces had grimaced and smiled and contorted. Their bodies had grown and their limbs had curled. They were afflicted with never-ending bedsores. The thought of Tonya's baby spending a lifetime like that, attended to by a succession of nurses charting changes as she graduated from one diaper size to the next, was so horrible that I almost vomited. "Of course I'm not all right, Peter. You basically just said Tonya's baby would be better off dead."

He studied me. "These things are very upsetting when they happen, Marti. But it's a real blessing that you're here. I'm sure you'll be very comforting to her."

My roles were colliding. "Is Tonya all right?"

"Medically, yeah. Her uterus is intact and she'll be able to have other children without problem. Emotionally . . . well. But she's fortunate the hospital provided her with an accessible social worker. To help her cope."

"Peter, I'm here on my own tonight. I'm not working. She asked me to be the baby's godmother." The expression on his face seemed to freeze a moment, and we exchanged a look of appraisal that shook me deeply. I could almost hear the ranks closing. "I don't understand what happened. I was in there and everything was fine. Nigel even came in and said so."

"Sometimes these things just occur—you know that." His voice had changed, become guarded. He crossed his arms. "If we had had an anesthesiologist on the floor, we might have prevented the extent of damage. But everybody was in it up to their eyeballs. Hell, Marti, I told you it was terrible here tonight when I saw you earlier."

"And what? We should've left and come back later?"

He cleared his throat. "Cord problems can happen without warning. Obviously."

He crossed his arms.

"Peter, would this have happened if Catherine hadn't ruptured the membranes?"

"What kind of a question is that, Marti?" His posture was defensive.

I remained silent.

"Marti, I'm sure you'll be the most help if you provide reassurance."

"Most help to whom?"

His beeper went off. "Look, I'm sorry. This has been a helluva day. I am terribly sorry about what happened. But I'm sure you"— doctor's wife, hospital social worker—"can appreciate how upsetting this kind of thing is for all of us. Various tests will be performed on the baby. Of course she'll be transferred to a pediatric neurologist. I'll be available to answer questions about the delivery. As will Catherine. But I believe that we should concentrate on the baby's well-being. I'll talk to you soon." He started out and then came back. "Had Miss Maines considered adoption?"

"What difference does that make?"

"We're all on the same side here, Marti."

Right.

A disembodied voice came through the little speaker clipped to Peter's breast pocket, urgently calling him to the OR.

"We'll catch up later, Marti."

I was momentarily distracted by Natalie Hill, who walked past me, carrying a clutch under her arm as though she were on her way to a morning meeting instead of a midnight trespass.

The bed was stripped and returned to its prone position. Mrs. Harris, whose back was to the door, was gathering Tonya's things, carefully placing them into a blue plastic hospital-issued bag, restoring the quarters to its original impersonality. She picked up the teddy bear.

"I'll take that, Mrs. Harris," I said. "Tonya doesn't need to see it right now."

Mrs. Harris turned and shook her head.

"What a terrible thing. Everything happened so fast . . ." Her voice trailed off.

"Mrs. Harris—can you explain what happened?"

"What's that?"

"How come everybody kept saying everything was fine? How did the cord get twisted?"

"It wasn't that the cord was twisted. It was 'cause it came out first."

"What? How did that happen?" There was a long silence. "Did Dr. Stamp do something wrong?"

"Let me ask you something, Ms. Trailor. Before I came back in the room, did Dr. Stamp perform a manual exam?"

"I'm not sure I understand what you're asking."

"Did she check Tonya vaginally—with her hand?"

"No. She used that instrument to rupture her water."

The nurse hesitated, cleared her throat, and held my gaze. "Tired, inexperienced kids have no business delivering babies by themselves."

"What do you mean?"

"I'm right sure Dr. Stamp broke Tonya's waters before the baby's head was engaged in the birth canal. It wasn't flush up against the cervix. The part of the cord that came out stopped the blood—and oxygen—from getting through. It's called umbilical cord prolapse. It's like bending an air hose. If Dr. Stamp had checked, she would have realized the baby wasn't in the proper position."

It was textbook malpractice.

Mrs. Maines suddenly ran in, terror pinching her face. She was still wearing her waitress uniform, the apron ties swinging by her narrow hips. "Where's Tawny?"

I walked toward her.

"Tonya's fine, Mrs. Maines. She's going to be okay. I'm so sorry, but the baby—the baby's really sick. She was without oxygen for a long time. The doctor is terribly concerned about her brain."

Tonya's mother slumped against the door.

"It's a girl?" she asked.

I nodded.

"Where's Tonya at?"

"She's in recovery, sugar. I'll bring you all to her," Mrs. Harris said, opening the door for us.

We walked past the nursery. A couple of the babies were crying.

Tonya was lying in the bed. Various tubes were attached to her, an IV pump clicking noisily as it dripped clear fluid into her veins. Beneath the sheet, her knees swayed from side to side.

"Mama!" Tawny cried, her body heaving. "Camra ain't going to be right! It's because I didn't want her at first. It's my fault!" She was sobbing. Mrs. Maines scooped up her daughter as well as she could and began rocking her. Peter Hayden and another doctor walked in. Peter was carrying a clipboard. "I'm Dr. Hayden. Remember me?"

Tonya nodded and tried to sit a little straighter.

"This is Dr. Rooker. He's a neonatologist. I hate to interrupt you right now. But this should only take a minute and we need to go over a few things."

Dr. Rooker, a young-looking black man of about forty, whom I recognized from various department events, nodded at me grimly. He walked toward Tonya. "Miss Maines, I'm terribly sorry to meet you under these circumstances. I've just spent some time with your daughter and I truly regret that what I have to tell you isn't good news. She appears not to have any brain activity—which means she is completely unable to breathe on her own. I don't want to give you any false hope. I believe she will spend her natural life attached to a ventilator."

Tonya sat up with a confusing look of excitement on her face.

"Well, that'll be okay! I know people on oxygen tanks." She looked to her mother for encouragement. "Like Ms. Garston from church! She told me it weren't nothing more than a inconvenience! She even named it."

Mrs. Maines said nothing to her daughter. She just kept rubbing her back.

Dr. Rooker shook his head. "Miss Maines, Tonya, if I may, excuse me for not explaining better. The ventilator is different than an oxygen tank. It is actually a machine breathing for her. As a result of the lack of oxygen to her brain, the evidence strongly suggests that she will be profoundly damaged and will need to have many different machines to keep her alive. She will require constant medical attention. It's unlikely that she will ever leave a hospital."

The sounds of the monitors amplified.

"Is there something you need from Tonya?" I asked when it seemed that the silence was going to go on forever.

"Yes, actually." Dr. Rooker held his hand out for the clipboard that Peter was holding. "What we need from you is to decide whether or not to sign a Do Not Resuscitate order for your daughter. I hate to impose this on you now, but it really cannot wait in terms of treatment. Even for the rest of the night."

"What is it?" Tonya mumbled.

"In situations like this where there is no hope, many people choose to let their loved ones go. Die peacefully, rather than have them resuscitated to live a life of questionable quality."

"You mean you're going to kill her?" Tonya asked flatly, as if nothing else could surprise her.

"No, no!" Peter jumped in. "This is only if her heart stops beating on its own. Which could happen now—or years from now."

"But maybe there could be a cure? Not right away, but someday?"

"I'm afraid not," Dr. Rooker said.

"Okay. I understand. I'll sign it. It don't make sense to bring her back if there's nothing to come back to."

"You're making the right decision, Tawny," Mrs. Maines said quietly.

An unfamiliar forcefulness came over Tonya and she sat up as best she could. "But I don't want nobody messing with her if she dies. I don't want nobody cutting on her little body. I want you to write that down next to what all I have to sign."

"Tonya, that's something we can talk about later," Dr. Rooker said softly.

"No! I want that on this contract. I'm eighteen. And I'm her mother. I've got rights, don't I?"

She looked to me for support. "Don't I?"

"We'll have time to address that later, Tonya," Peter said a little condescendingly.

Which set me off.

"Oh, for God's sakes! If she doesn't want an autopsy—then respect her wishes!" I erupted, surprising everyone, including myself.

The two doctors looked at each other.

"I ain't signing nothing until you write that down," Tonya exclaimed. "She ain't going to leave this world looking worse than when she came into it. She's going up to heaven all in one piece. Or I'm going with her."

Dr. Rooker nodded. "Okay, Tonya. I'll write a special clause that you refuse an autopsy. Okay?"

She leaned back, exhausted. "Okay."

Tonya signed the forms, initialing the added clause on all three copies. As soon as the paperwork was completed, she asked to see the baby. Peter arranged to have a nurse bring Tonya and her mother to the neonatal intensive care unit while I sat in the guest chair in her room. I spent the whole time rehearsing what to say about my conversation with Mrs. Harris.

When they returned, subdued and shrunken, I took a deep breath and started talking. I explained about the cord prolapse, using the hose analogy. I talked about how tired Catherine was and how she should have done the exam before rupturing the membranes. I remembered Peter's admonishment not to get things going too early, and then I said that it just seemed to me to be a horrible, horrible case of malpractice.

Tonya was so dazed that her mouth stayed open, revealing a pocket of saliva in the curl of her tongue.

"Sweet Jesus," Mrs. Maines said before lapsing into silence. Eventually she came toward me and said, "Look, Mrs. Trailor, you go on home. Me and Tonya have some talking to do. Your news ain't going nowheres. You look like you could use a good night's sleep. Go on home to your family. We'll see you in the morning."

Mrs. Maines's suggestion that I go home to my family was a jolt. I hadn't thought of them in hours. At the elevator, I was startled by the fuzzy fur of the bear when I reached into my bag for the keys. I took a deep breath and doubled back. I pushed open the NICU's silent door and saw Peter on the phone. His back was to me and I caught part of the conversation.

"To paraphrase Nigel, basically she even screwed up fucking up." Peter paused to listen to the person on the other end. "Oh, much more this way. And we both know anybody who took a deep breath on this floor tonight could get named."

I stood still, but the slow door closed, its click commanding Peter's attention. He saw me and disengaged from the call.

"Marti?" he asked, coming forward, genial again.

"I want to put this with Tonya's baby," I said, recoiling a little. "I'm sorry. I'm just so exhausted. I, uh . . . just wanted to drop this off."

"You look wiped out. Do you want me to give Elliot a call and have him come get you?"

"No. I'm fine, Peter." I avoided eye contact. "Thank you."

"The baby is through that curtain," he said, pointing to the back. "I've got to go. Try and get some sleep?"

I nodded and walked to the other end of the bright, busy room, through a heavy drapery into a semidarkened area, where classical music played quietly from a radio on a supply table. Two isolettes lay side by side. Above cheery name tags decorated with storks, "Do Not Resuscitate" was handwritten on wide pieces of white adhesive in thick black ink. I shuddered when I realized where I was and found myself tiptoeing toward them.

My eyes were drowning. Camra was on her back, a tube secured in her mouth. A piece of adhesive taped above her head ordered, "No Autopsy!!!" The steady breaths of the ventilator made her dusky chest rise and fall, while another machine kept flashing ALARM OFF across its screen. Every once in a while, a huge tremor would shake her perfect little body and then she would go still again. I put the bear near her feet, and watched her, and wept. I don't know how long I stayed there with her. Long enough to run out of tears, I guess.

CHAPTER TWELVE

Tonya has virtually no memories from the night of Camra's birth. Leland says that even if she did, the pain medication she'd been given would make her testimony impeachable. He is explaining this to me while Shane sets up the TV screen. I accept the bad news stoically. I accept all news stoically. My powerlessness has mutated into apathy. A uniformed policeman is sitting in the corner of the conference room, guarding against evidence tampering. Shane slips the DVD in.

"I haven't been in any hurry to show this to you, Marti, since it doesn't provide any exculpatory evidence in terms of a timeline," Leland says.

"What do you mean?" I ask.

"Well, if, for instance, the time stamp showed you leaving the floor at midnight and the baby's death was recorded at twelve thirty, then obviously you would have to be exonerated."

"But?"

"But the ECG alarm had been shut off since the infant had a Do Not Resuscitate order. So the actual time of death is not known. Unfortunately, all the security film really does is prove that you had been in with her."

"Oh," I say, and watch as I appear on the television screen. My hair, still long, is hanging in disheveled curls. I pull open the door, my purse swinging and the teddy bear's head poking out from it. I disappear and then reappear, shoulders bunched, face contorted, fumbling with my bag. As the camera captures only the public entryway and about ten feet of the hall behind it, I quickly withdraw from view. According to the clock in the corner of the screen, I spent six minutes inside the nursery.

The clip ushers defeat into the room, heavy and oppressive. Even the already silent cop seems more subdued.

"What were you doing with your bag there, Marti?" Leland whispers so our conversation does not become testimony, courtesy of the policeman.

I match his hushed tone. "Looking for my keys."

"Bad timing," he mutters. Then I realize the prosecution is going to suggest that I was shoving a syringe inside it. I open my hands in a kind of shrug.

Shane interrupts to break up the negativity. He does this a lot, offering conversational diversions from conflict, gently rerouting discussions. I wonder if he is a child of divorce.

"Leland," he says softly, "I was finally able to speak with my friend in Hospital Security. He said it's an independent system that doesn't feed into the main monitoring office. It's nearly obsolete. Just records pictures. And the tapes are recycled. Actually, it was almost erased before anyone thought to impound it."

"What good is it, then?" I ask the blushing Shane. "I mean, if it only provides proof after the fact?"

"I would wager," Leland offers, "that the hospital put the camera up as a placebo for nervous parents. But since they don't really believe critically ill newborns are in danger of being kidnapped, they saved a few bucks by not hooking it up to main control. More than likely, the more monitors you have going, the more people you have to pay to monitor them."

"Oh," I answer. But my brief interest is already flagging.

The three of us watch the footage a few more times. And then Shane erupts.

"What's that!" he exclaims, the tips of his ears flaming.

We look at the corner of the screen where he is pointing. Almost disappearing into the dark curtain folds covering the window, a figure is hidden in the intersection of the nursery glass and wall. Intentionally or not, the prosecution has made no mention of this possible witness. Shane does some high-tech tuning and brings into focus the passerby. I let out a little yelp of recognition. And for the first time in a while, excitement appears on Leland's face.

I, too, allow myself unfamiliar hope.

I left the hospital in slow time, experiencing everything as though dreaming. I collected the car, fed my parking card into the automatic gate lift, obeyed traffic signals, and made my way home, all with a lethargy that was like walking through wet cement. It was arduous coming up with an action plan while simultaneously working to block out the horror of the evening. Calling Win to tell him about Tonya and her baby seemed to be of the first order. Next would be my brothers for legal and medical opinions.

And moral support.

I opened the door and waited for the desperate Batman to relieve himself in the front yard, locked up behind us. The house was freezing. I went to grab a sweater from the closet beneath the stairs and flipped on the light switch. First Elliot's immaculate row of clothes came into view, then mine. And then a large, dark shadow that scurried between the bureaus. I screamed. Because even though I caught only a glimpse, I knew it wasn't merely a fall mouse that had come in for the season.

My fight-or-flight response kicked in.

I tried to call Colby to go to her place, but she didn't answer her phone. I took a deep breath, called Win.

"Marti? Is something wrong?"

"Yeah. There is. I know it's late, but could you meet me somewhere?"

"Sure. Of course." He suggested Jillies, an all-night diner within walking distance of his place. He was already waiting at a table with an old jukebox mounted next to it.

"Hey. Here. Get started on this drink and then tell me what's going on."

I did as I was told and welcomed the vodka's slow burn down my throat.

"Thanks, Win."

I took a deep breath and then launched into a description of the evening's events, interrupting my narrative to answer his questions, wiping away tears when I talked about Camra's beautiful little face.

"What a tragedy. Where does everything stand now?" Win asked, his eyebrows pulled together in a pyramid of concern.

"Tawny signed a DNR. She was also adamant against an autopsy should that become a question." I used my napkin to blow my nose. "Her mother is staying with her tonight. And I guess they'll figure out what they're going to want to do in terms of the malpractice."

"You told them everything the nurse said?"

"Shouldn't I have?" I said anxiously. "Oh, you know what? Screw it! Of course she has the right to know."

"Absolutely. I wasn't saying that. We're not in the business of filtering information. But we're going to have prepare ourselves for playing defense. In terms of the hospital." He reached across the table and put his hand on my wrist. "You didn't do anything wrong, Marti. There's no road map for this. Okay?"

Win motioned to the waitress, who quickly brought over fresh drinks, then he asked about the responses of the different doctors involved. "What does Elliot say about all of this?"

"He's um . . . he's in Annapolis. With the kids." I looked up at him, at first resisting eye contact and then surrendering to it. "Win, he's moving out. It's gotten really bad between us. He, uh . . ." My voice grew quieter. "There's someone else."

I bunched up my shoulders in an attempt to achieve a what-are-you-going-to-do shrug that immediately shifted into a pathetic spasm of shame. Then the room got really hot and really loud. "And, to complete this day from hell, there's a rat in my house."

He knew about my phobia. "C'mon, kiddo. Let me take you to my place and pump some coffee into your system. We can look up exterminators." He threw down a handful of bills and led me out.

The walk to his apartment was eerily quiet. I was shivering so hard, my ribs hurt. His place was filled with plants, books, and pictures of his daughter. I sat on the adobe leather sofa, curling my feet beneath me, leaning back to enjoy its feel against my skin. Win went into the kitchen and I closed my eyes, dozing off for a moment.

"Hi," he said softly. "Feeling any better?"

"Relatively," I answered. "I don't feel like hurling anymore."

"Have some caffeine." He handed me the cup and sat down. "Hey, Marti? I know how hard everything is for you right now."

"I just don't know what I'm going to do."

He lifted his feet onto the big pine chest he used as a coffee table. "When I found out about Lydia's affair, I didn't think I would get through it. I don't think I even wanted to. It's an indescribable hurt. It blew me away."

"I just feel so stupid!" I exclaimed. "After the Brices' party he told me he wasn't having an affair with Claudia. She was just a friend. And I believed him. What an idiot I am. Jesus Christ. 'I did not have sex with that woman.'"

"Marti, the last thing you are is an idiot."

"God, Win. He makes me feel so shitty about myself. And it's insidious, you know, the way it chips away at you? Death by daily censure. Chronic disapproval. Colby tried to point it out to me before—I didn't see it, though. But it's true. He criticizes me constantly. In subtle ways. In ways that leave me defensive and off center. He hates my disorganization—kicks the laundry basket if he can't find what he's looking for. One time he even said my feet looked old. Well, he didn't say it like that. He said something about the veins on my instep getting so prominent."

Abruptly, finally, I realized what I was doing—advertising my shortcomings. In neon. I stopped short, ashamed.

"What's the matter?" Win asked.

"Trick question?" I tried to smile, couldn't pull it off.

He reached over, gently pushed a curl behind my ears. His fingers brushed my cheek. His touch was electric; my whole body felt charged from the contact. "Elliot's an asshole," he said softly. "You deserve much more, Marti. You should be with someone who makes you feel good. Not somebody who makes you question who you are."

"Who am I?"

"You should not have to ask that," he said sadly. "You, Marti Maxwell-Trailor, are incredible. Funny. Smart. Pretty. Compassionate. Wickedly witty."

The compliments made me self-conscious. "Smart and witty. Hm. No credit for synonyms."

He laughed. "Okay, how about welcoming?"

"Welcoming? Like a restaurant hostess?"

"No. Like the one person I'd want to sit next to at a crowded party." He took my hand. "I've been insane for you since the first time I made you blush."

I was still drunk enough to ask when that was.

"The night we met." Win's voice was low, thick. "I'm not blowing smoke."

Our thighs were touching. I could smell him. His aftershave; his warm breath. And suddenly sex didn't seem like a remote possibility. It was imminent, a gathering storm—rattling patio furniture, tossing plastic toys across the lawn. Pure longing scattered my thoughts. I wanted to kiss him so badly, my tongue paced behind my teeth.

Then, from nowhere, the room was no longer a constant. I closed my eyes. Waited for the queasiness to pass.

"Win, I—I'm really not feeling too great. I need to lie down. Or throw up. Maybe both. I don't even think I can go home right now. Can I just lay on the couch for a while?"

"Well, that wasn't quite the response I was hoping for. Let me put you to bed in my room. I'm sorry about this, Marti."

"Oh, Win, everything is such a mess." I started crying again. He passed over a napkin to blow my nose.

"C'mon. Let's get you to bed."

I allowed myself to be led to his room. A green-and-white quilt was heaped at the foot. Something moved in the corner of my eye near the bathroom. I startled. An aged retriever with an almost completely white muzzle lifted its head. Briefly.

"It's just Fanny."

"Watchdog?"

"Not often." He paused. "Certainly not tonight."

I punched him as gently as I could without throwing up. "How old is she?"

"Fifteen. I have to carry her down the steps for walks."

"That must be awkward. She's big."

"We go way back." Win pulled the blanket up and bent to grab one of the pillows. "Just for the record, if I had had any intention of seducing you, I would have made the bed."

"And I would have shaved my legs," I admitted.

Our eyes met and we grew quiet. Muted by the drapes, the streetlamps gave off this gentle glow that softened everything, including my resolve. My breath caught and I had to look away. The physical attraction between us felt like the field around a speaker with the bass turned up. Way up. And it wasn't just that my whole body quivered from being so close to his. It was knowing that noth-ing would have felt better than being in the arms of a man who liked me. He bent to kiss the top of my head. "Sleep well."

I fought the overwhelming urge to pull him down—and into me. "You too," I whispered. I desperately wanted to call him back. And was desperately glad I didn't. Adding guilt to the mix would have finished me off. I tried to sleep, but images looped behind my eyes. Tonya's baby. Her little body shuddering in the isolette. My own kids. How scared they looked when they saw Elliot and me fighting.

A train wailed mournfully in the distance.

I listened for Win in the next room. He coughed sporadically, and the leather couch creaked beneath his weight. I wondered what he looked like asleep. I wondered what making love with him would be like. Occasional headlights slow-danced across the walls, and a long time later I eventually slid sideways into sleep, listing like an unsteady sailboat, before finally slipping under altogether.

I woke in the morning to the urgent splash of pee hitting water. At first I thought it was Elliot. My pulse quickened as the unfamiliar surroundings came into focus and I remembered the night before.

As soon as Win tiptoed out, I bounded into the bathroom. I tried to close the warped door and couldn't. In any other circumstance I would have just held it, but my stomach was a mess. I turned the water on and sat on the toilet. My head down, I prayed that Win couldn't hear. The cramps subsided. I flushed, quickly stripped, and climbed in the tub. The nozzle came on with violent force. I barely rinsed off. I discovered the door open and my underpants missing, the retriever lying next to the bed, her nose buried deep in the cotton crotch. Humiliation definitely seemed to be the theme for the morning.

Fanny growled as I approached. I didn't care. I grabbed hold. She held her ground. It was a struggle, but there was no way I was giving up. I gave a serious tug and landed on my ass, underpants in hand. I stuck them in the pocket of my jeans.

Win was in the kitchen.

"Hi," I said.

"Hey there, beautiful woman."

"Boy, that's some shower you've got. It's like acupuncture with a nail gun."

"Yeah, every morning I try and convince myself that there's nowhere to go but up. Come have a seat for a sec." He pulled a ladder-back chair from the table. Its legs scraped the floor. "We just got some bad news, kiddo. The hospital called a little while ago. Tonya's baby died last night."

"Oh, God. When?"

"It couldn't have been too much after you left. It was Nate Rooker who phoned. He tried to call you. It's probably a blessing, Marti."

"I know. But it's so horrible. Such a waste."

He put his arm around me and I leaned into him.

"Also, Marti, Colby called last night."

"Here? Why?"

"She had her phone off but saw you'd tried to call. She was worried when she couldn't reach you."

"What did you tell her?"

"The truth. You had a crappy day, had too much to drink, and I insisted you come here and sober up. I told her you fell asleep and I didn't see any reason to wake you to go home to an empty house. She said for me to tell you to answer your goddamn cell phone. Also to check out the front page."

He handed over the *Richmond Daily*.

STOCKER MEDICAL—CALL GIRLS INVITED?

Last night, Stocker Pharmaceuticals sponsored a medical education dinner for urologists. The mostly male attendees at the River Run Hotel represented the predominately male field. According to a police department source, however, the invitation-only event was also attended by six women with arrest records for prostitution.

Following a dinner presentation about new Stocker products, the atmosphere at the reception became more relaxed. A bar opened and a steady stream of attendees disappeared into the various breakout rooms off the main auditorium. They were gone for brief periods.

Through the use of a data-mining service, Stocker is able to study and reward the prescribing habits of individual physicians. Targeted marketing is a common practice.

Several prominent physicians from area hospitals were among the 200+ guests. Many of the attendees are considered heavy hitters and are rewarded with a variety of perks. These benefits include airfare to meetings and expensive meals at restaurants.

The company also compensates physicians for lecturing colleagues about the benefits of various medicines and products. Payment for these efforts start at $1,000 per appearance.

Stocker's problems are not limited to payola.

The Redeem Erectile Dysfunction device, which was fast-tracked for approval when developed by RJ Health, a company subsequently purchased by Stocker, has been blamed by a former patient for the chronic pain that ultimately led to his heroin addiction. Other Redeem device recipients have reported similar intractable pain resulting in drug dependence.

Tomorrow: Part Two—Data Mining and Your Physician's Prescribing Habits

"Nigel was there last night."
"Jesus."

"He checked on Tonya before he went. I may feel guilty that I didn't warn him."

"He's a big boy."

"Not really."

Win laughed. "You're merciless."

"I better go home, let the dog out."

In the empty hallway he put his cool, dry hand to my face. It smelled of lemon soap. "Marti, no matter what happens, you'll always know where to find me."

I moved toward him and reached up on my tiptoes. To kiss his cheek. Or maybe his mouth. I truly don't know. But that is how I was standing, with my hair shower wet and my underpants bulging in my pocket, when Carter-Randolph Hayes pulled open the door to the adjacent apartment. I replanted my feet and wished my life over a thousand times in that instant as I felt her take in the awkward sight.

"Well, hey, Marti Trailor!" she oozed, all Junior League enthusiasm, inscrutable and agitating. "What a . . . surprise."

"Hi, Carter-Randolph."

"Marti, this is my baby sister, Kara." She turned and said, "The Trailors live next to us. And I guess you live next to her . . . friend. What a coincidence. So what's new, Marti?"

Let's see . . . my husband has been having an affair with a nurse whose cousin is responsible for killing my client's baby, and I'm about to become a single mother, and you, the Mouth of the South, are under the impression you caught me in a compromising position and will no doubt broadcast your discovery to the whole freaking city even though I exercised unbelievable restraint.

"Not too much. I wish we had time to chat, but there's an emergency at the hospital. Nice meeting you, Kara."

"Well, that was awkward," Win said after our silent walk back to my car.

"You think?"

At home, I discovered that Batman had gotten sick after rummaging in the trash. My first reaction was to be relieved that Elliot wasn't there. My second was to cry. After I cleaned the floor I marshaled my dwindling resources and phoned Michael to have him explain umbilical cord prolapses. Just to be sure. Despite Win's attempt to allay my fears, I wished I'd done this before saying anything to Tonya and her mom. In keeping with my usual pattern of act first, obsess later, the worry of Mrs. Harris being wrong was starting to play like an unbidden song lyric. William was visiting Michael, so we had a three-way conversation on speaker. I described the events at the hospital and asked for their opinions. Michael confirmed the plausibility of Mrs. Harris's theory.

"Was the baby early?" he asked.

"Yeah. Almost a month, I think. I mean, we had just started the childbirth classes."

"Well, I'm not exactly sure if that's early enough to contraindicate the amniotomy—"

"The what?"

"The artificial rupture of the membranes. To accelerate labor. But that's something to look into. Anyway, it sounds like the cord came out with the rush of amniotic fluid. If the baby's head had been properly engaged—if the doctor had waited—the head would have sealed the canal and the cord would have followed the baby."

William gave me the name of Sharon Hanover, a local malpractice lawyer.

"She's impressive," he said. "A pit bull of a torts attorney. I heard there's a hospital down there that's been trying for years to get her on retainer just so she'd never be able to go up against them."

"Thanks. By the way, it was Catherine Stamp. The doctor, I mean. The one who—"

"No!" Mikey exclaimed.

"There's something wrong with her, though. She was bordering on hostile. And so tired she seemed stoned." I tried to organize my impression of her.

"Do you think she was?" William asked.

"I don't know."

"Well, write down your perceptions of everything that happened last night. They may come in handy," he instructed.

"Okay." And then, digging my fingernails into my palms, I said, "Um, there's something else. Elliot and I are splitting up."

Silence separated us while I stared out the window at the dreary day. Dingy gray clouds roosted above the roof of Carter-Randolph's house.

"Oh, M-Marti," Mikey said.

Which almost got me. I forged on without acknowledging his concern. "Things have just been deteriorating for a long time. I guess I wasn't ready to recognize the symptoms. But I have now. Please don't tell Mom or Dad, yet. Okay? I don't think I can bear to have my temperature taken every fifteen minutes."

"Is there anything we can do for you, Mart?" William asked. He sounded sad, not surprised.

"I don't know. Just don't be nice. I can take anything but aberrant behavior."

We hung up and I tried to reach Colby but again got only the machine. I left a low-key congratulatory message about her article, dealt with Batman, called an exterminator, then headed back to the hospital.

Nigel pounced as soon as I got off the hospital elevator.

"Why, Mrs. Trailor! Just the person I was looking for!"

"Really?" I said stupidly. "Why?"

"I believe the two of us need to have a little chat. Shall we?" he asked as he held open the heavy fire door for me. I followed him through the tunnel that connected the hospital to the professional office building, trying not to feel like an errant child, as he kept a steady three paces in front of me. He unlocked the door to his office and turned on the light.

It was a fussy English study. Red leather chairs with shiny brass tacks faced an enormous desk with neat stacks of paper, a short Waterford vase full of pens, and a telephone. Prints of hunts and cowering foxes hung above a short bookcase holding leather-bound volumes of obstetric texts. An antique stethoscope was aligned with a sterling-silver frame featuring Leslie and baby Tara wearing matching blue-flowered Laura Ashley jumpsuits. Nigel's other four children glowered from their own frame. I wondered about the moment when he exchanged the picture of Mrs. Hill-the-First for Leslie's. Was there any sadness, any regret? Had Leslie's likeness just been slid in over Natalie's like some archaeological clue?

I took a deep breath and then went on the offensive. Beatbeatbeat, went my heart. "What can I do for you, Dr. Hill?"

"I believe you have some question about the course of treatment that was chosen for one of our patients."

His smile was patronizing.

"I assume you're talking about Tonya Maines," I said. "Yes, I believe her water was broken before the baby's head was engaged."

"And what gives you that idea, Mrs. Trailor?"

Oh shit, I thought, realizing I shouldn't say anything about Mrs. Harris. "I'm not at liberty to discuss that at the moment, Dr. Hill."

"Well, that's a fairly incredulous leap to make for a layperson, isn't it? Your training is in the field of social work, I believe."

"That's right."

"As I have already spoken with the doctors involved, as well as with your husband—"

"You called Elliot?"

"That's right. For a variety of reasons. Not the least of which is his role on the quality improvement team. I can only assume that the information you are spreading came from a nonphysician. Someone unqualified to make such an assessment. As such, I would appreciate it if you wouldn't spread your little story any further, Mrs. Trailor. You are a hospital employee." He extracted from his top drawer a manila folder with my name on it. Which totally unnerved me.

"Dr. Hill, it's not a 'little story.' A baby is in the morgue right now. She should be with her mother."

"I can assure you, as is always the case when there are unfortunate incidents, an internal investigation will be performed."

A noise escaped my lips. Nigel's face became a canvas for unmitigated fury.

"As I was saying, a preliminary discussion has occurred. And it is entirely possible that the hospital might agree to a package. Mind you, no fault is being acknowledged. But we can see that the circumstances were confusing enough to cast doubt. All of this is provisional, based on Miss . . . your client waiving her choice to pursue anything through the court system. Or making any written complaint or claim through the insurance company."

"Wait, what? Are you offering me a bribe to take back to her?"

An old clock ticked. Nigel put the folder on the corner of his desk, crossed his arms. "I hear you and your husband have been having problems."

"What?" My eyes widened at the non sequitur.

Nigel smiled, revealing the tops of overlapping teeth. He stayed quiet.

"Dr. Hill, I'm not sure what you're talking about."

"Truly, Mrs. Trailor?" He arched his eyebrows in overdone surprise. "It's been fairly common knowledge around the department that your marriage has been on the rocks. Predictably."

"Predictably?"

"While I don't presume to know the intricacies of your particular situation, I do know that when extramarital activities occur, they are symptomatic of a diseased relationship."

"My marriage has no bearing on any of this, Dr. Hill." I felt like vomiting.

"You can't be serious, Mrs. Trailor. You are, in a particularly unprofessional manner, manipulating your client in order to harm your husband. By attacking the institution. And, of course, Dr. Stamp. You're allowing negative personal circumstance, your deteriorating marriage, to dictate your actions." He paused to clear his throat and then added in a voice full of false compassion, "For all I know, Mrs. Trailor, you may not even be aware of what you are doing. But I have no intention of allowing you to disrupt the workings of my department. Or to crucify Catherine Stamp. I strongly urge you to seek professional help. And by the way, when I say professional, I mean medically trained."

"What are you talking about?"

"Perhaps the guilt associated with your son's accident is also having an impact. It would certainly be understandable for your thinking to be affected by some variant of traumatic stress. In any event, if you don't halt this nonsense, I'll be forced to release a statement to the press outlining the personal motivation for your behavior."

"Which is what?"

"That you are orchestrating a smear campaign of the worst kind to vilify your husband's mistress."

The walls tilted. "What?"

"Come, come, Mrs. Trailor. You don't really need me to spell things out further, do you?"

I barely had time to assimilate this information before a tiny ball of anger grew inside of me.

"You know what, Nigel? I don't care what you think or what you do. But I've got a hunch that if I hadn't been there, you and your department would be steamrolling this girl. And I don't think it's incidental that she's poor and black."

"Oh, we're playing the race card now, are we? Trying to jerk my chain by accusing me of prejudice? Let me remind you that my department is consistently ranked in the top one hundred nationally. And the primary beneficiaries are poor and black." He smiled indulgently. "My dear, surely you can do better than that?"

"How about telling the hospital administration that you were at the Stocker dinner last night? With the hookers?"

For the briefest of instants, the vein in his temple pulsed. "Yes, that's true, Mrs. Trailor. I was at the dinner, as a first-time invitee. But I left prior to the unseemly events. To come back to the hospital for an emergency."

"How convenient for you. You pig."

I turned on my heels and practically ran all the way to my office. As soon as I got there, I bent over the garbage can and heaved.

Win rushed in.

"Oh, whoa," he said. "Let me help." He held my hair back as I bent forward. Another wave of vomit came up, some splattering on his shoes. "Nice shot," he remarked, wiping off my mouth with his ever-present hanky. "You okay?"

"I'm upset."

"Do you always barf when you're upset?"

I nodded.

"How adorable. What's going on, Marti?"

I told him about Nigel.

"Whew. We're going to really have to think all this through." He led me into his office and handed me his leather travel kit. "We've got some work to do. I got a feeling we're not in Kansas anymore. There's a toothbrush in there."

I emerged from the bathroom just as Joel Levine barged into the office. He was wearing his white lab coat with "Director of Social

Work" stitched above the pocket. He couldn't have buttoned the two sides together if his life depended on it.

"What is going on over here, Win?"

The question was obviously a formality. He clearly knew. Before Win could formulate an answer, Joel put up his dimpled hand like a safety patrol stopping traffic. "I just got off the phone with Kensington Wickham. Who was in a hell of a state over a rumored lawsuit."

"Actually, Joel, I e-mailed you the whole incident report. What's happened so far, anyway," Win said calmly.

This seemed to mollify Joel somewhat and he sat down in the chair across from the desk. It groaned. He wiped his brow with the back of his hand. "I'll tell you what I know. Ken basically intimated that he'd pull his matching funds for the New Moms program if you all align yourselves with the claimants."

"Who is Kensington Wickham?" I asked.

Win answered, looking upset. "He's on our board and helped get the start-up funding together for the program. I'm not sure what you mean about aligning—"

"Is he a tobacco Wickham?" I interrupted.

Joel answered, "Yeah. Not the ideal funding source for a hospital-based program. Then again, beggars can't be choosers."

I jumped in again. "Catherine Stamp—the resident who screwed up last night—is from a tobacco family, too. Not the Wickhams—"

"Are you suggesting this is a conspiracy, Marti?" Joel asked, leaning back in his chair and assuming the body language of a therapist talking down a disturbed client. He was probably thinking that an altered mental state might be just the ticket to isolate me from New Moms.

"Look, Joel, I know that sounds crazy, but I grew up around powerful people. And a lot of things get worked out around country club swimming pools. It's hardly a stretch to think that Catherine's daddy contacted Wickham. Just because they make different brands of cigarettes doesn't mean they don't know each other. They're probably neighbors. Their children probably danced together at cotillion."

"Marti, what are you talking about?" Joel asked.

"It's just that things are the same in Washington. The fiercest congressional enemies sit next to one another at their kids' Christmas pageants. My dad calls them pissing pals. Favors get passed back and forth between adversaries because they run into each other all the time. In restaurants, theaters, and bathrooms. Their lives are totally interwoven. The community of powerful people is tight. I could even call up the governor because our kids are in the same school."

"Marti's father is Congressman Maxwell," Win interjected.

I glanced back at Joel and saw he was ruling out the need for major tranquilizers and a leave of absence for me. Reluctantly.

"Anyway, at this point we don't even know if Tonya is interested in pursuing anything legal," I said.

Joel shrugged his shoulders nervously. "Well, I wouldn't bank on that. Look, I'm not sure about the protocol for any of this. This is a new one on me. But my advice—and I use that word euphemistically—is for the two of you to run everything by the hospital attorneys. Okay?"

We agreed.

"Good, I'm glad we're all on the same page, because this thing has bad news written all over it. The last thing I feel like doing is engaging in a wrestling match with OB-GYN and Nigel, you know?"

After Joel left, Win and I waited a few minutes and then walked to Tonya's room together, Win carrying a vase of roses he had bought on his way into the hospital. The flowers, a dozen newly opened buds, were a mournful shade of burnt sienna, the color of a sunset's shadow. There was no baby's breath in the bouquet, just ferns from distant forests.

The door was ajar and I stuck my head in and was surprised by a small group of visitors clustered by the bed. Tonya's mother, still in her uniform from the night before, approached.

"Good morning. Come on in."

I introduced Win, and then we entered the room, where we were met by two people I didn't know. "This is Mr. Dugid, my caseworker," Mrs. Maines said. "And this is his friend Sharon Hanover. She's an attorney."

I smiled at the very same lawyer whom William had recommended just a couple of hours before. Her earnest face and loosely bunned hair and sensible shoes made her seem more Quakerish than a legal attack dog.

"Nice to meet you," I replied, shaking her hand.

Andy Dugid was sitting next to Tonya. With broad shoulders, flat stomach, and graying crew cut, he resembled a character actor specializing in drill sergeants. His forehead was carved by years of active eyebrows pinched together in concern. In contrast to his deeply tanned skin, his sky-blue eyes were startling. Easily in his fifties, he was still a very handsome man.

"Why, Ms. Trailor, I'm honored to put a face to your lovely Yankee voice," he said, and smiled.

"Nice to meet you." I smiled back.

"You're going to have to excuse my manners, but it's not too often that I get the chance to hold hands with a girl as pretty as Tonya. So I'm going leave it right where it is, if you don't mind."

"Not at all, Mr. Dugid. I understand completely." I bent over and pushed the young girl's hair off her face. "How are you doing, sweetie?" I asked.

Tonya tilted her head. Just then the catheter snaking out from under the blanket began to fill with urine. A deep red color rose from the top of Tonya's chest, reaching her face, turning her brown cheeks almost maroon.

"Excuse me," she whispered.

"No one's responsible for anything they do when they're in a hospital bed, sweetheart," Mr. Dugid said, his deeply southern baritone soothing. He patted her arm.

"Thank you," Tonya said, her words almost lost in the whispering sheets as she rocked slightly from side to side.

Sharon spoke. "By way of explanation, Andy called early this morning to come over and see about Tonya. Andy and I are in the same rowing club. Anyway, as I told him, I'm glad to oblige, but I'm on my way out of town for a couple of days to be with my mother, who is ill. So if you don't mind, I'll start the ball rolling now, and then if it looks like we have cause, I'll pick it back up just as soon as I get back. So . . ." She clasped her hands. "I'd appreciate anything you can tell me to help get started."

Win and I looked at each other. This was exactly what Joel had warned us not to do. Win lifted his eyebrows in a *you decide* expression.

I did. Fuck the hospital.

I relayed the story Mrs. Harris told me, Wickham's warning, Nigel's veiled offer. The only thing I couldn't repeat was what Nigel had said about Catherine and Elliot. It was too humiliating.

"Good grief," Sharon said. "This is a real can of worms. Well, let me gather my thoughts a moment. Let's see . . . Tonya has agreed that it would be in the best interest of the case to have an autopsy performed on Camra. Otherwise, we run the risk of the hospital suggesting that the baby was suffering from congenital defects that caused her death. Without an autopsy there would be no way to refute that."

I was surprised by Tonya's change of heart. She had been so determined to prevent the procedure just hours before.

"If the results show hypoxia," Sharon continued, "I'll file suit downtown. As I explained to Tonya and her mom, the parameters of the case have changed with Camra's passing. If she had lived, she would have been eligible for benefits through the Catastrophic Birth

Program. That would have covered all medical expenses. Her death, though, is capped at a hundred thousand."

"It's not about money," Tonya said quietly.

"We know that, sugar," Andy said. "We all understand."

Sharon's strategy basically consisted of deposing me and Tonya, Mrs. Harris, Catherine Stamp, and Peter. She wanted to do this as quickly as possible, ostensibly to gather fresh memories. But also to avoid contamination by the hospital's handlers. Tonya grew restless and edgy, her hormones raging with no payoff. I had to go into the bathroom so she wouldn't see me cry. When I came out, everyone was getting ready to go.

The four of us walked into the hallway together. I turned to Sharon.

"You know what's funny? My brother gave me your name to give to Tonya when I called him this morning."

"Is he an attorney here?"

"No, in D.C."

"Who's your brother?" She laughed when I told her. "My God, there really are only a hundred people in the world. I was just on a panel with him. He's quite the charmer."

"I suppose that's one way of looking at it."

Sharon laughed again and then engineered it so that she and I were walking side by side. "Listen, Marti. I was told that your husband is on staff here. Will that pose a problem for you?"

"Actually, um . . . we're separating."

"Oh! Well, I'm terribly sorry about that."

I felt a dangerous press of tears. Sensing her concern was having a deleterious effect, she resumed her business voice. "Anyway, before I leave town I'll be getting in touch with Mrs. Harris. Before anyone else does. This won't be the first time Dr. Hill and I have tangled, you know."

"Really?"

"Most recently when I sued the hospital on behalf of a woman on whom a resident performed an abortion. She'd gone in for an amnio."

"You were the attorney for that case?"

"Yes. We'll make sure that the hospital does right by Tonya." She cleared her throat. "Now, Marti, I'm not your lawyer so I can't really offer any advice, but I would like to suggest that you avoid talking to the press. It's not a bad idea to avoid unsupervised discussions with the administration, either. There's a lot at stake here. So not much would surprise me. We don't want them to be able to control the spin. We must be very organized in our approach."

"Okay." I smiled. "I'm grateful to have someone guide me through this."

"It'll be a team effort. I hope that both you and Win are cognizant of the potentially precarious positions your jobs will be in. You'll basically be going up against your employer."

I nodded.

"Attrition through intimidation is a common happenstance in the legal system. I'm going to make sure that Tonya understands the cost/benefit ratio of going to trial before I file anything. The hospital will fight to the death in the courtroom, but I have a hunch we'd be able to recover substantial damages from them without ever leaving the medical campus."

"You mean Nigel's offer?" I asked. "His *bribe*?"

Sharon's eyes crinkled in amusement. "Think of it as a mutually beneficial agreement. It is certainly something that I'm going to investigate. After the abortion fiasco, I'm sure that the powers that be will grab at the chance to make all this go away as quietly as possible. Everyone needs to understand what's at stake if we go the court route. You too. My guess is your Maxwell pedigree will be of interest to the press."

I felt weak.

"That doesn't look like it sits too well with you."

"Unlike William, I do my best to stay out of the public eye."

She laughed.

My pathological aversion to scrutiny developed in middle school, when my parents' divorce became media roadkill. The idea of being involved in a potentially high-interest case was grotesque. But I would have to suck it up. "Listen, there's something else. I just learned that Catherine Stamp and my—"

Andy Dugid came up right then. I asked Sharon for her card, told her I'd get in touch. In the elevator's mirrored door, I saw Nigel's distorted reflection. He was staring at us from the nurses' station. At first I thought he was looking at me, and then I realized it was Sharon who held his attention. His expression was frightening. I pressed the elevator button and studied the floor.

Colby called just as I got home.

"Jesus, Mary, and Joseph, Martha Helen! What in God's name is happening?" She was going full tilt before I could even say hello. "I'll have you know I've been so sick with worry I haven't had a moment to contemplate what I'm going to wear to pick up my Pulitzer!"

"Oh, Cole . . ."

"What, Marti? What? Is it one of the kids?"

"No—they're okay. I'll tell you. But it's off the record," I said, announcing the compromise I had reached between not talking to the press and needing my best friend.

"Sounds bad."

"And it's just starting, I think."

The telling was getting easier with each rendition; pretty soon the language would have traveled far enough from its starting point that the words would be free of all emotional content. They'd just be little empty suitcases. Colby waited until I finished speaking, a seasoned reporter not wanting to derail any forthcoming information. When I was quiet she said, "Well, I suppose we knew it was always a matter of time, right? Exhausted residents working around the clock. God knows how many mistakes never even come to light." She paused for a moment and then added, "Lord, Marti! This has wire service written all over it. Does the attorney think there's a strong case here?"

"Yeah. But slow down, Colby. I'm not even supposed to talk to you. The best thing would be if you just call Sharon Hanover. Tell her someone saw her in Tawny's room. Leave it at that. See what she wants to say."

"Gotcha. If there's enough there, everything you said would be not for attribution, okay?"

"What's that mean?"

"It's different than off the record—I use what you say, but I don't attribute it to you. I'll do some discreet nosing around." She paused and then added, "As for Elliot—fuck 'im. I'm hating the cheating bastard right now."

With that, my own near infidelity tumbled out of my mouth.

"Yeah, I kinda figured as much. Win's voice definitely had that close-but-not-quite ring to it when I called last night. I can't wait until you finally succumb."

"Why?"

"To find out."

"To find out what?"

"If he has a big one."

"Only you would think of that in the middle of an apocalypse."

"Look, Marti, I really don't mean to be blithe about this, but I'm at the end of my chain here. I'll tell you what, if it had been me, I'd have dumped Elliot Weeks Trailor like a bad habit a long time ago. Tested the waters with the man from Michigan last summer. Gotten on with things." I could barely hear her above my screaming primal fear. "Are you listening?"

"I'm so scared, Cole."

"Of what?"

"Ending up alone," I choked out, ashamed. "Elliot will remarry, Win'll go back to his wife, and I'll never get out of my bathrobe."

"Oh, for the love of God, Marti. You don't even *own* a bathrobe."

"It's what I've always been most afraid of. My whole life, I've been waiting and now it's happening. I'm going to end up like my mother."

"What's wrong with being like your mother? She's talented and working and spending time with people she wants to."

"Yeah, now. All these years later. She was a basket case for most of my childhood."

"Well, you don't have that option. You may not know it, but you're tougher than that. You're going to pull yourself together!" Colby snapped. Then softly, "Look, honey, you've been alone in your marriage a long time already."

"Colby, Elliot wasn't always bad—"

"You listen here, Martha Helen. We've been through all that. Deal with who he is now. Self-centered, arrogant, and dismissive. You wouldn't keep wearing a ratty dress just because it looked good when you bought it." She laughed. "Well, *you* might. Anyway, 'long as I'm still kicking, you'll never be alone. Now, you get yourself straight for your children. It's going to be rough for a while. They're going to need you in control. Okay?"

"Okay," I whispered.

"I'm going to give Sharon Hanover a call. I'll keep you posted."

"She's going out of town for a few days. Hey, Colby—did you see Nigel there? At the Stocker thing?"

"He was there?"

"Yeah. That's where he was going when he left the floor."

She whistled. "I'll call you later."

I spent the rest of the day substituting housework for thinking. I gutted cabinets, stripped beds, and scoured tubs. And only for a moment while I was cleaning the bathroom, when an image of Win invaded my thoughts, was the tactic unsuccessful. I actually had to rest my head against the cool tile of the shower as I remembered him touching my face. The memory took my breath away.

I was putting the vacuum back in the hall closet when the handle got caught on one of Elliot's jackets. I tried to untangle it and a piece of cream-colored stationery poked out of the pocket. I froze when I recognized the rotund vowels of the private school script. It was a letter from Catherine Stamp.

"Darling E. I'm so sorry I sent the soldiers. I only did it because I thought it would bring him some smiles. I never meant to upset Martey. I think my judgment was clouded from lack of sleep. (I'd also taken something, which probably contributed.) Anyway, I love you darling and am very, very sorry. C.

She'd drawn a simple outline of a sailboat next to her initial.

Rage pumped through me.

How dare she send something to my child? And how dare Elliot lie to me about it? I ran and yanked open the closet door, fury overriding rat threat. I grabbed his well-organized clothes off the compulsively spaced padded hangers, made a mountain of his jackets and pleated pants, snatched belts and ties by the handful, tangling them together like necklaces in a jewelry box. I jerked wooden stretchers out of shoes, ripped suit coats from their separate bags. I moved on to his bureau, scooping up socks, underwear, and tennis shirts by the handful. When everything was in a pile, I shoved all of it into garbage bags, some already half-full of real trash. Holding open the one that held the newspaper I'd used to clean up the dog's mess, I dropped Elliot's watch, cuff links, and nail clippers to the bottom of the bag. Then I slid my wedding ring off and released that, too. And I carried them, one by one, to the front porch.

CHAPTER THIRTEEN

I truly believed that Shane's discovery was going to turn everything around. But it was more like reaching an emergency exit and finding it locked.

Natalie Hill, whose shadowy image was captured by the hospital's security camera along with my own, is not in the country. The one person who may have witnessed the benign nature of my nursery visit is gone. As soon as I identified her, I remembered the note of support she had written me. I told Leland about it and he actually stopped our meeting and drove me to Colby's to get it. He must have been driving his little sports car twenty-five miles over the speed limit. While he tapped the steering wheel in anticipation, I dug at my cuticles, praying that I hadn't thrown out the card. We spoke only when I gave directions. He screeched to a stop in front of the Kusiks' and we both ran inside, my heart thumping like a wild animal against my ribs. To my amazement, the letter was lying between two books on my bedside table like a rose being dried as a keepsake. I handed it to Leland and allowed myself a little smile as the gold-scripted *KH* glinted in the light.

Fool's gold.

Natalie Hill is back in England. Drinking again. Leland got a subpoena for her, but he might as well have rolled it up, stuck it in a gin bottle, and pitched it out over the Virginia Beach breakers toward Britain.

When the kids walked into the house, I gathered them in my arms and didn't relax my grip until Simon complained the cast was crushing his chest. Elliot was standing in the doorway, his sunglasses on, his linen pants hugging his ankles, exposing newly tanned skin downed with brown hair turned gold. He was working the insides of his cheeks as though trying to grind his molars into dust.

I gave each child a final hug and then offered them five dollars apiece to walk Batman. While Simon and Poppy argued over who got to hold the leash, Nina announced she didn't feel like going. Duty bound to prevent a full-scale blowout between her parents, she lay down on the couch, arms straight at her sides. The rigid posture reminded me of times from my own childhood when I thought my physical presence alone could cancel a fight. I walked over, knelt, and kissed the top of her head. The smell of the ocean rose to meet me.

"Sweetie, I need you to go for a walk. Everything is going to be fine."

"I don't believe you," Nina whispered hoarsely. "I heard Daddy talking to Grandma and Grandpa."

"Nina, I mean it. Please."

Little pinched furrows appeared above her brow as she hesitated endlessly on the adolescent side of noncompliance. When she finally stood, she jammed her hands in her pockets and sighed. The act was so full of sadness and resignation that I could barely stand it. I watched her inch down the hallway, shoulder rubbing against the wall to slow her departure. She was walking away from her past life—and she knew it.

The door slammed. That was Elliot's cue to talk. "I want to know exactly what is going on at the hospital."

"Well, then perhaps you had ought to call the hospital," I bristled, angrily brushing stray bangs from my face. The smell of cleanser stung my eyes. "I don't want to talk about work. I want to talk about us."

"First I want to find out what's going on."

"Beyond the fact that Tonya has hired a lawyer and Nigel has threatened my job, I don't know."

He shook his head, staring at me from behind his glasses, arms crossed at his chest. His fury and smug posture incited me.

"You're mad at me? Your girlfriend"—the word made him recoil—"killed a baby! What should Tonya do, forget about it?"

"In the first place, Marti, we don't know what happened to the baby."

"Well, there's going to be an autopsy, so we will. And I'll testify to the fact that Catherine didn't examine Tonya before she ruptured the membranes."

He flinched. "I don't know what's happened to you, Marti. Your behavior is utterly irrational. Nigel warned me."

"Nigel warned you?" I tried to maintain the same tone of voice, but nothing can make you feel crazier than someone suggesting that you are.

"You've lost all perspective, is what that means. You're reacting as though this thing happened to a family member. On top of which you're exploiting the tragedy to get back at me."

"I didn't even know who you were sleeping with until your boss told me. I thought it was her dipshit cousin. As for the baby, I was there when she was born. I cared about her. I care about her mother. What's the matter with you that you don't get that? Who *are* you?"

"I'm sorry the baby died." He took his glasses off and sat down on the arm of the couch. "I'm also sorry that I wasn't honest with you about Catherine. But I'm in love with her."

"Oh well, as long as you're in love with her."

"You've gotten so harsh."

At that moment I could remember nothing good that had ever transpired between us. No conversations, private jokes, or passionate lovemaking. No music. Or vacations. Nothing. He could have been anyone. Our whole history together had been obliterated, the years of marriage erased. He leaned toward me, trying a different tack.

"Marti, I know I could have done this better. I wish I had done it better. But you realize these are separate issues, don't you? Look, if somebody is responsible for what happened during the delivery, it was a terrible accident. But an accident is just that—an accident. I know you don't want to hear this, but Catherine is a wonderful person. All she's ever wanted to do is help women have babies."

"How ironic."

He glared at me, said nothing.

"I want you to leave, Elliot. For good."

When the kids came back, we sat in the family room. The girls and I on one couch, Elliot and Simon on the other.

Iiiin, I inhaled. Ouuut. "Guys, Daddy and I have some sad news."

Simon whimpered. "Did somebody die?"

Poppy began crying so hard, she started hiccupping. I pulled her closer.

"No, honey. Nobody died. But it's something hard that we're going to have to get through. And we will, with each other."

"What?" Nina asked.

"Daddy and I have decided we aren't going to live together any—"

"But you promised," she shouted. "You promised you'd never get divorced!"

"Oh, Neens," I whispered. "It's not something we wanted to have happen, sweetie. Sometimes bad things just do."

"Go to a guidance counselor," Simon suggested.

Elliot leaned over and put his mouth on top of our child's head. It wasn't so much a kiss as an attempt to breathe him in. It hurt my eyes.

"I know this is because you don't love us anymore," Nina said, standing and addressing Elliot. "Because you have a girlfriend. The one from that restaurant when you took us out for breakfast that time. I know you're going to marry her and have new children."

I tried to remain calm.

"I love you all very much," Elliot said quietly.

"Even Mommy?" Poppy asked.

"Of course. But we think it would be best if we lived apart for a while. We'll always be your parents and we'll always love you."

Simon calculated. "Does this mean we'll have double toys?"

"What's wrong with you!" Nina screamed, escaping my reach and running out of the room.

"What did I do?" he asked, covering his face with his good arm. I went over and pulled him in for a hug.

Everything was swirling beyond my control. Even my breathing was erratic. Once Simon left my embrace, I went into the kitchen and took two hits off my puffer, trying to regain order from the inside out. Three different kids with three different responses was so overwhelming, I didn't know how we were ever going to set things right again. I went to find Nina. She was on her bed, face-down, hair fanned out on the pillow. She had literally passed out. I kissed her head and slipped off her little sneakers. The sight of the soles of her naked feet undid me. They were so vulnerable. Pale and smooth, like the inside of a seashell. I had to bite my lip to keep from crying out at the damage we were inflicting on our babies.

Downstairs, I found Simon offering to help carry Elliot's bags to the car. Using all of his third-grade strength, and only one arm, he hoisted the sack with the dress clothes. And dog shit.

"P-U!" he exclaimed loudly enough for me to hear through the closed window.

Elliot came back in, seething. "Impressive job with my things, Marti. That was very mature. Thank you very much."

"I guess I missed the etiquette chapter on 'Packing Your Spouse When He Moves in with His Girlfriend.' "

"The dog crap was really clever."

"I thought it fit nicely with a certain theme." He closed the door behind him. Permanently.

I didn't feel equipped to be the designated mature adult. I wanted to receive comfort, not provide it. But I pulled it together, suggested to the kids that we play Monopoly. The four of us spent the rest of the afternoon negotiating, building, and trading. None of us had fun, but we kept busy. In between turns I stared out the window, past the maple tree that had carpeted the little plot of lawn with red and orange leaves, past the street filling up with second cars. I looked out into the future, trying to envision life without my husband.

It was like a buffet put on by the Anxieties. Each worry a separate entrée with its own side dish. Would Elliot try to screw me with support payments? Would we have to move to an apartment that might not let us have a dog? How would I survive three teenagers? Who would back me up on curfews, driver's licenses, and dating? What would it be like at the activities that command parent appearances? Would Elliot bring Catherine? What about teacher's meetings?

I caught myself. Elliot hadn't been to one yet.

For dessert, I got to envision people calling me Mrs. Trailor-the-First.

"Pay attention, Mom," Simon instructed. "Nina just landed on Boardwalk and owes you rent."

It took me a minute to refocus. "Sorry. Pay up, Neens."

The doorbell rang.

"Daddy, Daddy!" Poppy screamed, upending the game, running to open the door.

When she swung it open, another familiar male voice bellowed, "No, sunshine! It's your grandfather!"

I walked slowly toward the commotion and found my brothers and parents setting down suitcases in the hallway.

"So much for secret keeping," I whispered into William's chest as he cradled me.

"There's a time limit. You know that, Martyr Helen."

"Fifteen minutes?"

Once the initial flurry of excitement died down, everyone dissolved into tears. It was not an easy evening; the kids got agitated by the influx and kept getting into annoying squabbles. My parents were so solicitous, their concern was intrusive rather than reassuring. Mikey and William, in their attempt to normalize things, broke the family portrait during a game of couch ball when a returned serve over the coffee table went astray, knocking it from the mantel to the floor.

The symbolism was lost on no one.

In order to prove that I was all right, I insisted on preparing dinner. I shopped for the late cookout as though on speed, racing through the store's busy aisles like an ambulance weaving through traffic. I bought tubs of potato and pasta salads, presliced carrot and celery sticks, hot dogs and hamburgers, chicken breasts and sausage, soda and cupcakes, huge containers of condiments, and cheerfully decorated paper products.

I spent almost two hundred dollars on picnic food for eight people.

Then, because I was so freaked out by my mania, I carried the bags into the house through the back door so no one would see. It was when I brought the plate of meat to the yard that I froze. I could no more have turned on the propane grill than fly an airplane. Outdoor cooking was Elliot's culinary domain. So I stood helpless before the shining control panel of the monstrous barbecue, not only terrified that I might somehow ignite the whole neighborhood, but shaken by another aspect of separated life. For a crazy second I thought of wheeling the microwave to the patio. Fortunately, my big brother appeared, saying, "Step aside, step aside, let a real chef show you how."

When I had gone back into the kitchen, my mother pushed my

bangs off my forehead the way she used to when I was little. She asked what the children knew. I tried to answer, but all I could do was shake my head and bury myself in her soft bosom.

"It'll be okay," she said over and over, until eventually I pulled away.

Later that night while the kids chased their uncles, spitting watermelon seeds embedded in progressively larger chunks of pink fruit, my parents pummeled me with questions about my plans, immediate and long term. My father listened calmly to my pronouncement that I was just going to take it a day at a time.

"I think you and the kids should come back up to D.C. I can help you find a job on the Hill. We'll all be around to—"

"Dad, really," I said much more calmly than I felt, "I have a life here. My kids' lives are here."

He argued. I interrupted. "Please don't be bossy right now. I know you're just trying to help. But please don't Congressman me."

He looked over his half lenses, nodded.

Skipping baths, dental hygiene, and bedtime stories, I put the kids to bed, reassuring each of them of dual parental love. Poppy also made me promise that they would always live with me, a commitment as easy to make as promising the sun would be back up in the morning.

I went downstairs and found everybody in the kitchen, a smell of garlic hanging in the air, offering a mistaken impression of domestic tranquillity. My mother was browning ground beef and boiling noodles for a succession of husbandless dinners. The wrapped casseroles reminded me of my childhood, when she would grudgingly accompany Dad on the campaign trail, preparing dinners in advance for the sitter. I used to finger paint on the icy aluminum canvases and perform superstitious rituals while watching the prints disappear from the foil. If I could say the whole alphabet before the little heart or flower vanished, then my parents would be getting along on their trip.

I pulled the crumbled letter from Catherine out of my pocket and laid it on the table.

"Look what I found."

Everyone read it. My mother was the first to react, focusing on the hard proof of infidelity and bursting into tears.

"She's the woman who delivered the baby," I explained. "And the hospital is trying to say that it's a personal vendetta—me against her—motivating my involvement in the case."

"Son of a bitch," my father muttered.

"Let me see that again," William said, reaching for the paper. "Look at this—" He pointed to her line about taking something to stay up. "I wonder if anyone has thought to do a drug test on her. That would certainly explain a lot. Have you shown this to Sharon Hanover?"

I shook my head.

"I think we should give her a call. She may even want to come over and pick it up."

"She's out of town for a couple of days. I haven't told her about Catherine yet. I was going to send an e-mail."

"Well, that shouldn't wait. I'll give her a call," William said. "It's the kind of thing that should be over the phone or in person anyway."

Dad nodded.

Michael said, "I could be wrong, but I th-think the letter points to irresponsible scheduling, too. The lawyer should get her hands on the call schedule for the past few months. Even if her mental state was affected by amphetamines, she may have felt f-forced to take it in order to do what she was supposed to."

"God," I said excitedly. "I have some of the schedules. Elliot keeps them in a hard file. His desk stuff is still here. I'll pull it all together for Sharon."

By the time my family headed back up to D.C. the next day, I was at least thinking about moving forward. I had made an appointment with Sharon's secretary. I even planned on asking for a referral to a divorce lawyer.

Then I was arrested.

CHAPTER FOURTEEN

So here I am.

My days have taken on an underwater quality. Everything is muffled and foggy. I pick through the remains of my life in a stupor, waiting to wake up. I'm sure I use the bathroom, eat, and dress. On the other hand, if someone were to tell me I'd stopped doing these things—that would be believable, too.

My world is filled with appointments and press stakeouts. Depositions and talk of evidentiary discovery. Last week voir dire took place; the jury was selected. "With peers like these . . . ," I whispered to Leland. He shot me one of his warning glances that I am all too familiar with.

My kids have had therapy sessions and a meeting with a squat Child Protective worker with teeth so uniform, they looked filed. He evaluated my suitability for unsupervised visits. I asked if he knew Andy Dugid. He said yes in a way that slammed the door on any extracurricular conversation. Then he recommended my time with the children be chaperoned.

I was booked, my picture taken, my fingertips rolled side to side on a scanner by a surly woman in a uniform that smelled like spray starch. When I was allowed my one phone call, I had a moment of utter panic. Whom to call? Who would answer? I dialed my dad's emergency number at the Rayburn House Office Building. His legislative assistant tracked him down. Colby posted bond and I was out by midnight. My brothers and parents were there to greet me.

But I can't go home.

Elliot's ongoing betrayal guaranteed that.

"In your view, Dr. Trailor," the judge had asked at the preliminary hearing, "does your wife pose a flight risk?"

"I honestly don't know" was how my husband had answered, costing me my children. I had to relinquish custody for the duration of the trial, to remain free.

After the hearing, the Trailors awkwardly followed us onto the elevator.

"Elliot?" I said when the doors slid closed.

"Yes?"

"Go fuck yourself."

Mrs. Trailor gasped.

"Courthouse sex," Colby announced. "Happens all the time."

She pressed L with a freshly manicured finger and we descended in silence.

The first days after Elliot moved back into the house and I moved out were spent curled on the Kusiks' couch. My mother sat next to me, her cool hand stroking my forehead like she did when I had the mumps in fifth grade. My dad and brothers have been tag teaming it here. Mom has pretty much been down for the duration. Which in reality hasn't been that long. In fact, there's speculation about why I was put on the docket for such a quick trial, particularly since I wasn't waiting in custody. On the message boards that I can't stop myself from reading, opinion is divided into two camps. Some say it's because of Dad's clout. Others contend it's because the prosecutor wants to use the case in his election bid. It doesn't matter. I swing between relief and terror over the rapid advance to trial.

I'm down to hours.

Yesterday Colby declared it was time to shop for appropriate courtroom attire. She said this as if it were a standard category of wardrobe, like a trousseau or layette.

"I have lots of clothes," I argued.

"I'm not going to dignify that with a response." Colby handed me my coat. "Come along, Martha Helen. John and Charlie are going to the Science Museum, the rest of your clan can entertain themselves, and you and I are going to the mall in Short Pump."

"Why there?" I actually whined. The excursion felt insurmountable.

"If we go anywhere closer, we're likely to run into one of the neighbors."

"Oh."

Ever since the press had appeared like mushrooms in the front yard, Colby's neighbors had been on a rant. Some even circulated a petition to have me evicted. Colby had read the paragraph and the signatures out loud, ripped it in half, and handed the top back to the woman on her porch. She said she'd keep the autographs for future reference. From my frozen position in the hall, I heard my best friend lean in close to the whisper-thin brunette and enunciate very clearly: "Ruthie, if you so much as put one foot on my property ever again, I will personally tell my colleague—the bearded guy over there by the mailbox—about the little gathering your son hosted. The one with the Ecstasy. The one with the cheerleader passed out on your lawn. Wasn't it sweet little Jonathan who posted pictures of her?"

Ruthie made a fast retreat. I offered to move into a hotel.

"Girly-girl," Colby said hotly that afternoon, "I will pretend you didn't say that."

At the store she pulled together enough outfits for weeks of testimony, selecting conservative ensembles: three midcalf-length skirts (one bone, one navy, one black); a bluish-gray tweed jacket; five different blouses; two cashmere sweaters. Everything smart without being flashy.

"Nothing like the misery diet," Colby said about the fact that I was down to a size four.

She claimed her courtroom experience had schooled her in the real nuances that affect rulings and swore that inadequate eye contact, rude body language, and unfortunate fashion choices could stymie an innocent verdict as much as evidence.

"I'm telling you," she said, presenting me with moderate black heels, "you wouldn't believe how much this stuff comes into play. The last thing you want to do is show off in front of the jury."

Then she paused and dropped her voice. "And the next to last thing you want to do is look so . . . disheveled they'll think there's something the matter with you."

"I look that bad?" I asked, startled by the assessment.

"Not bad, Marti. Just seriously . . . upset."

She was being uncharacteristically gentle. I looked like shit. Or I did until yesterday. Dark brown smears filled in the hollows beneath my eyes, and unruly brow hair was scattered above them. My lips were critically chapped, and the ten pounds I had dropped left loose flesh behind.

Also, I seemed to have pimples—pimples!—on my forehead.

"And while we're on the topic," Colby went on, "you need to stop scrunching up your face. You'll be as wrinkled as a scrotum by the time we can put paid to all of this."

After lunch Colby talked me into a makeover, which I eventually realized had been prearranged. The aesthetician waxed and squeezed, then smoothed a cool cucumber cream over my face, all while humming along with a Pandora playlist of Dave Matthews music.

I was a little alarmed by the red streaks that had taken the place of superfluous hair—but then I remembered what was going on in my life and went back to not caring.

As soon as the facialist left, a stylist materialized to rework the cheap haircut I had impulsively gotten after my arrest. She thinned, shaped, and conditioned, chatting about other famous clients like the governor's wife.

She didn't get that I didn't want to be recognized or that I had stopped responding to the conversational come-ons. At the end, though, it was worth it. On the way to the parking lot, I caught sight of myself in a full-length mirror. I looked like a new person. Someone thin and fragile, perhaps, but no longer a woman who might have missed her last dose of Thorazine. Colby put everything on her credit card. I'd had to relinquish mine along with my passport. My indebtedness is so profound, it no longer agitates me. The loss of my children dwarfs everything else. If you have a gangrenous wound on your foot, you don't notice sunburned shoulders.

I wonder, though, where the smaller pains actually go.

"Thank you," I whispered over the car's roof.

"That's enough of that."

Which triggered a muddy stream of new mascara down my cheeks.

"Oh, for God's sakes," Colby drawled. "Now look what you've gone and done!"

"Thank you for never asking if I killed Tonya's baby. . . ." Sobbing, I ducked down between her Volvo and a Lexus, not wanting to provide material for a lurking camera phone.

"Why would I ask you that?" she demanded, coming to my side of the car, hugging me. "Let's go home, Martha Helen. You just gotta keep on keeping on. It's only a little longer now."

The only thing that has kept me going is knowing that I don't have to keep on keeping on. There's an emergency exit tucked in the lining of my suitcase. A bag full of out. There are blue pain capsules left over from Charlie's cancer procedures; orange tranquilizers of Colby's, remnants of the same. White mystery tablets. For insurance, I have a full bottle of red-and-yellow over-the-counter headache pills. They're supposed to be a horrible way to go, but the other drugs will take the edge off.

It would be wrenching for my children, but dying is better than jail. Saying good-bye on weekly visiting days would be worse. Little Poppy in particular couldn't take that. Last year, before she had tubes put in, she kept getting ear infections that caused a constant ringing. The noise bothered her more than the ache.

"Don't you hear it, Mommy?" she asked. When I said no, she pulled me down and put her ear next to mine. "Do you hear it now?"

We are so connected, I think I did.

After our shopping trip, my family met us at the door with Chinese. Ironic, I thought to myself. This whole nightmare started over sweet and sour. Sometimes I wonder if Elliot was with Catherine on the night of the Spring Fling. The evening he was supposed to be helping out at the hospital. The night I met Win. The night the ball began rolling into the street.

Everyone was subdued at dinner. Not just me, for once. Even my brothers were unable to stage a pep rally. I've been logy for weeks and weeks. More than once Leland ordered coffee for me without asking. If he could order electric shock therapy, I'm sure he would.

"Girly-girl," Colby said, putting down her chopsticks, "I cannot stand to watch you stir your food around on that plate for one more second. Come with me, I want to talk with you anyway." I followed her into my room and she sat next to me on the soft guest bed, her hip and thigh pressing into mine. It was a surprisingly comforting sensation. She picked up my hand. "Listen, Martha Helen. I just wanted to tell you, so you could be prepared in case they're there together."

"Who?"

"Elliot and Catherine. They're out of the closet."

"Oh. How come you didn't tell me before?"

"You mean today when we were having our special girls' day out?"

Which made us both laugh and laugh, until we cried.

I asked her to say good night to everyone for me and just crawled under the covers without changing out of my clothes. Then I shoved a corner of the blanket into my mouth to stop myself from screaming.

CHAPTER FIFTEEN

Help. Help. Help. Help. Help. Help. Help. Help. Help. Help. Help.
Help. Help. Help. Help.

My heart is frantic, thrashing so violently inside my chest that it
occasionally bounces into my throat. I can barely breathe. My right
shoulder has started shrugging at random intervals as if a small animal burrowed under my collarbone while I was sleeping. Nothing
is beyond the realm of possibility anymore. Nothing.

John eases the car into the ominous weather. The heater is no
match for the chill and I bunch the jacket across my chest, startled
all over again by my stripped ring finger. After so many years with
the diamond-studded band, it looks naked and sad. There's an in-
dent below the knuckle. I avert my eyes and tune back into Colby's
patter.

"That stuttering columnist from the *Times*—do you think he
stammers on the keyboard?"

She'd normally never say anything like that, given that Mikey
stutters. I don't respond. I don't need to. Ever since she helped me

get ready this morning, her mouth has been going nonstop. Her anxiety is coming out in brutal critiques of her brethren. I don't think I've ever seen her like this. I am sitting in the back, imagining her remarks as pebbles marking a path home.

"Word on the street is Patreee-cea from WZZZ is just a blow job away from a larger affiliate. And did I tell y'all Chanly the Weasel is being considered by the state GOP for press secretary?"

I lean my face against the window. It is so cold that it hurts.

"Well, he is!" she plows on. "You want to talk conflict of interest? At most papers that wouldn't be tolerated. He'd be given his walking papers. Not here. No, here there's no firewall between the press and partisan politics. No ethics problem at all. Just yesterday I saw the weasel yukking it up with two of the head honchos. You'd think the son of a bitch just won something."

I say nothing.

"No offense, darlin'," John offers, "but Marti and I are both aware that sleaze and journalism are not that far apart on the radio dial."

Just as he finishes saying that, a media mob comes into view. They're in front of the courthouse, waiting. A cluster of miscreants clad in Civil War attire is also huddled on their periphery.

"Great," I mumble. "General Lee's inbred descendants are here."

They've come for my father's benefit, not baby Camra's. He's been on their shit list ever since supporting the installation of the Arthur Ashe statue on Monument Avenue. The paper ran a string of vitriolic editorials suggesting, "New York Liberals"—Jews—"tend to their own business." The columns were so inspiring, a group of itinerant Confederates drove up 95 and picketed Dad's office on Capitol Hill. Being who he is, my father actually ordered them coffee and bagels.

"Assholes," I say.

Worry, thick as rope, uncoils between Colby and John. I can almost grab hold of it.

"Whatever you do, Marti, do not engage with those people. Spin is everything."

"I know."

Why is she telling me this? Does she think I've become a loose cannon, my own worst enemy? Suddenly I'm afraid that I am, that I may do something outrageous in the courtroom. What if the only thing I still have—self-control—is disappearing? My shoulder goes back to doing the hokey-pokey. I wonder if Tourette's can be latent, brought on by stress.

"I'll go find a space," John says, releasing the door locks. He puts his arm behind Colby's seat so he can rotate his bulky frame. "Marti, look at me."

I do.

"You have to be strong," he says hoarsely.

I can't speak.

"Marti! Think of the kids!"

"No," I whisper.

"You can and you will," he commands.

We squeeze through the gauntlet of frenzied correspondents on our way up the stairs.

"Mrs. Trailor!" a photographer shouts. "Smile!"

"Think you can get a fair trial?" someone else demands.

"How are your own babies doing?" a woman screeches. "Breathing?"

"Don't react," Colby hisses. "They want you to look bad. Trust me, Trailor. Just keep going. It's a fucking game. Don't smile, don't grimace. Just move. It's about the optics."

I rub the back of my arm where someone's pinched hard enough to hurt through the coat. A couple of black cops are leaning against the iron handrails witnessing our difficulties, arms crossed.

I am momentarily confused. Then I remember.

I am the white woman who murdered the black baby.

"Nice work, fellas," Colby proclaims. "Thanks for your help."

Before going through the metal detector, I hand my purse to the guard. She slams it down on the table with such force that two pens, a half-dressed tampon, and an inhaler are belched out. A flash goes off. My cheeks flame as my private mess is exposed and recorded. The blend of dislocation and acuity is making my head hum. It's like the dentist's Novocain. You don't feel the pain and you're hyperaware of his stomach noises.

Leland and Shane meet us in the hallway and we travel toward the courtroom en masse. They're wearing dueling aftershave. I breathe through my mouth.

"Got your game face on, Marti?" my lawyer asks. He doesn't wait for a response. Which is good. I can concentrate on walking.

We round a corner. Tonya is sitting with her mother, Sharon Hanover, and Andy Dugid. Tonya has lost all of the softness she had during pregnancy. She's almost gaunt. I desperately want her to look up. To give me some kind of sign. She doesn't. After my arrest I tried to call Mrs. Maines at the restaurant, but she'd quit. When I mentioned this to Leland, he got mad.

"You want to be accused of witness tampering?" Now he just increases the pressure on my arm. A cluster of lawyers is cracking up outside an open courtroom, while orange jumpsuited prisoners parade through a side door. Both groups still when they see me.

"This way," Leland says, pushing open the heavy door at the end of the hall. I follow him toward the front of the packed room. He pulls out the chair to the table as if he's my date, says something quietly. I can't hear him because I am suddenly gripped by a seasick-like nausea.

"You're going to have to pay better attention. I'll guide you, gal—but you're going to have to walk. I can't carry you. Do you understand what I'm saying?"

I have no clue what he is talking about.

"I'll try to do better."

"Good. Now if you have anything you want to tell me about

somebody's testimony, anything you think I should ask, you'll need to write it down. Remember, this judge doesn't tolerate distractions. She may look like Miss Virginia, but she's tough as old steak."

I want to tell him that's a redundancy, not a contradiction. I don't. Instead I rock a little in the upholstered chair, which has the same give as a movie theater seat. It's surprisingly comfortable.

"You like ballpoints or would you rather have a pencil?"

"How about a razor?"

"None of that, now. No Marti-isms. Your task is to stay focused. Be positive."

There is a rustling behind us and my mother's blue-veined hand grabs my arm. She squeezes and I lean into her without turning. Leland glances back at the audience. Is it like at a wedding? I wonder. Do people announce whose side they are on by where they sit?

And then it starts.

The bailiff is a large black woman with a complicated hairstyle. She instructs us to rise, her bead-tipped braids tapping against one another as though she's peeking through a curtain.

I grab hold of the table to compensate for my knees, which seem about to buckle.

"Breathe," Leland whispers gently.

I try.

The Honorable Dorie Hermann strides in. There's a noticeable bump under her blousy black robe. I feel panicky.

She's pregnant? Isn't that some kind of conflict?

She sits and the rest of us follow suit. I rock while the jury is given their instructions. Nine black, three white. Eight women. With the exception of an elderly, stoop-shouldered man whose craggy skin looks like it's been cured in a tobacco field, everyone else is south of fifty. About a third are studying me, some furtively, others with brazen curiosity. I try to smile but am only partially successful. Half my mouth is reeled up on a fishhook, the other half remains in place. I'm thinking I may be having a stroke.

Two women in particular give me the creeps. One has a mullet of orange hair and looks an awful lot like Larraine. She pulses hostility. The other keeps cutting her eyes at me without turning her head. It is an impressive economy of motion. She emits an aggrieved officiousness that brings to mind every bureaucrat I've ever bumped up against.

A jurocrat.

They are here because Leland used up his preemptory challenges during voir dire on potential jurors who were even worse.

Wycliff stands, buttons his jacket.

"Ladies and gentlemen, I'm Chappell Wycliff for the Commonwealth. I want to thank you for performing a sacred civic duty by being here. I'm going to start right off the bat by admitting this case is circumstantial. But as I'm sure you know, that is the nature of some courtroom dramas. My job will be to show you how, like drunken motorists merging onto the expressway, three factors came together with terrible results."

He crosses his arms. "With the testimony of witnesses and the presentation of a wealth of evidence, you will see that Martha Maxwell-Trailor murdered Camra Maines, a defenseless baby." Wycliff takes a few paces toward the jury box. "Now. What are the factors?

"Factor one"—he points a finger toward the ceiling—"the character of the accused. Who is Ms. Trailor? Ms. Trailor is what my mother, God rest her soul, used to call an interesting woman. A complicated woman. Ms. Trailor is the daughter of a very famous congressman. A man who has fought for civil rights his entire career."

By alluding to Dad without condoning his work, Wycliff has figured out how to play the race stuff without angering either the blacks on the jury or the deep-pocketed Right-wingers in his campaign circle.

"Impressive," I write on the top line of the yellow legal paper.

"Marti Trailor," he continues, strutting, "is a woman barely over the upset of seeing her son hit by a car not too long ago. In fact, Ms. Trailor is a woman so notoriously messy in deed and thought that she needs medication to stabilize herself.

"Marti Trailor is a woman who on the very night she murdered a baby, went out drinking with her boss and then spent the night with him."

As the room gasps, the skin on my face seems to shrink, pulling tighter and tighter. If Carter-Randolph hadn't come upon Win and me that morning, I probably wouldn't have admitted to the police I stayed in his apartment. But as Leland says, nothing proves a lie like being caught. Wycliff continues his assault, thrusts up his hand, making the victory sign.

"Second factor: Professionally, Ms. Trailor is a woman with a history of trying to control her clients. I'd wager that's because she thinks she understands more than the rest of us." He opens his arms to include himself and the jury. "I don't know—maybe growing up the daughter of Congressman Maxwell, attending those fancy private schools up in Washington, taught her things you and I never learned. Things about having more power than regular people. More sense than the rest of us.

"Folks, what I can tell you is this: Ms. Trailor has manipulated— although I'm sure she'd say guided—clients into surrendering children for adoption. She has paraded her pro-abortion sentiments. And in Camra Maines's case, Ms. Trailor was heard saying that this baby would be better off dead."

The prosecutor, now with three fingers up, walks closer to the jury box, speaking in an exaggerated whisper, letting his new best friends in on a secret.

"The third and final factor that contributed to the tragedy? Ms. Trailor was nursing a vendetta against the physician who delivered poor Baby Camra, accusing her of malpractice. Why? Because Ms. Trailor's husband is in love with her."

He pauses to let this sink in.

"I submit to you that the defendant saw the perfect opportunity to destroy the woman she despised."

I am momentarily intrigued by the fact that I am upholding decorum, practicing proper courtroom etiquette, when I could so easily lose my shit altogether.

"So. To review. We have an emotionally unstable woman with a pattern of controlling behavior confronted with a handicapped baby. Now if you'll allow me to interrupt myself for a moment, I would like to say that, yes, Camra Maines would have been handicapped. But my friends on the jury, one of my little nephews is handicapped. And bless his heart, you'll never meet a happier child. I don't know what would have happened to Camra. But neither did Ms. Trailor."

His words clap across the room.

"No! Ms. Trailor decided that this baby wouldn't even get a chance. Whether she was motivated only by a warped sense of supremacy, or by revenge against the woman she held responsible for the ruination of her marriage . . . I will leave up to you. But the facts are that she was the last person recorded leaving the crime scene and syringes were found in her possession—a syringe being the instrument of murder: the weapon that was used to inject air into that tiny baby's intravenous tubing. Which ended her life. I will present a long line of witnesses—including Ms. Trailor's own husband—who will walk you through the horrible circumstances that make up this case."

Tears are leaking from my eyes, little acts of nature.

To my left I hear some rustling. It's Leland's turn. He stands.

"Ladies and gentlemen, I, too, would like to thank you for taking time out of your busy lives to listen to this case. As we discussed in voir dire, your responsibility is to ensure that Mrs. Trailor is found innocent unless the Commonwealth proves beyond a reasonable doubt that she committed the crime for which she is being tried. Let me repeat that. Beyond a reasonable doubt. It will be my job to show you that the circumstantial evidence that Mr. Wycliff alluded to is coincidence. Or just plain wrong. An example? My client did not learn of her husband's affair with Dr. Stamp until after the baby's death." He pauses. "I'd hazard a guess that Mr. Wycliff's factors are nothing more than accusations fueled by political ambition. Now, if you'll indulge me for a moment, I'd like to tell you a little story."

He is settling into his southernisms, his folksy accent picking up. It's amazing how interchangeable the two lawyers sound. In a dark room I'm not sure I could distinguish between them. Which could be the punch line to a dirty joke. Leland alights on the corner of the table, leaning his weight atop a few inches of the polished wood. My eyes follow the line of his back. Someone has carved *mother-fucker* into the mahogany veneer.

I am awed by the audacity and run my finger over the cut. Did the author make a game of it—adding to the project whenever no one was looking? Or was it a brutally fast scarring, undertaken as a last act?

Leland clears his throat. On he goes.

"My story is about a gentleman named Mr. Stone. Now Mr. Stone, an affable man of some years, had a new suit, which he took to the dry cleaners one day. When he picked it up and brought it home he discovered a fresh burn mark on the breast pocket that hadn't been there before. He became angry and planned to return it the next morning. On his way to do this errand he bumped into a neighbor who inquired about his health. Our friend Mr. Stone said, 'I was fine until that damn dry cleaners ruined my suit.' So the two neighbors chatted a while longer and then Mr. Stone went back to the cleaners. He walked in the open store, but no one ever came out from the back room to help him, so he took his suit and left."

My lawyer stops his allegory and heads over to the jury box, where he places his hands on the short wall in front of the members.

"Well, ladies and gentlemen, unbeknownst to Mr. Stone, the dry cleaner had been killed just a few minutes before in a failed robbery attempt, and was lying behind the counter on the floor. Now, this would have been nothing more than a sad coincidence. However, the neighbor remembered Mr. Stone's anger at the dry cleaner and told the police. And someone else volunteered that Mrs. Stone may have been spending a little extra time having her husband's shirts starched. So our friend, who was guilty of nothing more than being in the wrong place at the wrong time, was arrested."

I flash on my brothers, imagining them making fun of Leland. Mikey would say something like, Couldn't he just have defined circumstantial? William would respond that it's a courtroom tactic, getting the jurors to die of old age.

"Now, good people, it will be shown over the course of the trial that there are explanations for all the pieces of so-called evidence. And we will go through them one by one until you realize the frightening way things can be wrenched out of context and spun into an indictment against an innocent person."

He turns and points toward me. My face flames.

"In this case, against a woman who would never dream of doing what she stands accused of. This case should terrify you. Why? Because it could be any one of us sitting in Mrs. Trailor's chair. This is the greatest miscarriage of justice that I have ever seen. And I guarantee that you will come to the same conclusion.

"You will find that there is a good explanation for everything my good friend Mr. Wycliff tries to lay at my client's feet. For instance, the tape that he described only tells half the story. He neglected to mention that the camera only records the public entrance into the nursery area. He forgot to tell you there's another door through the nurses' station. He also forgot to tell you somebody else had a great deal to lose if the baby survived."

Almost from the outset, Leland decided to scuff up Catherine. To paint her as a spoiled party girl—now an impaired physician with judgment clouded by sleep deprivation and amphetamine use. He's going to suggest that when she learned there'd be no autopsy, she thought she could make the malpractice problem go away. Hasten the baby's death. Because the only issue then would be the circumstances leading up to the birth. It would be my word against hers about her not performing the manual exam.

"But what if it wasn't her?" I'd asked when Leland laid out his plan.

"All I need to do is introduce doubt that you did it, Marti."

"By offering somebody else up?"

"That's right."

In another life I would have been horrified.

"Oh" was all I said.

Leland takes his seat and looks to the judge, who is bookended by the American and Virginia flags. "Thank you, Counselors. Now, ladies and gentlemen of the jury, unlike some of the televised cases I hear about, I run a tight ship. I expect this to rest in the next four days." She turned back to face the tables. "Understood, gentlemen?"

Both lawyers nod.

"I don't look kindly on theatrics."

The jury giggles over the thinly veiled criticism of my lawyer. Some probably because they're embarrassed for him, others because they don't mind seeing somebody as suitish as Leland getting reprimanded.

Wycliff calls his first witness.

Both Leland and the medical examiner stand simultaneously.

Leland stipulates to the autopsy results that the prosecution is about to introduce. He thanks the coroner for his testimony, says he has no questions, and asks to just enter the statement as evidence. Leland told me before that he wants no pictures of Camra in the courtroom.

The coroner is excused.

"One down," the judge cracks to a lot of laughter.

I command myself to stop rocking in my chair. The predictability of the motion is definitely comforting, but I'm sure I look unhinged and push my thighs up into the bottom of the table to slow down. The pressure feels good. The prosecutor calls Wyatt Slope. He's only marginally familiar. With his tortoiseshell glasses and preppy looks, I could have met him anywhere in Richmond. But I can't place him.

"What is your profession, Mr. Slope?" Wycliff elicits after the witness is sworn in.

"I'm a CPA."

"And you are acquainted with the defendant how?"

"Through the OB-GYN Department."

"Goodness, that's an alphabet soup. Can you tell us what the initials stand for?"

"Sorry. Certified public accountant and obstetrical gynecology."

"And in what capacity do you know the defendant?"

"My wife is interning at the same department where Mrs. Trailor's husband works. I've met her at a few functions."

"And did you hear her say something that has relevance to the case?"

"A small group of us at a party were talking about a newspaper editorial that had just come out about right-to-die cases. About whether withholding sustenance and orders not to resuscitate are the same things."

"Mr. Slope, what did the defendant say that was remarkable?" The prosecutor crosses his arms.

"That she believed in euthanasia for bad haircuts."

A man on the jury chuckles.

"What else did the defendant say, Mr. Slope?"

"That she didn't believe in prolonging life for people in vegetative states."

I try not to move.

"Thank you, sir."

Like a piston, Wycliff sits and Leland stands.

"Mr. Slope, I seem to remember that editorial. Caused quite a flap, I believe. About a man's right to die. He'd been kept alive for years following an accident, if I'm not mistaken. Fell off a roof he was tarring, I believe?"

"I think so, yes."

There is a stirring in the jury box. I guess some of them remember the case. I wonder if this means anything. I'm pretty certain that trying to read their body language and facial expressions will trigger florid paranoia.

Stop, I tell myself. Don't look.

"And his wife, who was herself ailing, she asked that nature be allowed to take its course?"

"Yes."

"I believe in that tragic case she argued that her husband's condition was medically hopeless and that the emotional and financial cost of keeping him alive in name only was bankrupting her. She could no longer even make the hour trip to visit him. Is that your recollection?"

"Yes."

"And she just wanted to let him go?"

"Yes."

"And you heard my client voice the opinion that she believed in the man's right to die?"

"Yes."

"Are you suggesting, sir, that my client is the only person in this great commonwealth—other than the courageous woman who argued her husband's right to die—who doesn't believe in prolonging permanent vegetative states?"

"No. But my religion teaches that like abortion—"

Leland puts his hand up to command quiet. "Just answer my questions, please."

"Sorry."

"Now listen to my words before responding." Leland told me in his office that he wanted to keep all abortion talk out of the courtroom. Because of the photo of me giving the finger. I guess he wasn't expecting it from this witness. Or so soon.

"Do you believe, Mr. Slope, that simply holding the opinion that prolonging vegetative states is wrong, equates with murder?"

"No."

"You're excused."

It's very tense. Whatever gloves were on have come off. Slope walks past, pretending not to know I'm there.

Wycliff calls Rene Leboeuf.

She is carrying a clipboard, looking bulky in an unflattering brown pantsuit. When she raises her hand to be sworn, the jacket rolls under her arm and the maroon shirt pulls at its gold buttons.

"Ma'am, could you please state for the record your place of employment?"

"The James River Adult Chronic Care Group Home."

"And what is your title?"

"Case manager."

"And who are your clients?"

"Mentally challenged adults."

"And you have had contact with the defendant?"

"Yes."

"What was the nature of this contact?"

"We both worked with the same client."

"A pregnant client?"

"Yes."

"How did the defendant become involved?"

"A doctor or nurse from the clinic must have made a referral for services to the New Moms program." Frown scars pull at her lips like the dark lines on the mouth of a ventriloquist's dummy.

"You didn't think the referral was necessary?" Wycliff asks.

"Not at all. Prudi was being taken care of."

"What was your impression of the defendant?"

She scowls at me. Waits a beat. "That she had her own agenda."

Wycliff is pacing. "And what, in your opinion, was the defendant's agenda, Ms. Leboeuf?"

"To get Prudi to put her baby up for adoption. She used her training to impact Prudi's decision."

"And was Ms. Trailor's counseling effective?" Wycliff asks gently.

"Yes."

"Your client is without her child?"

"Yes."

"And how is she doing?"

"My professional opinion is—not good. Some days I can't even get her to participate in Independent Living Skills sessions. She used to really enjoy cooking. Now I have to coax her to participate in everything."

"So would you say she is grieving?"

"Yes."

Wycliff thanks her. While taking his seat, he adds, "I'm sure your clients are quite fortunate to have your professionalism and concern."

"Thank you."

I am suddenly struck by something and feel adrenaline kick in like a shot of asthma medicine. I elbow Leland and scrawl:

"Ask how a group home resident got pregnant!"

My lawyer reads, stands, and repositions his tie.

"How long have you been employed in this position, ma'am?"

"Eight years."

"And what is your training?"

"I have a bachelor's of social work."

"And how long was the client in question a resident at your facility?"

"Three and a half years."

"How many clients are in the group home?"

"We have a census of eight." She laughs a little, turning toward the jury. "With a long waiting list."

"And these mentally challenged adults live full time in the facility?"

"That is correct."

"Ma'am, as a caseworker you are responsible for the residents' well-being?"

He crosses his arms and then stands very still.

"Yes," she says.

"Their emotional well-being?" Leland prods.

"Yes."

"Their physical well-being?"

"That's right." Her nostrils are flaring.

"Could you then explain to the court how one of the residents in your care turned up pregnant?"

Wycliff erupts, "Objection!"

"Sustained."

"Withdrawn." Leland keeps going. "Were you aware that Mrs. Trailor had been in close consultation with her supervisor about the case?"

"Yes, but—"

"And that there were serious, indeed very serious, concerns about your client's intellectual—and therefore parenting—limitations?"

"Yes, but—"

"And are you aware of the negative effects of being raised in a severely limited environment?"

"I explained to Mrs. Trailor that I would have helped Prudi take care of the baby!"

"I see. Are you married?"

"No."

"Objection!" shouts Wycliff.

"Sustained."

"Do you have children of your own?"

"No."

"Objection!"

"So you were hoping to raise this baby? Unofficially adopt it?"

"Your Honor!" Wycliff explodes.

"Sustained! That's enough, Counselor."

"Apologies," Leland says. "Miss Leboeuf, what would have happened to this child if your client kept it but you changed jobs?"

"Excuse me?"

"What would have happened if you quit, for instance? Or been fired? What would have happened to the baby then?"

The woman's cheeks mottle, streaks of white raging against high crimson.

"Ground Leboeuf," I write. Then guiltily cross it out.

"Your Honor, please instruct the witness to answer the question about what would have happened to the baby if she left her position," Leland requests.

"I don't know," the witness says before the judge responds.

"I thought not. No further questions."

But the woman just sits there. Nobody seems to know what to do. The bailiff looks questioningly at the judge. Then the witness bursts into sobs. Huge, shoulder-rolling sobs.

This cannot be good.

This cannot be good at all.

Both Leland and Wycliff jump to pour water for the woman. Everyone on the jury looks wildly uncomfortable while she drinks. Finally the caseworker stands and makes her way out.

"Damn," Leland whispers.

"This is as reasonable a time as any for our break," the judge declares. I glance at the clock and am panicked by how fast the time is going. What if the whole trial passes as quickly?

"Need anything?" Leland asks after the judge makes her way into chambers.

"No. Can we just stay here, though?"

He pats my hand solicitously. "Sure."

Seeing Elliot in the hallway would finish me off. I sit with my back to the people who love me, pretending to be scrawling something of import while Leland goes through his notes, checks his phone, and occasionally asks questions about Peter Hayden. I tell him what I know. He produces a few protein bars from his briefcase, offers me one. I shake my head.

"By the way," he says. "Great catch about the pregnancy! That place ought to be shut down."

I make a weird sound instead of answering.

The bailiff with twitchy hair orders us to rise. Then Peter is called. The courtroom door opens behind us and then he is passing through the gate near my seat. He's wearing a double-breasted sage blazer over a white shirt and deep green slacks with cuffs that nearly cover his dark cowboy boots. His teal tie is dotted with little blue spruces. As usual, he looks Hollywood handsome. He offers a winsome smile while being sworn in. His eyes travel the audience, probably calculating potential for a nooner.

"Dr. Hayden, could you please illustrate your duties as a chief resident?" Wycliff asks.

"Among other things, I'm in charge of the scheduling of house staff, liaison work between faculty and residents, and setting up educational meetings."

"This is a position of prestige?"

"Yeah. On paper. In reality it's a lot of headaches and scut work."

Quite a few appreciative chuckles from the audience. Probably fans of medical dramas. Or maybe everybody just needs to let off some of the tension after the last witness.

"Describe, please, your contact with the defendant following the birth of baby Camra Maines," Wycliff encourages.

"Yes, sir. After it was clear that the infant was terribly ill, I told Marti that I thought she'd be a great help to her client in terms of coping."

"And what was Ms. Trailor's response?"

"She said that she wasn't there, at the hospital, as a social worker."

"Really?" Wycliff asks, the disingenuous bastard. "Then why was she present?"

"She said she was there because she was the baby's godmother. Although it was confusing because earlier in the evening she'd told me she was on the ward with a client."

"Excuse me, did you say godmother?"

"Yes."

"In your experience, in four years of medical school and four years in residency, is it common for hospital social workers to also offer themselves as godparents to their clients' babies?"

"No, sir."

"Were you surprised by this?"

"I thought it was a little unprofessional, yes, sir."

I pick up the pen, write: Asshole. Then shade the letters so the word looks three-dimensional.

"Did Ms. Trailor say anything else that might have relevance to this case?" Wycliff asks.

Leland objects from his seat.

"No, I think I'll let the witness continue for a moment or two, Mr. Powell," the judge says. "The doctor might not be an attorney, but he seems smart enough to me."

Everyone laughs. I swear she is flirting.

"Thank you, ma'am." Peter smiles. "Anyway, after the brain injury was discussed, Mrs. Trailor asked rhetorically if I didn't think the baby would be better off dead."

"Dr. Hayden, would you mind explaining for this unworldly lawyer what you mean by 'rhetorically'?" the prosecutor asks.

A couple of the female jurors nod appreciatively. Wycliff is amazingly deft at passing as a humble citizen. I feel like jumping up and revealing his membership in the Virginia Country Club; pointing out that if most of the jury ever made it onto its guarded grounds, they'd be ushered in and handed applications for employment.

"Sorry, sir. What I meant was even though she asked if the baby would be better off dead, it was obvious she'd answered her own question."

"And that answer was?"

"Yes."

"Objection, Your Honor!" Leland is up this time. "Next young Dr. Hayden is going to tell us he can read minds, too."

"Sustained. Please stick to what was actually said, Doctor."

Wycliff walks closer to the witness box. "Did the defendant say or do anything else that struck you as odd?"

"Yes."

"And what was that?"

"She argued against an autopsy."

"Because Tonya didn't want one!" I scratch, pushing the pad to Leland. He glances at it, turns his attention back to the front of the courtroom.

"Excuse me, Dr. Hayden," Wycliff says theatrically. "Did you say a hospital employee, someone who should have been at the very least neutral, argued against a scientific investigation that may have laid to rest questions about the child's condition?"

"Yes, sir."

"And when was this?"

"Shortly after the baby's mother signed the Do Not Resuscitate order."

"Interesting." Wycliff has put on his thinking face, eyebrows closing in on each other, two sharp mountain peaks against a rippled sky. "Very interesting. Well, thank you, Dr. Hayden."

The orange mullet is studying me.

Suddenly a terrifying thought ricochets alongside my pulse.

How will I know when it's time to check out?

I promise myself that starting tomorrow I'll slip the plastic bag of pills inside my shoe. At this I feel relief.

The prosecutor sits.

"My goodness, Dr. Hayden," Leland says by way of introduction, "has anyone ever told you that you're a dead ringer for a young Tom Cruise?"

"I've heard that people tell him he's a dead ringer for me."

The courtroom laughs. The judge smiles.

"Point taken." Leland grins good-naturedly. "Now, if I might, I'd like to go back to the evening of the baby's birth. Could you please describe the conditions on the ward that night? Was it busy? Calm?"

"It was very busy."

"Would you say you were short staffed?"

"We didn't have as many hands on board as usual, sir."

"Why was that?"

"Scheduling issues, sir."

"And who did you say makes the schedule?"

"Me. I do—for the house staff." For the first time, Peter looks a wee bit uncomfortable.

"Objection," Wycliff offers from his chair. "Irrelevant line of questioning."

"Hardly, Your Honor," Leland said. "I will show that the schedule is quite relevant to the case."

"Overruled. You may proceed."

"Is it not true, Doctor, that your department is understaffed because one of the residents is in drug rehab?"

"Objection!"

"Sustained!" This time the judge nods at Wycliff and scowls at Leland. "Stay on point, sir," she commands.

"Your Honor, I am trying to paint a picture of an overworked, overtired staff that was not only capable of misunderstandings—but also tragic mistakes."

Even though I'm waiting for Wycliff to blow up at this statement, I still startle at the sound.

"Your Honor! Perhaps my colleague here needs to be reminded that the scope of this trial is to determine what happened to that baby *after* she was born. The circumstance leading up to birth is of no relevance."

Leland stands straighter.

"Oh, I beg to differ. Your Honor, in order to determine the plausibility of the Commonwealth's case, we not only need to ascertain the conditions surrounding the death of the baby, but also her birth. It is my intention to prove the existence of a suspect with a real motive. Furthermore, Judge Hermann, when my esteemed colleague suggested my client fabricated malpractice claims as a form of revenge against Dr. Stamp, he opened the door to this line of questioning. The very nature of the term *medical malpractice* refers to activity that occurs while a patient is alive. And the prosecutor invited it in."

The judge pauses and then says, "I'll allow it. Proceed, please."

Leland picks up as though never interrupted. "So. Dr. Hayden. Can you explain what 'twenty-four on/twenty-four off' is?"

"It's a scheduling term. A full day on, a full day off."

"And during the time in question, Dr. Catherine Stamp was on this pattern?"

"Yes."

"So she'd be scheduled to be in the hospital for twenty-four hours in a row?"

"Yes."

"Awake?"

"Probably. You never know if you'll have any downtime to sleep."

"You also go on this schedule?"

"Yes."

"How often do you get to sleep at work?"

"Not often."

"And on this pattern it's always twenty-four in the hospital?"

"More or less."

"Well, surely it couldn't be less, Doctor?"

"No, I guess not."

"Because then there wouldn't be enough doctors on board, right?"

"Right."

"But it could be more?"

"Yes."

"In what circumstances?"

"Hand-off report at the beginning and end of shifts. Emergencies. Meetings . . ."

"So, my figuring after looking at the schedule has Dr. Stamp working a ninety-six-hour week for the time period in question. Does that jibe with your calculations?"

"It's possible. Yeah."

"Does this strike you as excessive?"

"It's within the guidelines of the ACGME."

"The what?"

"The Accreditation Council of Graduate Medical Education."

"It's my understanding that the council rules are for a maximum of eighty hours a week. Could you explain how a ninety-six-hour workweek falls within the regulation?"

"It's eighty hours averaged over a four-week period. Which is allowed."

"I see." Leland inclines his head toward the witness box. "And just because something is allowed makes it sound medical practice?"

"Objection!" Wycliff interjects. "Dr. Hayden's opinions about the national guidelines are irrelevant."

"Overruled. You may answer the question, Doctor. I'm interested in your response."

Peter's between a rock and Nigel Hill.

"I guess I don't believe that everything that is allowed is good practice. No."

"Thank you. Tell me your assessment, please, of what happens when people don't get enough sleep?"

Peter clears his throat. "They get tired."

"Very good. And does this affect performance?"

"In what?"

"In anything, sir!" Leland booms. "Adding numbers, painting straight lines, understanding directions!"

"It can."

"So getting back to the night in question. What was happening with Miss Maines's labor?"

"She was failing to progress. We were going to facilitate the labor by performing an amniotomy."

"Which is?"

"Breaking the bag of waters to speed things up."

"And who was going to perform this procedure?"

"This is where there was some uh, confusion. I . . . I told Catherine—Dr. Stamp—that if she ruptured the membranes in the immediate future, while I had to run in to deliver another patient, she'd end up without a dance partner. It was a poor choice of words on my part. I, uh, thought she understood."

"Understood what?"

"That I wanted her to wait for me."

"So you're saying that you had a misperception about Dr. Stamp's level of understanding?" Leland is on a roll.

"I suppose so," Peter mumbles.

"How long had Dr. Stamp been on duty at the time of the baby's birth?"

"I don't know exactly. Probably around fifteen hours."

"Actually, according to your own records, sir, she was in the hospital for eighteen."

"Okay."

"Please speak up, Doctor."

"I said, okay. Yes."

"Thank you. Do you think she was tired?"

He's shifting again in his seat. "I don't know."

"I find that hard to believe, Doctor. But be that as it may, in light of the misunderstanding between yourself and Dr. Stamp, would you now say it is possible that you also misunderstood the rhetorical question Mrs. Trailor asked about the baby being better off dead?"

"I suppose so."

"And why did you want to be present when the bag of waters was ruptured, Doctor?"

"I've had more experience."

"Did you question Dr. Stamp's ability?"

"No. I've just had more experience."

"And you wanted to be in there?"

"Yes."

"I understand, Doctor, that there is dispute over whether or not young Catherine Stamp performed a particular exam that might have changed the course of treatment—and therefore the outcome of events?"

But it doesn't matter. Wycliff objects anyway.

"Hearsay. Dr. Hayden was not present."

"Sustained."

"All right, let me turn to something else, Doctor. When Mrs. Trailor argued against an autopsy—was that out of the blue or in response to something?"

Peter takes a sip of water.

"It wasn't out of the blue. No. Miss Maines had said she didn't want one done."

Leland cocks his head, as if perplexed. "Funny, from your earlier testimony it almost seemed like declining the autopsy had been Mrs. Trailor's idea."

Leland has made Peter out to be a dissembler. Discomfort passes over his face. "I didn't mean to."

"I certainly hope not." My attorney walks toward our table and slides two papers out of his folder, goes back to the witness stand, and hands the top sheet to Peter. "One more thing, Doctor. Your hospital uses both electronic and written charts?"

"Yes. Occasionally we have trouble with our computer systems."

"Who doesn't?" Leland commiserates, passing a piece of paper to the judge. "Your Honor, I'd like to ask the witness to identify the handwriting on this medical chart by reading the signature at the bottom."

"You may."

"It's Dr. Stamp's," says Peter.

"And on this private letter addressed to Elliot Trailor?" he asks, first passing the sheet to the judge. "There is no signature, but would you say the cursive is the same?"

Wycliff is spitting mad. "Objection! Dr. Hayden is not a hand-writing expert!"

Leland manages to speak before the judge opens her mouth. "Your Honor—as you yourself said, Dr. Hayden seems smart enough. I think he can make a fairly educated comparison between the very distinctive writing samples on the two pages."

The judge asks Leland if he's planning on calling Dr. Stamp to testify.

"I am."

"Then you may question her about the handwriting. Objection sustained."

"As you wish. No further questions, Doctor."

Leland returns to the table, worrying the inside of his cheek. He places his papers in a neat stack. I think he wanted to introduce Catherine's drug use here but got shot down. My fingers massage my eyelids. I stop myself, though. I don't want anyone to say I looked tired or bored. And therefore guilty. I go back to a tightly controlled, barely perceptible rocking.

Detective Lee is called to the stand. He describes the medication he found in my medicine cabinet and the two syringes that were discovered in my office and purse. He explains that he and his partner were the arresting officers in the case.

"And were the defendant's fingerprints found on the hypodermic needles?" Wycliff asks.

"On the one in her purse, sir. The other one had been wiped clean."

"Which leads you to surmise?"

"That the one in her desk was the one used in the crime."

"Thank you, sir," Wycliff says.

Leland stands.

"Are all people who take medication for anxiety murderers?" he asks, approaching the stand.

"No, sir."

"Well, that's a relief," the lawyer says to laughter. "So, Detective, what significance is the Xanax in terms of the crime?"

"I guess none, sir."

"And is there any way to determine if either of the syringes were in fact used in the commission of the crime?"

"No, sir."

"And were Mrs. Trailor's fingerprints found on the IV tubing in which the air was injected?"

"No."

Leland starts to turn away, and the detective adds, "Because the tubing was disposed of. It was medical waste and there was no evidence that a felony had been committed when the infant expired."

"Thank you. That will be all, Detective." It's clear that my lawyer does not want to draw attention to what the witness offered. Leland has obviously made a mistake.

"Redirect, if I may, Your Honor?" Wycliff asks.

"Proceed." The judge smiles, showing even white teeth. "I was wondering if you were going to jump in."

I hate everything about her.

"Detective Lee, in your years of public service, have you ever discovered syringes on a suspect that were not used for either medical purposes or criminal activity?"

"No, sir."

"And again, why was the IV tubing disposed of at the hospital?"

Leland taps his finger silently on the table.

"Because no one knew it was part of a crime scene. No one knew the baby was murdered until the autopsy results came in."

"Ah," Wycliff says.

The jury nods in recognition.

Wycliff calls up a parade of quick witnesses, establishing the timeline of Camra's birth and death and my location during both. He brings up Carter-Randolph, who describes our grotesque meeting in Win's building. Leland gets her to acknowledge that extramarital kissing does not add up to murder.

"No further questions, Your Honor."

"I have a housekeeping note to take care of," the judge says. "As I'm sure all of your backsides can attest, I've let this session run a little long. And unfortunately I have a small scheduling conflict in the morning, so we will resume tomorrow at noon sharp. Eat lunch before you come. Have a good evening."

"What!" I exclaim.

"Shh!" Leland hisses.

I scrawl:

"How can she do that and still say the trial will last only four days?"

Leland lifts himself up. "Your Honor, I just want to be sure that if the trial is time limited, that the missing session will be made up as needed?"

"I'll take your request under advisement, Counselor."

We go back to the office. Shane has brought in sandwiches. The smell is making me gag.

"How do you think today went, Leland?" Shane asks.

"Could have been worse. That incident with the social worker was a first for me. I thought we were going to have to have her physically removed from the stand. That's one for the books. Getting old Dorie to let in the testimony about the birth was a win.

"Now comes the hard part, though." He turns to me. "Both Elliot and Catherine will probably be called tomorrow. You're going to have to take care to paint the picture of her unraveling over the evening," Leland says. "'Impaired, compromised, and impatient' all need to be said. Preferably more than once."

"Okay."

"As for Elliot, I'm going to do my best to have him excluded. But I wouldn't count on it, Marti. I have no idea what he's going to say. Do you?"

"No." I burst into tears. Shane looks away and Leland pats my back softly. "You going to be okay?"

"Is that a rhetorical question?"

Shane laughs.

Leland walks me to the door while I put on my coat.

"Bundle up, now. It's cold out. Get a good night's rest, Marti. With the speed this thing is going at, it's not impossible that you'll take the stand in the afternoon. Sleep well."

Sleep hasn't been a problem. My depression has ensured solid slumber. And on the few nights it hasn't, I've made judicious withdrawals from my cache of medications.

Back at Colby's, my parents and brothers are eating ice cream and cookies. They have apparently conferred and decided to speak about everything but the trial. I know they are probably all dying to dissect the day's events, but I am profoundly grateful for the sidestepping. We rate ex-girlfriends of William's and Mikey's. We talk about the brilliance of *The Wire* and whether racism was to blame for its lack of Emmys. My parents gossip about old friends. You'd never know I was on trial for murder.

I go into the kitchen and call the kids. Simon answers. Though just a few miles away, it is a distance of forever. We talk school and homework and his weekend plans to see a movie with Charlie. When he finishes with his daily update he gets Nina, who tells me about how Mr. Brandt sent a girl from the cafeteria to the office for teasing. "Then he said I could come eat lunch with him at his table!"

I smile at this first crush. "Nina?"

"Yes?"

"Do you know how much I love you?"

"Yes."

"Do the other guys know how much I love them?"

Her voice catches. I've scared her. I didn't mean to. Or maybe I did. To prepare her.

"Yes."

Poppy takes the phone. I have a hard time hearing her, as she is whispering. "Mommy! When is this going to all be done?"

"Soon, Poppyseed. Soon."

"Well, because, Grammy is so vewy terrible! The only thing she does is turn on things."

"What does that mean, sweetie?"

"The TV, the computer."

I laugh. "Oh. Well, try to be patient with her. Grammy is a . . . getting older."

"So you are going to be home soon?"

"I hope so, Poppy."

"Promise?"

Ah, shit.

"I want you to promise."

My mother-in-law instructs my distraught baby to say good night.

My parents and brothers are waiting in the hall to say good-bye. Their hugs are fierce.

I fall into bed.

Even with the abridged session, I don't want to take any chances.

In the morning I lock the door, fold the plastic bag of pills into a little cushion, and then slide it under my right instep inside my stockings. I will be aware of it throughout the day, comforted by its presence. I put on my makeup and see that a couple of errant brow hairs have already reappeared. I remember Colby's admonishment about my appearance and fish out the tweezers from my little bag.

In the kitchen Colby thrusts a paper plate at me. "Here, I'll allow you to eat in my car. This once."

"What is it?"

"Avocado with lime on toast," she says.

I smile. It's my favorite.

She hands me a travel mug with some juice. "You've got to keep your strength up."

"Thank you."

The three of us drive to the courthouse. This time the only soundtrack is public radio. For some reason we are all calmer. I eat. We park. We go through the metal detector single file. I gasp. My husband is sitting on the long wooden bench outside the room. Sitting close to him is Catherine. They look like a loving couple waiting for news in a hospital. A violent shudder shakes my body. I have hurried past this scene whenever anyone tried to bring it up. Now I can't. My husband is here to testify for the prosecution. He volunteered.

"Come on," Colby demands, pulling me forward. Then she turns around and hisses, "You're both despicable."

In the courtroom, Wycliff calls Tonya to the stand. She looks unsteady as she walks down the aisle. Her sleeves are too long. She is sworn in and takes her seat. I curl my toes down inside my shoe, feel the pill bag.

Wycliff introduces himself. "Let me start off, Miss Maines, by offering my deepest condolences to you on the loss of your beautiful daughter."

"Thank you." Tonya, crying, speaks so quietly that the bailiff gets up and adjusts the microphone, twisting its neck closer. Today her braids are corralled in a complicated twist.

"I won't prolong this, dear," Wycliff says, passing Tonya his handkerchief. "I just have a few questions. If that's all right?"

She nods.

"Do you remember when the doctors came in after the baby's birth and spoke with you about signing a Do Not Resuscitate order?"

"Yes."

"Did you ask for anything from the doctors before signing?"

"I told them I didn't want them to do an autopsy on her when she passed."

"Was Ms. Trailor present during this discussion?"

"Yes."

"After the doctors left, did Ms. Trailor tell you something about Baby Camra's condition?"

"She said it was on account of Dr. Stamp doing something she shouldn't of."

"Did she now? And did she use the word *malpractice?*"

Tonya nods, so slightly. She is crying.

"I'm sorry, dear. I need you to speak your responses. Did she use the word *malpractice?*"

"Yes." The word is whispered, reluctant.

"When you hear the term *malpractice,* do you think of lawsuits?"

"I guess so."

"And was this also when Ms. Trailor told you that her husband was having an affair with Dr. Stamp?"

Tonya squirms. "No."

"When did she tell you this?"

"She didn't."

Wycliff lets this hang for a moment, then says, "Again, my deepest condolences, Miss Maines."

Tonya looks at me, shakes her head in despair.

Leland stands, buttons his jacket in a respectful motion. "I will also keep this short. My client was your coach in your birthing class?"

"Yes."

"And she helped you find a place to live?"

"Yes." Her eyes are so red, they look like they're bleeding.

"And did you ask her to be the baby's godmother because you wanted her to always be a part of your daughter's life?"

"Yes. Can I have a break? Please? Please? I don't think I can do this anymore."

"Your Honor, I move to release the witness with permission for recall at a later time," Leland says. His concern is genuine.

"Fine, Mr. Powell."

He helps Tonya from the stand. She's weeping. My heart breaks for her all over again. She looks at me and mouths, "I'm sorry."

Leland walks her all the way to the courtroom door, their footsteps loud in the quiet.

Elliot is next up. Heads turn as he walks in.

I wonder if Catherine is still on that bench. I think I remember Leland saying something about her being sequestered. Or maybe I'm confused. As soon as my husband is sworn in, my attorney stands.

"For the record, I would like to note my objection to the Commonwealth's witness on the grounds of marital privilege. Testimony given by my client's husband should not be included."

"Duly noted," says the judge. "But as noted in my pretrial motion, the witness volunteered to appear and will speak only about those things that are not privileged—" She interrupts herself. "Right, Mr. Wycliff?"

"Yes, Your Honor."

"So, I am overruling the defense's objection. Again."

Wycliff leads my husband through his paces. Elliot seems calm and confident. He talks about his position at the hospital. His education and his training. Our separation. An errant tear lands on the table, stares up at me like a contact lens. I blot it with my finger, think about all the DNA I'm leaving behind.

"Now I'm going to ask some very narrow questions, if you please, Doctor. Nothing that would violate the sanctuary marriage provides for confidences shared within this union. Which is what my esteemed colleague is rightfully guarding against. How would you characterize your wife's feelings about your residency program?"

"Objection," says Leland. "Privileged!"

"On the contrary, Your Honor," responds Wycliff. "The defendant has been very vocal about her feelings."

"Overruled. You may answer, Doctor."

Elliot sits up straighter. "She's been fixated on the call schedule ever since I started. She even confronted Nigel Hill, the chairman of my department, about the program."

"Your boss?"

"Yes."

"When was this?"

"Not long after she started working at the hospital."

"And were you present for the exchange?"

"Not exactly. I was in the cafeteria with them, but not within earshot. I heard about it from a number of people who were, though. Marti basically told him his schedule was an accident waiting to hap—"

"Objection! Hearsay."

"Sustained," acknowledges the judge.

"Do you believe the defendant's long-held feelings clouded her read of the circumstances of the baby's delivery?"

"I think it's possible. Yes . . ." His voice drops. "Especially since the resident was Catherine."

"No further questions."

Leland gets up. "Let me get this straight, Doctor. You were not present at the hospital when the baby was born?"

"No."

"So what you're testifying to is the fact that your wife, a social worker, a hospital employee, harbored concerns about a brutal call schedule? On behalf of patients?"

"I would say they were more than 'normal' concerns. She's been obsessed with the subject for ye—"

"Are you a psychiatrist?"

"What? No."

"Then restrict your responses, please, to both the question and your field of expertise."

"Fine. As I said before, the schedule was a running theme between us. I was constantly on the defensive for doing my job."

"So, Doctor. Let me get this straight . . ." Leland pauses and cocks his head in consideration. "You volunteered to testify against your wife in a murder trial because she nagged you?"

A ripple of laughter.

"Your Honor!" Wycliff complains.

"Mr. Powell," Judge Hermann reprimands.

"My apologies. Dr. Trailor, you're the OB-GYN Department's representative on the quality improvement committee?"

"Yes."

"Could you explain to the court what this is?"

It's clear he really doesn't want to.

"Doctor?" prompts Leland.

"It's a multispecialty committee of physicians who are convened when there is an unexpected outcome or complication in the hospital."

"And the minutes of these meetings are public so that the affected patient or their family can take action?"

"No."

The ruddy-faced juror snaps his head up.

"Really? Why is that?" Leland asks.

"The goal is practice betterment. If the physicians thought anything that was shared might end up in court, it could eliminate meaningful reflection. And therefore improvement."

"In other words, the affected patient just becomes roadkill on the way to practice betterment?"

Elliot doesn't say anything.

"Doctor?"

"That's not how I would characterize it."

"Fair enough." Leland doesn't ask him to recharacterize it. "Was a meeting convened regarding Baby Camra Maines and the obstetrical delivery that your girlfriend ran?"

"Objection! Beyond the scope," Wycliff argues, standing.

"Sustained."

What? Why?

"Doctor, going back to the night of the baby's birth—you were out of town?"

"Yes."

"Where were you?"

"In Annapolis visiting my parents."

"Were your children with you?"

"Yes."

"But you returned to Richmond that night, the night in question, without them?"

My body jerks forward at this new information. An agitated rustling breaks out behind me.

"I did," Elliot says flatly.

"And then you turned around again the next morning and drove back to Annapolis to get your children?"

"Yes."

"And this had not been part of your original travel plans?"

"No."

"Why did you come back?"

"I wanted to be with Catherine. She was distraught."

"About?"

"The outcome of the delivery."

"Because she was responsible?"

"Objection!" Wycliff nearly shouts.

"Sustained."

"I'll rephrase. Is it common for physicians to be upset about outcomes outside of their control?"

"Of course it is. We're human."

"Is it common for physicians to be so upset their lovers make four-hour car trips to give them a hug?"

Elliot opens his mouth to answer but is T-boned by an even more vehement objection from Wycliff. The prosecutor looks as if he is about to leap over the table. "Move to strike! Your Honor, please remind the jury that Dr. Stamp is not on trial and that the defense's sarcasm demeans all of us."

"Your objection is sustained, Counselor. The jury will disregard. Mr. Powell, I am losing patience."

"Understood, Your Honor." Leland nods, rotates back to Elliot. "Did you make any other stops during your unscheduled trip to Richmond that night?"

"I'm not following your question."

"Dr. Trailor, did you go to the hospital after that poor baby was born?"

The avocado toast suddenly reappears in the back of my throat. I'm afraid I may vomit. I force myself to swallow. From someplace very far away Wycliff objects, but this time the judge tells Elliot to answer.

"I did not," the stranger on the stand says forcefully.

Not long ago I would have believed anything Elliot said. Any declaration. Any denial. Not anymore. Questions, half-formed and disorderly, start bouncing off one another in my head. Could he have done this? But why? To put the whole sad event in the past? So a handicapped child wouldn't follow his girlfriend—them—into the next chapter of their life? And he jumped on the It-Was-Marti bandwagon to protect himself? Could he hate me that much?

"No further questions at this time, Your Honor."

Elliot pushes open the short swinging door, glares at me, and storms past. Wycliff next calls Nigel, who struts into the room with the authority of an expert witness. He takes the stand, adjusts the mike like a pro.

"Could you explain your relationship to Ms. Trailor?" the prosecutor asks.

"The defendant's husband is one of my junior faculty. As you are aware, Mrs. Trailor was also employed at the hospital. I would occasionally see her on premises."

"And have you had any occasion to evaluate her performance?"

"Indeed I have."

"Please continue," Wycliff says.

"It was following her son's accident. I had gone up to the pediatric ward to pay my respects. Mrs. Trailor seemed very unstable to me. Granted, I'm sure she was riddled with guilt over her child getting hit by a car in a busy parking lot—"

"Objection!"

"Just answer my question, Doctor."

"My apologies. The occurrence involved her engaging in a verbal altercation with one of her clients who was also on the ward—"

"Objection!" Leland erupts. "This is completely prejudicial! Move to strike."

"Sustained. Jury will disregard."

He goes the humble route. "I'm sorry, Your Honor."

"Now, Doctor," Wycliff says. "Did you have a conversation with Ms. Trailor the day following the baby's tragic passing?"

"Yes. She was in a highly agitated state. I asked her to my office, where she threatened to work with malpractice attorneys on behalf of her client. I requested Mrs. Trailor just wait until I'd had a chance to review the case notes and she literally laughed."

"That's another lie!" I whisper urgently.

"It was my inference," Nigel continues, "that this was personal. Well beyond the purview of her professional responsibility. It was obvious to me that Mrs. Trailor had a great deal of animus towards Dr. Stamp."

"I'm sorry, sir, a great deal of what?" Wycliff asks.

"Anger. While not trying to put too fine a point on it, I obviously assumed the course she was taking was because of her husband's relationship with Dr. Stamp. Revenge."

The side door next to the judge's bench opens quietly and a police officer comes in. At first I think he has arrived with some official news. But he takes a seat up against the wall. He is just another observer to the final chapter of my life. The prosecutor keeps going. "I take it you are familiar with the expression 'Hell hath no fury like a woman scorned'?"

"All too well."

I think of Natalie.

"Prejudicial," Leland says again.

"Overruled."

I can't get a handle on the judge.

Wycliff moves closer to the witness stand to reassert command.

"Dr. Hill, please explain why you believe the defendant was harboring a vendetta towards Catherine Stamp, the resident who delivered the baby."

"Because the defendant's husband was having an affair with Dr. Stamp, which I believe was common knowledge throughout the department. Mrs. Trailor was utterly irrational about the subject. I would say 'gleeful' wouldn't be too strong of an adjective to use about her rival's situation."

"He's a LIAR," I scrawl, and push the paper back to Leland.

"So in your view, Dr. Hill, Ms. Trailor saw the tragedy as an opportunity? A vehicle, if you will, to get back at the woman she held responsible for ruining her marriage?"

"Precisely."

I glance up. The jurocrat is glaring at me.

"So you are suggesting that Ms. Trailor was angry enough at Catherine Stamp to fabricate her allegation that the doctor was derelict in her duties?"

"That is most definitely my assessment. Most definitely."

"And that she murdered the child in order to set up her rival?"

Leland is apoplectic.

"Objection!" he thunders. "Speculation!"

"Sustained."

Wycliff looks smug. And I remember it doesn't matter if the jury thinks I was a scorned wife on a murderous rampage or some sick angel of death. Or both. Because the only thing they have to decide is that I did it. Not why. My toes bend, feel the plastic bag, catch the sharp corner.

I force myself to breathe deeply, flip to a new page on the yellow legal pad, and begin notes to the kids.

"Simon, my middle child, my only boy. This will pass, darling. Be strong for your sisters. I love you with all my heart. Mommy. ps don't forget to use toothpaste when you brush. And remember that girls love gentlemen."

Moving on to Poppy, I print in fat letters: "Littlest one, my sweet gift, one way or another things will be okay. I swear life won't always be this bad, baby."

I skip a couple of lines and write: "Nina, my trial and error and first joy—"

But suddenly I am overwhelmingly agitated and edgy, every nerve in my body unsheathed and raw. I don't know what's triggered this intense disturbance, but it has something to do with the note to Poppy. My eyes go back to the print. Maybe I shouldn't be promising that things will get better? But I don't think that's the root of the internal riot. It's more like I'm trying to understand something, trying to grasp what's just out of reach. I stare at the words.

Littlest one, my sweet gift, one way or another things will be okay. I swear life won't always be this bad, baby. Won't always be this bad, baby.

Bad. Baby. Bad baby. And then the whole world stops. The bad baby law! Oh, my God! What do I do?

"Leland," I whisper frantically, turning toward him. "I need to talk to you!"

"Write it down," he intones like a ventriloquist.

I try, but my hand is shaking so hard that the pen jumps and skitters across the floor. I start to get up to get it, but Leland restrains me. My heart is pounding so hard in my throat that it feels as if I've swallowed it whole.

"It's an emergency! Leland!"

"Quiet," he commands under his breath, handing me his own heavy pen. "Sit back!"

It trembles in my fingers, too.

"Call a . . ."

Shitshitshit.

I'm blanking on the word. It's like being in one of those nightmares where you have to run but your feet don't work. Screw it. Across the paper I scrawl: "A time-out!"

"A recess?" he asks, nearly silent.

"Yes. Yes! Do it. Hurry!" I plead in an urgent whisper, jabbing the pen into my palm to keep from begging louder. "I know what happened!"

Leland's studying me.

"Your Honor," he says, rising, "I would like to request a recess. I need to confer with my client."

Please, I will her with all my might, please be a human being. The judge checks her watch and then glances up at the wall clock, comparing and calculating.

"Can't this wait?" She aims her annoyance directly at me.

Leland nudges me gently.

"No, Your Honor," I answer, trying to mask my hysteria with manners. "Ma'am, it really can't."

"We won't be needing more than an hour, Judge Hermann," Leland offers.

"Fine," she finally consents.

The bailiff rises and commands the rest of us to do the same. After the judge and jury stream out behind opposing flagpoles, Leland grabs hold of my elbow and steers me into the hallway. My heart is still hammering to escape my body. Shane joins us in a little conference room reeking from leftovers.

Leland closes the door behind us. "What's going on?"

"It wasn't Catherine or Elliot—it was Nigel! He was the one who stood to lose the most if Camra lived. He was the one who killed her. Because of the bad baby law."

"The bad—are you talking about the Catastrophic Birth Program?" Leland asks, squinting.

"Yes. That's why Nigel is lying about me. To protect himself. He killed Camra so his department wouldn't be forever linked to that program." My breath is a little raggedy. I try to slow down. The last thing I need is a self-inflicted asthma attack. "Even before this happened Elliot talked about Nigel's chairmanship being shaky."

"Why?"

"Because of all the mistakes that have happened under him. But it wasn't until he started saying all that bullshit about me on the stand that I got it. What he was doing, I mean. Everybody else—all the other witnesses—what they said was subjective, you know? Their spin on things."

"Keep going," Leland says.

"What they were talking about were my acts seen through their eyes. But Nigel, Nigel was purposely twisting things to set me up.

First he was just going to finish off the baby to keep his department out of the Catastrophic Birth Program."

"Why would he do that?"

"Because it's had such bad press recently. If a reporter did a piece about it featuring Camra, that would probably be the end for Nigel. Every article would also mention the resident in drug treatment and the accidental abortion. Other claims and lawsuits. Nigel's crazy sched—"

I stop.

"Marti?"

"I just remembered something else. The national regulations governing the hours that house staff can work, it's all self-reported. Nigel puts residents in a double bind where they either get their work done or lie about their hours. Elliot would do his patient stuff but then would have to stay and complete charts. Sometimes he'd be in the hospital for, like, one hundred hours in a week. We've had lots of fights about that. He was like the walking dead for years. He and his friends used to laugh because the regulations strongly recommended 'strategic napping' in the eighty-hour zone. But Nigel let it be known that those who couldn't get all their work done wouldn't make it. So a lot of them felt forced to underreport their hours. It's just part of the culture."

Leland is absently pinching and then smoothing the skin under his chin, thinking. I plow on. "With Camra alive there'd have been a constant threat of media exposure. Updates. Every time the program got in the news Nigel would be afraid she'd be wheeled out for photo ops. But a dead baby disappears. Ask Sharon Hanover what she thinks! She's the one who handled that abortion case. And don't forget Nigel was at the Stocker convention the night this all happened. That would keep coming out in the papers, too."

"Goddamn," Leland mutters, writing something down and thrusting the whole pad toward Shane. "Get Sharon, run this past her. We need her input. It sounds plausible, but I'd like some kind of confirmation before I go in with both guns blazing. Hustle up, Shane. I'll go fishing when it's my ups. See if I can't get him on the ropes. We were going to pound on Nigel about Catherine anyway."

Shane's out the door by the time Leland turns back to me. "You're full of surprises, aren't you, young lady?"

A guard knocks to tell us it's time.

We head back. Nigel is reminded of his oath and takes the stand again. I am in a fog, barely aware of Wycliff's last questions or Nigel's answers.

Please, God. Please let this be right.

"Doctor Hill," Leland says, tucking his thumbs under his chin, forefingers pointing toward the ceiling. Then he says nothing for a long time.

"We're not interrupting anything, are we, Counselor?" the judge asks.

"I apologize, Your Honor. I'll proceed now, if I may."

"By all means," she says.

My pulse is skipping under my wrists. I can see it.

"Ladies and gentlemen. Before I begin I'd like to explain how I got the nickname Angler."

Something is moving in my peripheral vision. It's the bailiff's braids. They've escaped their clip and are dancing in tandem like tired marionettes. She's shaking her head just enough to keep them going. She's clearly heard this before.

"I'm called Angler not only because there's nothing I love more than going after the big one, but also because I sometimes go from spot to spot in the courtroom just like I do at my favorite fishing hole. Not just from place to place. But from subject to subject, too. Some of my colleagues think this is a mistake, that I risk confusing the juries. But I believe the opposite. I have great faith in your ability to follow."

Wycliff is up. "For Pete's sake, Your Honor—this belonged in the opening statement. If anywhere. And anyway, you and I both know it's nothing more than a delaying tactic. I've been friends with Leland Powell for going on twenty years now and I haven't heard anyone call him Angler yet!"

The bailiff and the judge crack up.

Leland puts his hand over his heart, wounded. "Your Honor, my good friends call me that."

There's laughter.

I am so tense that my legs are clapping inside my skirt, stretching the material taut. A couple of the jurors are looking. I squeeze them still.

"In advance, I thank you all for your indulgence for my methods," Leland says to the jury as he commences another circuit across the floor. "And you as well, Your Honor. I'm sure you will see that this is not courtroom theatrics."

"I'll be the judge of that," she says to some giggles. "Let me remind you, Mr. Powell, that the clock is ticking. We still have quite a few witnesses to get to."

"Yes, Your Honor. Dr. Hill . . ." He stops to the side of Nigel. "Being chairman of a hospital department is an important position in the institution, is it not?"

"It is."

"You command a great deal of respect?"

"I would certainly hope so. My department consistently ranks in the top hundred nationally."

"Well, I've heard those rankings aren't based on anything scientific. But let me congratulate you anyway, Doctor."

Nigel's vein is dancing.

"Sir, what is your salary?"

"Somewhere in the neighborhood of a half million."

"A year?"

"Of course a year."

Half the jurors move in their seats.

"Is it difficult, sir, for your residents to comply with your expectations?"

"What?" Nigel's clearly off balance.

"Do you want me to repeat the question?"

"No, I don't. For some residents, the program becomes a process of self-selection."

"Could you explain what you mean?"

"Occasionally, a resident will find that the rigors of my training program are too great. They are the ones who transfer to lesser programs or change specialties."

"I see. Isn't it also true that you have had residents who have become addicted to drugs because of the demands you place on them?"

"Objection!" Wycliff is on his feet. "What is the relevance of this?"

"Your Honor, I am trying to show that Dr. Hill has a reputation for imposing intolerable expectations on his house staff—which in all likelihood contributed to the tragedy in question. Dr. Stamp was too tired to be doing her job."

"Sustained. Neither Dr. Hill nor his departmental policies are on trial."

Still, I see a flicker of a smile cross Leland's M-shaped lips. He has released the intended information anyway.

"Dr. Hill, were you present when Miss Maines delivered?"

"No."

"But you had been there while she was in labor?"

"Yes."

"And then you left?"

"Yes. It was late in the day."

"To go where?"

"I'm sorry?"

"Where did you go once you left Richmond Medical?"

"The River Run Hotel."

"A private affair?"

"No."

"A work-related function?"

"Yes."

"Okay, Doctor. Let's stop pussyfooting around."

Little snickers at his word choice.

"What professional responsibility called you away from the hospital?"

He exhales fury. "The Stocker convention dinner."

A couple of people in the back burst into outright laughter, and Nigel shoots them a frightening look. If they were residents, he'd have them crucified.

"And why did you return to the hospital, Doctor?"

"I was paged by Dr. Hayden. He explained that there had been an emergency. I would like to say for the record that I left the hotel prior to any of the improprieties reported by the press. And that was my first—"

"Doctor, you'll need to find another pulpit from which to issue your disclaimers. Please describe the condition the infant was in when you returned from the Stocker party."

"She was alive." The vein is hopping on his temple.

Behind me the door opens and hallway sounds enter the room. Even before the noise is silenced, Shane appears at the table. The yellow pad quivers a little as he places it in front of his boss's seat. Leland strides over, picks up the pad. He studies it for a moment and then turns back toward the stand.

I'm not sure, but I think he winks at me.

"And while you were at the Stocker event—"

"Objection! Enough is enough, Your Honor!"

"Sustained."

"Had the baby already been examined by the neurologist?"

"Yes."

"And the diagnosis of a permanent vegetative state had been made?"

"With some degree of certainty. Yes."

"And were you informed that the baby's mother had decided to forgo an autopsy in the event Camra expired?"

"Yes."

"Who told you of this?"

"Dr. Hayden."

"Bear with me again while I switch gears, Doctor. It's that angler in me."

Nigel glares.

"Doctor, could you please describe what happens when a medical mistake occurs?"

"I don't understand your question." Nigel is speaking through clenched teeth.

"Forgive me. That wasn't clear. What I mean to ask is what procedure is there, if any, for recording or reporting medical accidents?"

"I assume you're asking about the National Registry?"

"Please."

"When an unfortunate event transpires in hospital, one that ends up in a claim being made or in court, it's recorded."

"And that information is searchable?"

"Yes."

"And the unfortunate event that took place in your department when an abortion was performed on a woman who didn't want one . . ." He pauses for the communal gasp. "And a subsequent malpractice claim was filed—"

"What's the question?" Nigel snaps.

"Was that recorded in the registry?"

"I would assume so."

"Were you the physician who performed that abortion?"

"I was not."

"But you were the attending physician of record, weren't you?"

"Yes."

"And you are aware that the young resident who performed that abortion claims he made the terrible error because he was so tired?"

"He was an incompetent."

"Well, you chose him to be one of your residents, didn't you?"

"I am one of several members of the resident selection committee."

"And members of your program can spend up to ninety-six hours at work in a week's time?"

"Yes."

"But sometimes they still can't get all their work finished?"

"What are you asking?"

"Okay, let's cut to the chase. If you put unreasonable demands on these young physicians, letting them know either implicitly or outright that if they can't fulfill your expectations they will be terminated from the program, do you think some might feel pressured to underreport their hours?"

"I can assure you that does not happen."

"Really, Dr. Hill? Should I call Dr. Hayden back to the stand and ask him if he's ever felt pressured to shave off hours when self-reporting? How about my client's husband? Shall we get Dr. Trailor under oath again and see if he ever falsified his records? Putting not only his patients in jeopardy, but also his career? As Dr. Trailor said, his wife had a unique perspective on your department's schedule. One afforded to a spouse."

"Argumentative!" Wycliff interrupts.

"Sustained."

"Getting back to the registry, Doctor. It can't be good to have one's name listed frequently, can it?"

"Being included does not necessarily equate with fault. Any time a demand for money is made, that's recorded. And all too often cases are settled when they shouldn't be. When wrongdoing hasn't been proved. But in our litigious society it's more expedient to just pay out. Be done with it."

"Kind of like when that musician paid a kid millions because he didn't abuse him?"

"Objection!" Wycliff shouts. "This is ridiculous."

"Withdrawn." Leland walks back toward me and then turns again. "Surely, Doctor, given their druthers most physicians would rather not be included on that list? I mean it's not exactly the *Social Register*. Wouldn't you agree?"

"I suppose."

"Do you have any idea how many times your name has appeared either in the national database or in the one kept by the commonwealth?"

"I do not."

"Is there a way of flying under the radar, so to speak, to avoid having to report unfortunate events that take place in Labor and Delivery?"

My lawyer's questions are pinging all over the place.

"Clarify yourself," Nigel snaps.

"Sorry." Leland smiles genially. "I know this sounds like a contradiction—but does your department ever pay people so they don't make a monetary demand?"

Nigel twists his neck as if trying to relieve a crick. "There have been times when we felt it more expedient to offer a direct settlement. In order to avoid the time and expense of litigation."

"So your answer is yes?"

Nigel stays silent.

"Doctor? Your response, please."

"Yes."

"Thank you. And would you describe this arrangement as keeping a second set of books?"

"No, I most certainly would not."

"Doctor, did you offer a settlement to Mrs. Trailor for her to carry back to her client, Miss Maines?"

Wycliff is up. "I really fail to see the relevance of this line of inquiry. This is a murder trial. And Dr. Hill is not the defendant."

Leland turns to the judge. "As I promised in my opening statement, I am providing an alternate explanation for what happened to Camra Maines. In order to do that, I need to lay out motive."

"But Your Honor—Mr. Powell is all over the map. I can barely keep up!"

"If you'll allow me the latitude, Judge, I'll speak slower for Mr. Wycliff." The room laughs. "Ma'am, a woman's life is at stake, I beg your indulgence."

Wycliff explodes. "Objection! The death penalty is not being sought!"

"You're right, Mr. Wycliff." Leland turns to the jury. "I meant her life as she knows it. As a loving mother of three young children. Simon, Nina, and Poppy."

Just hearing their names causes tears to seep from my eyes. The judge glances at me and then says, "I'll allow you some scope."

"Thank you. Doctor, getting back to the secret payments, do you know how many have been made?"

"No."

"It's not a public document?"

"No."

"Not published anywhere?"

"I've answered that."

"Sorry, I don't mean to upset you, Doctor. What is the purpose of the quality improvement committee?"

"To ensure superior care is provided."

"Is a meeting called when there has been an unfortunate event or outcome?"

"That is not its only function."

"Answer the question, please."

"Yes."

"So it convenes after a hospital stay goes bad?"

"Yes. In order that lessons may be learned."

"Objection, Your Honor. We've already been through this."

Leland points to the back of the room and says, "We've discussed this with the soldiers following orders. Now I'd like to hear it from the general."

"I'll allow it," the judge says.

"Why does the quality improvement committee convene after a hospital error?"

"When an unfortunate event occurs, the group gets together to make improvements when called for."

"Might secret payments ever be discussed?"

Hostility is rising like steam from Nigel. "They could."

"Who is your department's representative to this committee?"

Long pause. "Elliot Trailor."

"My client's husband?"

"Yes."

"Did Dr. Trailor ever share information about these meetings with his wife?"

"If he did, it would have been a serious breach of protocol," he declares furiously, his face crowded with tics. His determination to upbraid Elliot is unmistakable. "A serious breach."

"Dr. Hill, could you explain to the court what is meant by 'A malpractice jury reaches deeper for a wheelchair than a coffin'?"

"I have no idea."

"Well, Doctor, why do you think payouts might be greater for catastrophic malpractice injuries when a victim survives rather than dies?"

"I suppose to cover the cost of long-term care."

"Very good." Leland's sarcasm is so obviously enraging that I wonder if he's doing it intentionally, to get a rise. He reminds me now of jagged steel. "Which brings me to my next question, Dr. Hill. What is the Catastrophic Birth Program?"

"It's a state program that is separate from routine malpractice coverage. Its moneys are allocated for care of infants injured during the perinatal period."

"In English, Doctor—or I suppose American—could you try that again?"

"It's a separate insurance plan that obstetricians and delivery hospitals make financial contributions to. To cover the costs of long-term care following bad outcomes."

"I suppose that's better. So might this program have been petitioned on Camra Maines's behalf, had she lived?"

"Yes."

"To cover the cost of round-the-clock care for the rest of her life?"

"Yes. But coverage is not an automatic. Strict eligibility requirements are in place."

"The program has been in the news recently?"

"I don't know."

"I find that hard to believe, Doctor. The problems associated with it have seen their share of ink—"

"Objection. What's the question?" Wycliff interjects.

"I'll rephrase," Leland says. "It's not clear that everyone is happy with how the program is running, is it?"

Nigel shrugs. A little rivulet of sweat trickles near his ear.

"With words, Doctor. Please."

"I don't know."

"Nearly a million dollars was embezzled from the program recently. Money that was taken from severely injured children. It's within the realm of possibility that Camra Maines's case could have found its way into the papers, don't you think?"

"I have no idea."

"Is there a tracking system for how many negative outcomes are associated with a particular hospital?"

"Again, no idea."

"Again no idea? Really? You are the chairman of the department?" There is tense laughter in the room. Leland straightens his bow tie, walks back to the table, and withdraws a light blue note card from a folder. "Do you recognize this handwriting?"

Nigel's eyelid jitterbugs. "It is the writing of Natalie. My first wife."

"Were you aware, Doctor, that on the night of Baby Camra's birth—and murder—Natalie Hill was present on the maternity ward of Richmond Medical Hospital?"

"No." Nigel jerks his shoulders back as if scratching them against the chair. Then he leans forward. "But it doesn't surprise me. She is a very unstable woman. Very unstable."

"Could you please read it aloud?"

He scans first and then complies.

" 'Marti, I know that you are innocent. Please call me as soon as you are able. Mrs. Hill.' " Nigel turns the card over, but there is nothing else. He hands it back. All of a sudden he is nodding, as though the answer has finally come to him. "Are you suggesting that Natalie killed that baby?"

"No, Dr. Hill, I am not suggesting that your first wife killed that baby. But in terms of access, is anyone allowed to roam on the floor?"

"Not if the guards are doing their job properly."

"Yours is an urban hospital?"

"Obviously."

"Seeing many impoverished patients?"

"More than our share."

"Dr. Hill, do you think truck drivers should haul dangerous loads up 95 when they haven't slept in days?"

"Excuse me?"

"Or is it better for them to map their routes primarily through poor neighborhoods?"

"Your Honor!" Wycliff is furious. "Objection!"

"Sustained."

"Dr. Hill, do you think there's any correlation between who your patients are and the fact that your overtired residents are allowed to train on them, exhausted?"

"Objection!" Wycliff roars.

"All training hospitals do that," Nigel spits.

"Sustained!" Judge Hermann looks seriously angry.

But Leland saws on. "Doctor, are you in favor of the VIP wing at the hospital—the new one that provides segrega—separate care for people with money?"

Nigel's face goes eggplant.

And then he detonates.

"Of course I am! It's a way of getting insurance dollars into the hospital, to pay for the unending free services our usual clientele commands. The baby mamas. That girl's hand will be out again. Windfall or not. Mark my words."

"Dr. Hill, did you have access to Camra Maines on the night of her death?"

Instead of answering, he shouts, "Check back with that girl in ten years. She'll have a house full of illegitimate children. Her baby's death was a favor."

"No further questions, Your Honor. In fact, the defense moves for a directed verdict."

Wycliff stands. "Perhaps we could have a private conversation in chambers, ma'am? Hammer out the details?"

Someone is weeping.

Me.

CHAPTER SIXTEEN

The Spring Fling celebration is today. Instead of the traditional event at the Chinese restaurant, the new chair of OB-GYN has opted for an informal, family- and vegan-friendly picnic at Maymont. One of the hemp-and-Birkenstock-clad docs, she is doing her best to change the culture of the department. She even e-mailed to ask if I'd like to come with the kids. While I begged off, citing the move, I truly appreciated the gesture. It was the opposite of being disappeared.

Colby steps out of my closet. "Did you want to keep this thing?" she asks, holding up my favorite jade sundress between two fingers like a dirty diaper.

"I love that!"

"Hm." She's helping me pack by getting rid of most of my wardrobe. More things have made it into the giveaway bag than the boxes. "I can't believe we're going to be neighbors, Martha Helen. I hope I don't get sick of you."

I laugh. She was the one who called as soon as the FOR SALE sign went up two doors from their place. The Cape Cod has high ceilings and honey pine floors. From my bedroom I can see the James.

I plan on putting a rocking chair next to the window so I can watch the seasons frame the river. "Do you need to take a break?"

"Why, Marti? Just because I'm five months pregnant and it's hotter than Hades in your closet?"

"Did I mention you have stretch marks this time?"

She opens the trash bag and drops my dress in. "Geico wants you to know that you are incredibly rude."

One of the perks of the baby's arrival will be being able to bank the umbilical cord blood in the event (God forbid) Charlie ever relapses. This kind of insurance prompted Colby to give the infant a nickname from those famous commercials. I've already warned her that the second my goddaughter appears, the moniker vanishes.

The rest of the house is all packed up. At one point the task was so overwhelming, I felt like renting a Dumpster and just tossing everything in, starting over after the move. Nina was not impressed with the plan. "We'd just end up getting more of the same stuff."

"You are the most grown-up, newly double-digit person in all of Richmond." I smiled. "We'll be systematic about this. Or as systematic as I can be."

So we went through all our things. We set up a Barbie hospital in the family room and the four of us performed marathon orthopedic surgeries. Although Poppy flipped when her brother grafted a Ken arm where a leg should have gone, for the most part it had been a successful mission. At the end, Poppy suggested we keep the facility open for her friend's dolls.

I pretended to give the idea some thought.

When we moved on to Simon's belongings, he'd already piled his too-small clothes and the toys he wanted to give away. Included were the soldiers he'd gotten after he broke his arm. Though I'd never told him their origin story, I think things can sometimes hold their own history and somehow he just knew. Either way, I was only too happy to knot the little bastards in the trash bag.

Colby steps out of the closet again.

"I forgot to tell you," she says, folding a Rides and Park tee my brothers gave me for my birthday.

"What?"

"Mrs. Hill-the-Second is getting out of Dodge. John told me that she gave her two weeks. She's taking a job in Northern Virginia. Now that Natalie's got her kids back, Leslie is packing up Tara Corelle and cutting bait. Her time as live-in stepmom apparently left a bad taste in everybody's mouth."

"Well, that and being married to a murderer. I wonder if when Nigel gets out of prison he'll have enough time to make another single mother."

"Remember how he sneered 'baby mamas' on the stand? The irony."

"William and Mikey called last night to see whether I thought Nigel's courtroom performance was more reminiscent of Jack Nicholson in *A Few Good Men* or an unmasking on *Scooby-Doo*."

"Have you decided whether or not you're going to testify?"

"No. And stop bringing it up."

My dad's getting ready to hold hearings on the dangers of overtired doctors. Some wild stuff is going to come out about hospitals that send fatigued residents home in taxis so they don't get behind the wheel after working for twenty-four straight hours. As if exhaustion becomes dangerous only once physicians change out of their scrubs. Dad wants me to be a witness and describe what happened here with Catherine. I'd rather chew off a foot, but he keeps pressuring me.

Catherine switched specialties to pathology, where her only contact with patients is interpreting their biopsy slides. Which, in fact, sounds a lot less dangerous than it is. All sorts of bad shit comes out of those things being read wrong. Her new program is down in Durham, so at least I don't have to worry about ever bumping into her at the grocery.

"What time is Elliot dropping the kids off?"

"After supper. Did I tell you the counselor actually used the term *conscious uncoupling*?"

Colby whoops from the closet. "You're still liking the guy, though, right?"

"Yeah. He's been pretty helpful." After two sessions, I agreed to accept some of the responsibility for what went wrong in our marriage. But no more than fifteen percent. And truthfully, I feel pretty noble about that. Elliot asked me out for dinner a few months ago. I declined. I feel healthier and stronger than I have in years. Not measuring up is exhausting. The Anxieties are actually in semiretirement.

"What's up with Tonya?" Colby calls.

"I just got an invite to her graduation party. It'll be their first cookout at their new place."

"She still doesn't want to go away to school?"

"No. She's going to take classes here. She's talking about journalism."

"Really? Maybe I can get her to do some research for me this summer."

"That would be phenomenal, Cole. Being mentored by an award-winning journalist would be pretty damn cool."

After the U.S. attorney brought a criminal case against Stocker, charging the company president with paying kickbacks to prescribers, pointing to (among other things) the event Colby crashed, she was recognized by the Virginia Press Association.

"Apparently a lot of guys have responded to that ad the ambulance chaser is running on TV about Stocker's pumps. It'll be interesting to see if there are enough men to file a class action suit. Maybe then I'll get my damn Pulitzer."

I smile, even though she's still in the closet.

The doorbell rings and Win appears with a bag of sandwiches from our favorite lunch place. "I come bearing food."

I stand on my tiptoes and kiss his soft mouth.

We're taking it slow, Win and I. Not because either of us wants to. It just seems the right thing to do. At work we make each other laugh. Low, bellyaching, leg-crossing howls. He can look at me in a certain way that sends invisible fingers running over my entire body.

Ariana's been visiting him. They have a sweet thing going. He's gentle with her, sly and playful. My children love him, too. Just yesterday, they met us over at the new place and we walked by the James, all four kids and the two dogs. Win put his arm around me, which caused such a surge of happy shock, I froze. That happens often.

Because deep down I know all of this could have gone either way.

ACKNOWLEDGMENTS

Granted, I've done some things in between, but basically I've been working on *Best Intentions* forever. I finished its first iteration when my husband was a ridiculously exhausted young physician. And now many years later, he is an assistant dean of a med school, teaching slightly less ridiculously exhausted students and residents.

What this means is there is a lengthy list of people who have helped one way or another. Although shout-outs don't always end well, I've tried to pull up a roster of loved ones. (Indulge me.)

There's my wonderful, crazy, adored family (who always check out the acknowledgments whenever someone we know writes a book): Emily, Jason, Zack, Caitlin, Maggie, Asa, Gray (my spectacular grandboy), Baba, Lynn, Eden, Brandon, Jamie, Sarah, Hannah, Hank, Tommy, Tabitha, Noah, Heather, Daisy, Mariah, Boman, Kee, Mina, Jedd, Sarah, Tilly, Bobbie, Tammy, Gary, Emmet, Mary, Scott, Satzes, Paddens, Raskins, Lopatins. Wellses. Friedmans. Jenkins, Blooms, Maurers, and Randels.

GrAnn (most especially), Donald, Ben, Alena, Allegra, Lilliana, Claire, Alex, Penelope, Jutay. Cynthia.

Sally, Sam and Dickie. My mom. (One of the very last things we did together was look at an early version of these pages.)

I have been equally blessed in the friend department as I have in the family. Lynn Parker, Dukes, Crumbs, Joan. Chens, Norwoods. Helen, Bob Ax, Kelly, Paul, Greig, Carol, Bridget, Kate, Hal. Anya, Luke. Bill. Sarahdoyle, Nolan, Norah, Pam, Debdie, Debbie, Deborah (lotta variations from a particular name epoch), Jimmie, Sharon, Gar, Kari, Jamie, Borosage. Barnets/DiNovi. Wrights, Landa, Iantoscas. Kate O', Carolyn. KayKay. Meg. Alice. Deirdre. Abbie. Beryl, Christian, Brian. Lora. Milams. Cullens. Bob. Bruce, Miriam. Becky. Kathleen. Khalids. Kizzy. Bob, Carol. Jen. Wanda. Susan, Robbie, Jim, Obeirnes. Phyllis. Silvermans. Martha. Faye. Janet. Richard Bensinger. Bethany, Dan. Roxanne. Crews of *Streetlight Magazine* and Blue Ridge Area Food Bank.

The protracted birth of this novel also means that there've been many professionals who shared legal, social work, medical, and writing expertise along the way. While it goes without saying that any screw-ups are just mine, I got only good things from the generosity of: Ginny Diamond, Deborah Kelly, Amy Hereford, Charlotte Sheedy. Larry Weissman, Sascha Alper. Janis, Ginger, Stefanie, Lisa, Patrice, Patty, Jenny, Susan, Jen. Carol Clancy.

And Kate Garrick, my amazing agent. Brenda Copeland and Elizabeth Lacks, two wildly talented editors I was so fortunate to have. Sona Vogel, Michelle Ma, Maggie Callan, Katie Bassel—deep appreciation.

Gratitude, too, to open-hearted Martha Woodroof, who read the manuscript and gave it to her incredible agent (see above).

And of course to Keith, my dance partner, who has been with me every single step of the way. Forever.